A FRAID

to

FLY

New York Times and *USA Today* Bestseller
S.L. JENNINGS

a Fearless novel

Afraid to Fly
Copyright ©2015 S.L. Jennings

Editing by Tracey Buckalew
Proofreader: Kara Hildebrand
Cover design by Mae I Designs
Formatting by Champagne Formats

ISBN-13:978-1512346534
ISBN-10:1512346535

"There is freedom
waiting for you on
the breezes of the sky,
and you ask
"What if I fall?"

Oh but my darling,
What if you fly?"

— Erin Hanson

Chapter 1

I'D BEEN HERE BEFORE.

Exiled to a permanent state of loathing where pain reigns supreme, and I was but a lowly whipping boy, spoon-feeding the monsters of my past with my own guilt and shame. A place where those same feelings fueled my constant need for acceptance and love, causing the misery to corrode my morality, and left me to douse the burn with hollow, tear-stained lies. Where regret was my only friend, and he was a cold motherfucker.

I'd been here before.

No, seriously. I'd been here before.

I wouldn't call myself a regular at The Pink Kitty, but I was far from a stranger. The drinks were strong, the music loud and provocative. And most importantly, the girls were hot and impressionable.

There wasn't much more a guy like me could ask for.

"Dude, I can't believe you brought me here."

I looked over at Blaine Jacobs, the boyfriend of my best

friend/soul mate/former roommate, and shrugged with a sly smile. "Hey, you're the one who said you needed to get out. What'd you think men do on Guy's Night Out? Talk?"

"Well . . . yeah. I'm not saying I haven't contributed my fair share of singles to a few college funds but, shit, you know Kam will kick my ass."

Chuckling, I appraised our front row entertainment with hazy eyes, following the hypnotic, pendulum sway of her shapely hips. Cherri, two Rs and an I. Twenty. Virgo. Got her name from her fetish for fruit in some unconventional places, and her affinity for the color red.

"Relax, B," Blaine's cousin, CJ, chimed in, smacking him playfully on the shoulder. "Kami's cool. Besides, ever since you two moved in together, I hardly see your ass. Fuck, is her pussy made of gold or something? It better be, considering that you've been acting whipped as shit. What the fuck, man? It's not like you're married!"

Blaine leaned forward and set his elbows on his knees before his narrowed eyes connected with CJ's, brewing an ice storm of wrath. I could feel the temperature drop 30 degrees. Judging by the hardness of Cherri's nipples just inches from my face, she could feel it too.

"First of all, that's the last time you ever mention any part of my woman, especially the space between her thighs. I better not even hear an obscene word and her name in the same fucking sentence. Don't even think it. The second you want to spout off some dumb shit and utter her name—don't. Not unless you want to keep your teeth. You got that?"

Just when I thought Blaine would cause CJ to disinte-grate under the hostility of his glare, his expression changed from murderous to somewhat thoughtful. He leaned back in his chair and exhaled a breath into the cheap perfume and sex-scented air.

"And yeah . . . I do need to talk. So try to fold your wagging tongues back into your mouths for two seconds, ok?"

I turned away from Cherri's routine to "Sweet Cherry Pie" and gave Blaine my full attention. He was a pretty chill dude, for the most part. The seriousness of his voice had me on high alert, sirens and bells colliding with the bass vibrating my skull. He wasn't fucking around.

Blaine let out another breath and tugged at his wayward hair, before rubbing his inked hands against his jeans. "I'm going to ask Kam to marry me."

"What?!" CJ and I shouted in unison. I couldn't turn away from Blaine's ashen face, but I could bet my left nut that CJ's eyes were just as bugged out as mine.

"Yeah. I've been thinking about it a lot lately," he continued. "And, shit, I know I'll never want anyone else. There *is* no one else. And it's bad enough that we're doing things ass-backwards with the baby coming and all. I just want us to be a real family. For our baby to have parents that share the same last name." He moved his jaw like he did when he was nervous or deep in thought about some shit—usually Kami's shit—before grabbing his beer and tipping it back. He was already signaling for another before he slammed the empty bottle down.

I closed my gaping mouth and tried to stifle the odd, conflicting feelings churning in my gut. Kami and Blaine were definitely right for each other. He was patient, understanding and protective with her. Hell, he was a fucking saint to put up with all her varying degrees of crazy. And somehow, he made all the bad shit she had been through easier for her to digest. No, he could never fully take it all away—her past was what made her who she was. But Blaine loved her in a way that made it ok. He made her see that the past was just that . . . the past.

However, Kami was just as haunted by her ghosts as I was about mine. She was a delicate thing. One wrong move and she would be running, willing to give up on her shot at true happiness. And marriage was a huge step—something I wasn't sure she would ever be ready for. Shit, maybe she never *could* be ready for something like that. I know I couldn't.

"Dude, are you smokin' crack? Marriage? Are you shittin' me?"

Thank fuck for CJ and his big mouth. Blaine was more preoccupied with his cousin's insolence to notice my less than joyous expression. I liked Blaine—at least I did now. We had come a long way since earlier this year when he decided to insert himself in our lives and make our crazy little nutcase fall in love with him against her better judgment. But part of me would always feel like no one would be good enough for her. Whether they rode up on a big ass pick-up truck or a white stallion, Kami Duvall would always be too good for any guy, myself included.

Did I want to be good enough for her? Hell yeah. More than anything. But I gave up on that a long time ago. I loved her too much to burden her with my past bullshit when she had so much of her own suffocating her.

"Hey. Earth to Dom," Blaine said, waving a hand in front of my face.

I blinked my glazed eyes a few times before they focused on the guys. "Huh?"

"I said, I'm about to call it a night, fellas. I haven't had a Saturday night off in months, and I'm not about to spend it in a place like this. Why the hell should I be at a strip club when I have a drop dead gorgeous girl at home waiting for me?" He pulled out his wallet and slapped a bill onto the table. "Next round's on me."

"Yeah, yeah," CJ replied, waving him off. "More T&A for us." He returned his attention to the stage just as the next featured dancer's song began.

Shaking his head at his cousin, who was lewdly adjusting himself, Blaine turned to me. "So Dom, I just wanna get your take on all this. You're cool with it, right? Because if you're not, you know Kami will never go through with it. And I wouldn't even press the issue." Again, he tugged at the longer layer of hair grazing his forehead. "It just would really mean a lot to me to have your blessing."

I dropped my gaze down to the drink in my hand, not really knowing what to say. Shit, was I ok with this? With Kami being married? She wouldn't be *my* Kami anymore. She'd be his. *Blaine's* Kami. Fuck, to be honest, she already was.

"Yeah, man," I managed to smile, clapping Blaine on the back. "You got it. I wish you two nothing but the best. Congratulations."

Blaine exhaled the nervous breath he had been holding, and his face split into a cheesy-ass grin. He was a good one. Something I'd never be. And now he was even better because he was humble and considerate enough to ask for my blessing. "Thanks. That means . . . that means a lot. You have no idea."

"Of course," I nodded. I didn't have an idea. I'd never know that feeling of immeasurable pride and joy.

"Ok, cool. I'm outta here." Blaine jumped to his feet, suddenly anxious and enthusiastic to get home to the woman of his dreams. The woman of my dreams too. If I actually had dreams, instead of the nightmares that broke free and wreaked havoc on my subconscious almost every night.

I waved goodbye just as a waitress strolled up to our table, pen and pad in hand. "What can I get you guys?" she asked, popping her pink bubble gum. She captured my attention, seizing my senses with undiluted femininity wrapped in concentrated sex appeal. She was tall for a girl—slim, but curvy and soft in all the right places. She wore the usual cocktail waitress get-up of obscenely short shorts and a skintight tank top that looked like it belonged on the runway, rather than Hoe Stroll, North Carolina. Hell, she *owned* that shit. Confidence was practically oozing from the pores of her alabaster skin.

"Well?" she asked, looking up from her paper pad and pinning me with her bright blue eyes. Fuck. Me. She was gorgeous. Dark hair framed her heart-shaped face—a hauntingly beautiful backdrop for those remarkable eyes. She wore very little makeup, thank God, but her full lips were painted a shocking red. Just the sight of those lips had me licking my own.

"We'll have another round," CJ said before I regained vocal function, his eyes roaming her ass without shame. I wanted to tell him to back off. Wanted to knock those eager eyes to the back of his head. But the delicate beauty in front of me left me breathless, and ultimately, speechless.

What the hell was wrong with me? Um, *hello?* I was Dominic Trevino. *Dirty-fucking-Dom.* I wasn't exactly new to this shit. I never got flustered with any chick. Ever. I loved 'em and left 'em just as quick as I could bag 'em. And the girls . . . the girls knew the game. I didn't have to lie to them. I never fed them any false bullshit, nor promised them anything more than a few orgasms and maybe a meal or two. Sometimes it took less than that. Women were weak for my exotic good looks and Latin charm. It was a gift and a curse. Because, most of the time, that was all they saw.

So why was this chick looking at me like I had three heads, and all of them were butt-ass ugly? Hell, she was nearly scowling at me. Oh shit, had I already slept with her? And forgot to call or something? No. I would have remembered her. Definitely.

"Hey," I finally said, touching her elbow just as she turned to walk away. She jerked her arm away with so much force that her pen clattered to the floor. "You're new here."

"No shit, Sherlock. Now get your hand off me, prick," she snapped through gritted teeth.

"Whoa, whoa, my bad." I raised my palms up to show her that I wasn't a threat. That was the last thing I wanted her to think about me. "Sorry, uh, didn't mean to frighten you."

"You didn't," she sneered, her ethereal blue eyes sparkling like sun-filtered prisms under the multi-colored, neon lights. "I just don't want your hands on me. Got it?"

"Yeah, sorry, didn't mean to offend you." I furrowed my brow in confusion and dipped my head to one side, trying to unmask the reason behind her visible disdain. Despite the hardness of her scowl, there was something soft and graceful about her. Angelic, even. Like a lamb in lion's clothing. I just

7

needed to peel off all the layers. "Do I know you or something? Like, did I do something to upset you?"

She popped her pink bubble gum again, chomping on the gooey goodness like it was my manhood she was grinding to bits. My nuts ached, but I couldn't tell if it was from arousal, fear or some convoluted mix of both.

"Know me? Ha!" she laughed sardonically. "Like I'd ever associate with someone like *you*."

In the span of three seconds, I had somehow morphed into a two foot, yellow, Twinkie-like creature wearing overalls and goggles, because I swear, the only reply I could think of was, *"Whaaaaaat?"*

"Someone like *me?*" I snickered, shaking my head. "Funny coming from a chick in booty shorts and a top that looks like it was painted on . . . in a strip club, no less."

Hello, mouth. This is foot. Now choke on that shit.

Before I could open my mouth to apologize, the waitress let out a frustrated growl and stormed away, leaving her pen to die a slow, cruel death on the sticky, fluid-splattered floor.

"Dude, talk about crash and burn!" CJ guffawed, enjoying the sight of someone else getting beat with the rejection stick for once. I downed my whiskey to nurse the invisible wounds.

Before I could harp on the evening's odd turn of events, Cherri sauntered over to our table, depositing her nearly bare ass on my lap.

"I get off in two hours," she whispered, twirling a lock of her bright red hair.

I looked over at CJ just as one of the more seasoned dancers escorted him to the Champagne Room for a "private" dance. I shook my head. Hope he was up to date on all his shots.

I stroked Cherri's bare thigh, my fingers grazing the mound of hot flesh that only a thin layer of silk concealed. She moaned as my lips slid up her earlobe. "Yeah. I'll be here."

Chapter 2

I WOKE UP IN a humid, tangled web of naked limbs and tousled hair. Three sets of legs, including my own, were twisted in the sheets. Both blonde and red tresses tickled my face and chest. Two hands grasped my torso in slumber, yet one was decorated with fire engine red nail polish, while the other was painted a familiar powder pink.

I'd been here before too.

This scenario. This feeling. This regret.

Same shit, different day.

I unraveled myself from the erotic mosaic of my bed and shrugged on the pair of discarded jeans from last night. Fatigue was still heavy in my joints, so I sat on the edge of the mattress, running a hand over my sleep-matted hair, and trying to piece together the last several hours.

Shit.

You know what's worse than reliving some of the lowest points of your deviance? Being too fucked up to remember them.

A part of me wanted to do the Dirty Bird on the fifty-yard line of my immoral psyche. While the other part—the more rational, mature part that wouldn't be placated by random hook ups—knew that I was wrong. But how do you stop doing the only thing that gives you a sense of security? The thing that makes you feel connected and accepted by someone—anyone—if only for a few hours?

I wasn't jaded to what I was really doing—what I was really hiding under a collection of ripped panties, scratches on my back and dirty sheets. Yeah, the sex, the women . . . it was exciting and satisfied me physically. But it did nothing to fill the void of confusion and shame. Still, I was resigned to bury them both, no matter how impossible that feat seemed.

I trudged into the kitchen for my caffeinated wake up call. I was on my second cup when Angel emerged, dressed in a pair of my boxer shorts and a white, ribbed undershirt, sans bra. Without a word, she lumbered over and took my cup into her small hands, taking a long sip.

We stood in heavy silence as I worked to fix myself another cup. When two people shared what we did . . . there really wasn't much left to say.

"So . . ." Angel said, finally breaking the awkward tension.

"Yeah."

"Crazy."

More silence stretched between us as we sipped our brew. It wasn't that I was ashamed of what happened between us. Hell, it wasn't the first time. And it's not like Angel and I had had sex. But, I knew what we were doing wasn't healthy. It wasn't right. It was just a placeholder for the happiness we both longed to obtain.

"Let's keep this between us," I murmured. "We don't need Kami thinking we're falling apart over here. She'll pack her bags and be in her old room in a heartbeat."

"Would that be the worst thing in the world?" Angel shrugged. She was dead serious, although I could tell she regretted her selfish intentions. "Yeah, you're right . . . she'd flip. We promised her we'd knock it off last time. I *so* cannot sit through another one of her lectures."

I smiled, remembering the last time Angel and I stumbled into a little mischief. Kami nagged us for hours, and oddly enough, we let her. "That girl is more of a mother than she gives herself credit for."

"Shit, if I'd had a mother like her, maybe I'd be less of a train wreck," Angel added with a melancholy grin that didn't meet her cornflower blue eyes.

"Hey . . ."

Dismissing me with a wave of her hand, she shrugged and looked away. "It is what it is. We both know I was doomed from the start."

I wanted to wrap her in my arms. Wanted to take away whatever bullshit she was trying to label herself with. On the outside, Angel Cassidy, rocker extraordinaire, had bigger balls than any man I had ever known. But inside, beyond the make-up, money, and material things, she was a scared, lonely little girl. I had found her that way almost ten years ago. And somehow, the years, time and circumstance had aged her, but she had never truly grown up.

The piercing sound of stiletto heels against hardwood drew our attention, and we watched as Cherri made her way into the kitchen, her barely-there mini dress looking harsh and offensive in the morning light.

"Hey, guys," she smiled lazily. Remnants of black mascara creased at the corners of her eyes, and her hair was matted. She pressed her lips against mine before turning to offer Angel the same. "You two . . . wow. A girl could get used to this."

She grabbed Angel's mug of coffee and took a sip before she could object, then spun on her heel. "Last night was fun. Call me," she shot from over her shoulder. Neither of us even bothered to ask her how she was getting home, being that Angel had been our ride. I don't think we even cared.

We looked at each other with raised brows. "We gotta stop this shit," I finally said, more for myself than anyone else.

"I know." Angel's voice was feather-soft, just a wisp of a sound. It was hard to believe that three nights a week, she was the badass lead singer for AngelDust, the all-girl band that was quickly becoming a force to be reckoned with within the Charlotte indie rock circuit. But then again, I could believe it. Angel was as talented as I was when it came to keeping up appearances. We were cut from the same cloth of bullshit artists. We spewed our own deviated versions of the truth in order to camouflage the wars raging within. Our situations may be different, but the pain was the same. Misery didn't discriminate.

"I gotta run," Angel said, dumping the stripper-tainted remains of her coffee into the sink. "Got plans for lunch."

"With who? Your *giiirlfriend?*" I teased, poking her in the ribs.

I could almost feel the heat radiating from Angel's flushed cheeks. "Shut it, asswipe. Not my girlfriend. A friend. She's married, remember?"

"So?" I quipped with a cocked brow.

"Soooo . . . I don't fuck with married broads. It's bad ju-ju. I don't need karma taking a massive shit on me. I've got enough bullshit to deal with on my own."

I nodded, the memory of last night's news pressing its way to the forefront of my mind. I knew Blaine was confiding in CJ and I, and I truly didn't want to tarnish that. But I needed to vocally digest it. Maybe saying it out loud would make it easier to accept.

"Speaking of being married . . . something I need to tell you." I took a deep breath and exhaled my own selfish feelings, plastering on a smile. "Blaine is proposing to Kam."

Angel's eyes grew twice their size and glazed with shock and horror, which would have been my initial, honest reaction. "What?"

"Yeah. He told me last night."

"Fuck!" she shrieked, scrambling to the house phone a few feet away. "I have to call her."

"What? No." I grabbed her elbow, halting her pursuit. "You can't do that, Ang."

"Why? Why the fuck not? Wouldn't you want to be warned before someone ruined your life? Before someone took the only good and whole and sacred thing you have and destroyed it?"

I let her words sink in, hearing the desperation in her voice. She was genuinely scared for Kami. Shit, she was scared for herself. We'd all seen it firsthand—how fragile love could be. So beautiful, yet paper-thin and translucent. One wrong move, and it would crumble in your hand like ash, falling away into the wind like it was never really there.

"No. We can't," I forced myself to say. "We have to let her go. We gotta let her fly. If we hold her back, we'll be grounding her. Damning her to a life that even we don't want to live."

"Whatever," Angel replied, though she settled the phone into the cradle. "You know, you're usually less emo once you get some."

I shrugged, and quirked a mischievous grin. "Maybe I just need a little more."

I spent the remainder of my Sunday like I usually did—working out, lounging and thinking about my parents. About the life I could have had if they had survived that car crash twenty years ago. It seemed like so long ago—like a page out of someone else's story. Someone else's stolen memories. I never knew them—never knew what it felt like to be truly loved and cared for—but anything had to have been better than what I was left with.

That was all I gave myself. I didn't sulk and mourn. I didn't let my tear-stained past tear me apart. I swallowed it and pressed forward, telling myself that I was okay. I was strong. And I was safe.

That had been my mantra for as long as I could remember. The words I had been forced to hold onto in my darkest days, where there was no sun, no warmth, no reprieve for the pain. The words I repeated over and over in order to stay alive.

Chapter 3

ONDAY MORNING, I WAS catching up on case-
work when the center's program director, Amber,
knocked on my door. I massaged my temples as I
called for her to come in, the tension I had expended over the
weekend creeping back in.

"Hey, Dom. I know you're swamped, but I'd love your
help on a situation," she said, entering my tiny, shoebox of an
office. Amber smiled, fingering her short, naturally coiled hair
and took the seat across from me, sliding a file folder across
my desk.

"Ok, what's up?" I asked, hoping the irritation wasn't
present in my voice. Don't get me wrong, I loved my job. I
couldn't see myself doing anything else. But Charlotte was
definitely feeling the effects of the struggling economy. Working at a non-profit organization for at-risk and special-needs
youth was no easy feat, especially when funding was getting
cut left and right. The city was constantly growing, yet dona-
tions were becoming scarcer. It seemed like we were being hit

with high priority cases every other day, with no room in the budget to hire.

"We've got a kid coming in this week, but here's the thing . . . he doesn't speak."

"You're shitting me," I frowned, though I knew she wasn't. I could see it for myself right there in his file:

Toby Christian, age 12.

Tutoring for Math M, W, F. Language Arts T, Th.

Counseling services 3x a week.

Special circumstances: Selectively Mute.

"I wish I was," Amber replied. I could hear the exasperation in her voice, and I knew she was just as dumbfounded as I was on how to proceed.

"Wouldn't this be better suited for social services? Considering his handicap . . ." I flipped through his file, scanning the info provided on his home life. Single guardian home. I released a sigh and shook my head. Of course. And his poor mother was probably working herself to the bone trying to stay afloat while also caring for a special-needs child. I'd seen it far too often in this line of work, and my heart broke just a little every time I saw how starved for love and attention some of these kids were. They didn't ask for this life. They didn't choose to be born into poverty and substance abuse and over-crowded public schools, where they were left to slip through the cracks. And while we did what we could at Helping Hands, there were still so many kids out there that were waiting on someone—just one person—to open their eyes and give a damn.

I gave a damn, which was why I was here. And yeah, I could've put my degree towards something more lucrative that would fill my pockets. Still, nothing but this right here—knowing that I was doing something that could potentially save a life—would ever fill my soul.

"That's the thing . . ." Amber replied, a touch of hesitance in her voice. "They referred him to us. Medically, there's nothing wrong with him. Mentally, the kid's been through hell. About a year ago, he found his mom face down in her own vomit. Heroine overdose. Hasn't spoken a word since."

I exhaled back into my seat and closed my eyes, letting it all sink in. Dammit. No kid should ever have to face that type of horror. To see the person who was put on this earth to love you—to care for you and protect you—be so selfish with her own life. How heartbreaking for him to learn at such a young age that his mother loved her drug more than she loved him. Because that was what it came down to. She should have quit for him. She should have been there to cheer him on at Little League, or watch him in the school play, or help him with his math homework every evening at the kitchen table. Something—anything—but this.

"Father?" I asked, trying to get my head back in the game and stow my own personal feelings. It was vital in this profession, although I wasn't very good at it.

"Not around. His sister is his legal guardian."

Red flags. At that revelation, I sat up, leaning forward with my elbows on the table. "Sister? Is she stable?"

"Seems like it. Student and Certified Nursing Assistant by day, waitress by night. She's done everything she can to get him the help he needs through the school system, but as far as they're concerned, there's not much they can do for him. He's resistant to most authority, to the point that he almost shuts down. He can communicate non-verbally, but that's only when he wants to. Honestly, after reading his case file, I can't be sure that we even have the manpower to take on a case this demanding."

I looked back down at his file, reading what little info we had on the kid provided by his school counselor at the third school in the district he'd attended in the past year. Apparently, after hitting brick wall after brick wall, they referred Toby's sister to us. Poor kid. No one wanted to deal with him, so he was being passed around, leaving him to be someone else's problem. I knew what that felt like more than I wanted to admit. I, too, had been a problem that had been handed over to relative after relative, until I ended up in the care of the monster that completely destroyed my body and stripped my soul of its innocence. I couldn't let the same happen to this child. Not if I could help it.

"I'll do it," I said with an air of finality. I didn't know what I was getting myself into, but I knew that his file had landed on my desk for a reason.

"Great!" Amber exclaimed, clapping her hands together before nearly jumping out of her seat. Maybe she was afraid I'd change my mind. I couldn't be sure I wouldn't . . . or I shouldn't. "He'll be here this afternoon for his first tutoring session. Then I was hoping you could show him around . . . ? Make him feel welcomed? He's experienced some bullying with the little knuckleheads at school. A kid that can talk yet chooses to remain silent? Instant target."

I winced before nodding, totally feeling Toby's pain. Amber always thought of my empathetic heart as a gift—I could understand these kids like no one else, because I could literally feel the hurt and confusion they were dealing with. I'd always thought of it as a curse. To take on all those emotions and expect to part with them at the end of each day? Not likely. There was no magic switch to turn off the images of their dejected faces when some punk at school called them stupid or gay or fat. There wasn't enough liquor or women in the world that could make me *unfeel* their hurt and rejection when their parents forgot to pick them up from school or show up for awards assemblies or, shit, feed them fucking dinner.

It hurt. Every part of my job hurt like a bitch. But the reward—seeing those same kids thrive and blossom into strong, resilient, responsible young adults—was worth every frustrated tear I'd ever shed behind closed doors.

Not all parents were bad or neglectful. Actually, most of them were supportive and receptive of our suggestions. But every now and then, we'd get a mom or dad or legal guardian, whether temporary or permanent, that just didn't have it in them to care. So we tried our damnedest at Helping Hands to care enough for all of them.

I spent the next few hours dousing myself with copious amounts of caffeine and paperwork until lunchtime when I'd receive the reprieve I looked forward to every week—lunch with Kami.

Kamilla Duvall was indeed my best friend, a badass singer and musician, and the girlfriend/baby mama to Blaine, but she was also so much more. Shit, she was everything. For starters, she was undoubtedly the most gorgeous girl I had never had the privilege of sleeping with, which was saying a lot. Even Angel, who totally played on the All Girls Team—and had for as long as I could remember—had taken a dip in the Dirty

Dom pond. Let her tell it, I turned her gay. But come on, she probably knew that no other guy would ever be able to compare, so she just gave them up altogether.

The thing with Kami was that she was as meek and mild as a church mouse, yet probably the strongest person in the world. You had to be, to carry the heavy burden of a past like hers. The girl had issues—*didn't we all?*—but somehow it just made me love her more. She was a beautiful anomaly to me, which was why I had made it my mission for almost the last six years to protect her and give her the love she so desperately needed, yet rejected like the plague. She didn't love easily, but when she did, she did it freely and with every torn bit of her broken, little heart. And it just so happened that she was currently giving the best parts of her fractured love to Blaine, who happily took over my role as her sole protector and cuddle buddy.

I knew we'd be best friends for life, but to be honest, I was a little hurt that I'd been replaced so quickly. Of course, I wanted her to lead a happy, healthy life, and I knew for a fact that Blaine would provide it for her, no matter how much of a misfit he appeared to be on the outside with all the tatts and piercings. And after coming to grips with the reality that she and I would never, ever be, a long time ago, it would have been selfish of me to hold her back from the happily ever after she so deserved. So maybe I wasn't hurt. Maybe I was jealous. Of him, for cracking through the hard, cold shell around her heart. And of her for letting go of her past and choosing a different path—one that proved that storms were not everlasting, and that our pain didn't have to define us, no matter how deep-rooted and corrosive it was.

"Knock, knock," a sweet, melodious voice drifted from behind my ajar door. I glanced up from the files on my desk and my own tormented reverie, just in time to see Kami waddle in, glowing like that sun. Pregnancy really did suit her.

"About time," I jibed, hopping up from my desk. I made my way around it to wrap her still-tiny frame in my arms. After pecking her on the cheek—a concession I made for Blaine, who didn't appreciate our slightly inappropriate PDA—I stepped back to get a better look at her. "Jeez, Kam. What has that bartender of yours been feeding you? I swear, you gain another ten pounds every time I see you."

Rolling those exotic, almond-shaped eyes, she gave my arm a slap before patting my midsection. "Shut up, you jerk. I don't see you turning down any of those free meals at Dive."

Dive was the bar that Blaine owned and the place where the two had met over a couple shots of tequila. A couple weeks after that, Kami was his new bartender, and it didn't take long for the two of them to nix the googly eyes and actually make it official. Of course, Kam put up a good fight, but I had to give it to Blaine. The dude was persistent as fuck. Just another reason to hate/respect the guy.

"True enough. Shall we head on over now? I'm starved, and fish tacos are today's special." I couldn't help it; I was a fat boy at heart. Plus, Mr. Bradley, Dive's cook, could make a mean fish taco.

"Ugh. Do you mind if we go someplace else? I'm really not feeling that place right now."

I frowned. Kami loved Dive like it was her own. And soon, after she and Blaine tied the knot, it would be. For her to blatantly avoid the place that had brought her so much happiness and pride for nearly a year meant trouble. And when it came to Kam, I'd cross hell and high water to ease her of all discomfort.

"Something wrong?"

She shook her head, but the little frown dimples between her eyes told a different truth. Oh shit, did Blaine already propose? Is she torn about her answer?

"No. Yes. I don't know yet. Could be nothing or it could be a big ass, raging headache. Mind if we hit the little Mexican spot on Davidson? My treat?"

I smiled before leaning forward to kiss her forehead. There was no way I was saying no to that little pout. Or a free meal. "Sure. But only if you tell me what's bothering you."

We made our way to the restaurant, blasting AngelDust the entire way. Angel and her all-girl band (go figure) were gaining quite the following around town, and since they were based out of Dive now—voted one of Charlotte's newest late-night hot spots—there was a good possibility that some record label would be pounding down our door any day now. So the girls had picked it up a notch, and started recording some of their most popular hits in the homemade studio at our condo. And now that Kam had moved out and was official-ly shacking up with Blaine, Angel was more determined than ever to fill the empty space with music. She put her everything into the band, to the point where I had to wonder if she was even more affected by Kam's absence than I was. We were the Three Amigos, a dysfunctional Three's Company. We were the *"three best friends that anyone can have."* And then Blaine came along and fucked it up. You can't have a two-man wolf pack. That's not even a pack anymore. It's a duo.

23

But I wasn't bitter. Promise.

"So what's got you all pissy and forcing me to miss fish taco day?" I asked before taking a massive bite. The fish tacos here were good, but they weren't Mr. Bradley's. That old man could make roadkill taste gourmet.

Kami plucked a black olive with her fork and sighed. "So, remember I told you about Blaine's ex-wife, Amanda? The chick he married right out of high school?"

"Yeah," I answered around a mouthful of cod and mango salsa.

"Well, apparently, she's back in town. And you wanna guess what her first stop was when she got here?"

"You're shitting me." Shredded cabbage unceremoniously fell from my lips, but I didn't care.

"Yup. Dive. She heard through the grapevine that her ex-husband is now the owner. And she showed up with some bullshit excuse about wanting to "catch up for old time's sake,"" she said, using air quotes that somehow looked more like devil horns. She was pissed, and rightfully so. But knowing Kami, she didn't let it show. She just bottled it up and let it eat her alive until she could escape to a safe place to vent. And that safe place was me. I was her haven when real life shit got too tough to handle. When she felt the walls closing in on her sanity. Keeping Kami healthy and happy had been my top priority in life. Even above my own well-being.

"So what happened?"

"Well," she huffed out, making that single, inconsequential word sound like defeat. "She came in—all blonde hair and pouty lips and big, plastic tits—and she sat her sweet, southern ass at the bar like she was right at home. Like she belonged there. It was like a scene outta "Sweet Home Alabama" when Reese Witherspoon goes back home and everyone is shocked to see her, and awed by her holy presence—like she just floated down from the big Playboy mansion in the sky on a damn cloud. I wanted to barf, and it had nothing to do with morning sickness."

"That pretty, huh?"

She shrugged and rolled her eyes. "I should have known. Could you see Blaine marrying anyone other than a supermodel? And she has a kid, Dom! A kid! And she looks amazing!" Her green-eyed gaze then drifted down to her swollen belly, all humor zapped from her expression. "Look at me. I'm a house. What if I gain like a hundred pounds with this pregnancy? What if I have cankles? What if my belly is so scarred with stretch marks that it looks like a road map? You think Blaine will still want me? You think *anyone* would want me?"

Before she could utter one more word of self-doubt, I pushed our plates to the side, and reached over to take her hands in mine. "You stop that shit right now, Kami Duvall. Of course, he will. Even if you gain two hundred pounds—which is physically impossible for you, by the way—that man will still love you like it's his only purpose on earth. And if he turns out to be some undercover asshole, which we also know is impossible, so the fuck what. You have me and Angel. And let's face it—I'm pretty much going to be the best *tío* in history, so that little prince or princess will never be short of love. You can count on that. So no more worrying about shit that's not going to happen. *Comprende?* "

Taking a deep, cleansing breath, she swept her gaze up to mine. The smile on her lips was forced, but it would do for now. It was a start. A year ago, Kami was so riddled with anxiety and fear that she wouldn't even let herself get close enough to a man to allow herself to care about blonde exes with boob jobs. She just simply didn't permit herself the chance to *feel.* Now she was in love—the scariest fucking thing a person could do—and she was invested in it. She had allowed herself to fall despite her hang-ups and phobias. Despite her past and her fear of the future. She let it happen because she knew, undoubtedly, that Blaine would catch her and never, ever let her go.

I envied her ability to trust someone so wholly . . . so unselfishly with her whole heart. Just months ago, she was in a hospital bed, her body broken and battered after a gruesome attack by her disgusting POS sperm donor. Yet, even when that should have shattered her beyond repair, that heart of hers had somehow made it out alive. At a time when giving up seemed like the most logical choice, she did the unthinkable. She let Blaine in, because being without him was scarier than all her fears combined. That reason alone made her superhuman to me.

So if she could get through that, she could totally handle some ex-wife with a shady agenda. She had come too far to give up now.

"When was the last time you saw Dr. Cole?" I asked, my hands still holding hers.

"A week ago."

"Still seeing her regularly?"

"Yeah, Dom. You know I am." Huffing out her frustration, Kami slipped her fingers from my grasp and focused back on her food. She hated talking about going to therapy, but she knew it was necessary, especially now that she was pregnant. Her hormones were out of whack, and everything in her once perfectly predictable life had been turned on its head. And since meds were out of the question, she was seeing Dr. Cole up to twice a month.

"Well, did Blaine give you a reason to doubt him? Did he seem overly happy to see her?"

She frowns down at her half-eaten enchiladas. "No. Not exactly. He just seemed . . . surprised. Like, I could tell he was shocked. I just didn't know if that was a happy shock or an *oh shit* shock."

As badly as I wanted to be the hero in this situation and save her from even having to worry her pretty little head, I knew it wasn't my place. Kami wasn't mine. And it was about time I let that sink in. The first step in the process toward setting her free was to be honest. With her and myself.

"Talk to Blaine. Tell him how you feel, and ask him if Amanda's presence will be an issue for you two. I guarantee that he will be more than happy to soothe all feelings of doubt and insecurity. The boy loves you, Kam. He's insane for you. Give him a chance to show you that he's everything you thought he was the day you walked into that bar and handed him your tattered, patchwork heart. You weren't wrong about him then, so why would you think some chick would make you wrong about him now?"

At that, she smiled, her shoulders visibly relaxing under the dissolving anxiety. "You're right. Yeah, I should talk to him."

Before her renewed confidence could dwindle, I pulled out my wallet and slapped a few bills on the table. "Now. You should talk to him now. Come on, Miss Duvall. You've got a bartender waiting for you."

As we pulled up in front of my building, I made Kami promise to go straight to Dive and confront Blaine. Going home and sulking until she drowned in unspoken accusations and irrational doubt would have been the easy route for her. But actually facing her fears? That was an incredible feat for Kam. Hell, it was something I still didn't have the balls to do.

"Hey, Dom?" she said, halting me from closing the car door and allowing the chill of the overcast day to sneak in. It was just starting to warm up again in North Carolina, an unseasonably cold winter blooming into a hopeful spring.

"Yeah?"

"Thank you. I owe you lunch . . . again. And . . . and I love you."

I dipped my head to hide the grin on my lips. I was so damn proud of her. Six months ago, I never thought I would hear Kami utter those words to . . . well . . . anyone. And now, she made it a point to tell me every time we parted. The same went for Angel and Blaine, too.

"Love you too, Kam. Now go get your man and remind him just how much of a lucky bastard he is."

I closed the door and jogged to the entrance of Helping Hands still wearing that grin, although it felt wrong and forced on my face. I was truly happy for my best friend, despite the ache of anxiety in my chest. But, I was starting to realize that maybe it wasn't because I was worried for her. Maybe it was because I knew that for every step she took towards Blaine, she was taking another step away from me.

Chapter 4

AFTER SPENDING THE REMAINDER of my afternoon pouring over Toby's case file and brushing up on my American Sign Language, I totally forgot to check in with Angel. That was a must for my little blonde bombshell. She needed constant communication—constant interaction—like I do. What Angel sought was validation. She needed to know that someone out there cared for her and loved her just the way she was. I was in search of affection, which usually came in the form of countless, random hook-ups. Now that Kam was out of the house and I didn't have to feel guilty about my whorish behavior, I felt more starved for attention than ever before. Which was why my "dates" were becoming more necessary. Soon I'd have to resort to buying condoms in bulk from Costco.

When the center's activity bus arrived with the students from local schools around 3:30 pm, I was positivity buzzed with anxiety. I needed a challenging case to distract my mind and a new focus for my convoluted hero complex. It was true—I found purpose in being a savior. It took the attention off the fact that no one was there to save me, because I didn't need that. I was doing just fine on my own, despite the terrors that laid in wait behind my eyelids every night, or the emptiness I felt after every faceless hook-up. It worked for me. It was the only way I was able to get up every morning and put one foot in front of the other. It was the only way I could tolerate looking at my reflection in the mirror.

I went out to greet the kids like I always did, shaking their hands, asking about their day, complimenting them on improved grades and aced tests. That was the only interaction many of these kids received, and I made it a point to make every child feel special and important, even if for a couple minutes. I wanted them to know that they mattered, and that the world was waiting on them to grow into their best selves. It wasn't that I was blowing smoke either; I truly believed that. This was our future, and I had the privilege of guiding just a tiny speck of it.

"Mr. Trevino, I want to introduce you to one of my new friends," Amber said, bringing up the end of the line, gently guiding a small boy to follow. "This is Toby, and he'll be joining us after school. Toby, this is Mr. Trevino, and he is one of our mentors here at Helping Hands. He's also a pretty cool guy, and I think you two would get along."

"What's up, my man? Good to meet you. Glad you could join us today." I smiled at the boy, who looked more like the size of an 8-year-old than a middle schooler, and extended my fist. However, my jovial expression went unreciprocated, and my un-bumped knuckles were left suspended in mid-air. I couldn't even be sure the kid even heard me. He was com-

30

pletely blank.

I dropped my hand and recovered by running it through my oil-slick black hair. "Ok, well, Mrs. Owens tells me you're in some of our tutoring programs. Why don't I show you around before we get started? Cool?" Again, nothing, but I nodded at Amber, letting her know that I could take it from here. I could see the apprehension on her face—*how could we reach a kid that chose not to communicate?* Still, I wasn't quite ready to write him off. I was pretty damn positive that he had experienced enough of that in his short lifetime.

"Well, over here is our snack bar area. We've got lots of great snacks, sandwiches, pizza, juice. Any favorite foods you like to eat after school?" I asked, pointing over toward a small cafeteria-style area. I wasn't sure if Toby would follow so I walked slowly, giving him the option to join me. I was careful not to touch him. Most kids who had experienced trauma had an aversion to touch, or in my case, couldn't get enough of it. I wasn't sure which one was worse. Until Toby showed any signs of trusting me, it was best I kept all contact to a minimum. No one knew what the kid had to live through while his mom was shooting poison into her veins.

"And down this hall is our gym, complete with a basketball court. You play?" I explained, pressing forward despite his unresponsiveness. He might not have communicated, but I knew he was listening. He was walking beside me. And although he was wary and kept a safe distance, there was a chance I could eventually gain his trust, and maybe even his friendship. "I'm pretty awesome myself. Maybe we can pick up a game of one-on-one sometime?"

We turned a corner and entered another hallway that

housed the half dozen classrooms we used for group study sessions. I told him about the subjects we assisted with and how many of our students went on to earn A's and B's with lots of dedication and hard work. After that, I showed him the various tables around the facility that could be used for private tutoring if group study wasn't his thing. I had a feeling he was more interested in that anyway.

"So, do you have any questions for me?" I asked, leading him back to my office. I had an open door policy whenever children were present. I would never, ever close my door unless a student requested it for privacy. And even then, I let a staff member know that I was engaged in a counseling session and even recorded it. Not that I didn't trust myself—that was definitely not the case. I just never wanted a child to feel cornered or intimidated. Closed doors had only meant one thing to me once upon a time. They signified perversion and pain. They had instilled fear so deep inside me that I used to wet myself. I had gotten over my aversion, but the memories . . . they still lingered.

I sat down on the armchair opposite the small loveseat in the corner of my office. I rarely sat behind my desk unless I was doing paperwork or other official HH stuff. I wanted the kids to feel at ease with me, and posing as their superior was not the way to do it.

"Hey, I can read a little sign language if you'd like to communicate that way. Or I've got a pad and pencil. Whatever you feel comfortable with." I set the paper and pencil on the table beside the couch, as Toby mentally weighed the seating arrangements. Obviously, taking the sofa was the safest bet. He sat down and dropped his backpack to the ground. Still, I could see he wasn't comfortable. His small, frail frame was as stiff as a board, and he kept his alert eyes on me at all times. I didn't push for more though. This was progress. I could tell that if he didn't at least suspect I was safe, he would've fought his way out of here.

While he watched me like a hawk, I took the opportunity to assess him physically, looking for any signs of mistreatment or neglect. Yes, he was on the small side, but that could have been hereditary. He was thin but didn't appear to be malnourished. His pale skin and brown, shaggy hair appeared clean, as well as his clothes, if not a little nondescript. No name brands or flashy trends, which was the norm for most kids here. And according to his file, his sister was a student on a waitress's salary. I'd be alarmed if he *did* stroll in here with the latest fashions.

We sat there for what felt like hours, letting the silent screaming of trepidation fill the space like an invisible fog. It wasn't conventional, although it wasn't exactly uncomfortable either. I imagined Toby didn't say much even before his mother's passing. Kids in uneasy living situations rarely said more than they had to in order to fly under the radar. After my parents died, I learned to keep quiet, because I thought not being heard equated to not being seen.

I was wrong.

I inwardly prayed that Toby hadn't suffered the same delusion in his past.

At almost 5 o'clock on the dot, our vow of silence was broken by the sound of approaching footsteps and Amber's voice.

" . . . and this is the office of our assistant director, who also happens to be one of our most popular mentors here at Helping Hands. We thought he and Toby would make a great team, considering that Dominic—"

"*You!*"

The very second I heard her hiss that word, spitting it out like a curse, I knew that it had left the same cherry-painted lips I hadn't been able to stop thinking about since Saturday night. She was dressed in light blue scrubs, and her dark hair was pulled back in a simple ponytail. Once again, very little makeup, and her lips were lightly glossed in a soft pink. It was the cocktail waitress from The Pink Kitty. And the way she was scowling at me, those endless, ocean blue eyes tightened into thin slits, she remembered me too.

I tore my gaze away from the fire that burned behind hers and glanced over at Amber, who looked as baffled as I felt. "You two know each other?" she asked gesturing between us.

"We've met," I answered. It was true, although I didn't disclose the *wheres* and *hows* of that meeting.

Remembering herself, and present company, Toby's sister quickly schooled her features into something less controversial and nodded in agreement. "Yes. We've met. *Once.*"

"Ok, so I assume introductions are not in order," Amber replied skeptically. She continued to look at us with a touch of cynicism, as if she knew we were full of shit and was just playing along. I knew that smirk. It was the same one she wore when our students would try to pull a fast one, and she was on to them. She'd let them keep digging the grave for their lies, allowing them to believe they had somehow outsmarted her. Then, just as the feeling of victory had begun to set in, she'd wipe the smug grins right off their faces and read them from

34

A to Z.

That was exactly how she was regarding us at that precise moment.

I had two choices. Either I play dumb and get embarrassed by my boss in front of a kid and his (insanely hot) sister, or be real and avoid further confusion and/or a potential conflict of interest.

"Actually, our run-in was so brief, I'd hardly call it an introduction. I didn't even have the chance to get her name," I admitted. Ok, option 2 benefitted me too. I didn't catch her name, and I needed something other than the "sexy as fuck waitress in a strip club" when fantasizing about her in the wee hours of the night when no one was around to fill my bed.

"Oh. Well, Dominic Trevino, this is Raven West. Ms. West, this is Dominic. Now that we're all acquainted, Dominic will be personally mentoring Toby, and ensuring that his transition here is enjoyable and productive."

Raven.

It was like that name was specifically designed for her, and no other woman on this earth could ever bear it justly. From the black of her hair and the porcelain pallor of her skin to the mystery brewing behind those piercing blue eyes, she was a raven indeed. Yet, even knowing she despised me for some undisclosed reason, she didn't represent death and longing. She was the vastness of eternity, uncharted and unseen.

"Is that right?" Her face was amused, but the sharpness of her voice could cut like a knife. This wasn't residual annoyance from Saturday night. This chick genuinely hated me. Shit. Maybe I *did* sleep with her already? But even that wouldn't explain her distaste for me. I was always crystal clear about my intentions with women. I could get them off, but I would never lead them on. Still, there was always that one who swore she could change me. Like her pussy had magical powers that could instantly transform my indifference into uncontrollable worship for her.

There was no such thing as a magical pussy. Trust me. I've looked.

Even if we had indeed already done the dirty, there was still no rational explanation for my lapse in memory, or her disdain. First off, I would have remembered. Funny as it sounds, I remember all of them. The way they felt underneath me, so soft and supple and warm. The noises they made when I pushed inside of them. The way they tasted on my tongue— some sweet, some tangy. Those were the memories that got me through the night. The memories that stilled the shakes that followed the terror of my dreams. I had been building my psyche's catalogue for some time now, hoping that one day it would be too full of enjoyable remembrances to contain the old ones. The ones that still haunted me every fucking minute of every fucking day.

One day, it would work. One day the only connotation attached to sex would be pleasure. And that feeling would last beyond the initial act. It wouldn't dissipate the moment my lover for the evening left my bed, leaving me in the cold darkness of my own thoughts. At least that's what I was counting on.

Even on the off chance that my memory failed, there was no way Raven could have forgotten *me.*

Let me just put it out there: I'm un-fucking-forgettable. And that's not an issue of opinion. It's a goddamn fact.

I had been with a lot of women. *A lot.* And during that time, I had learned and perfected the art of making love, which was precisely what these women felt with me—loved. Worshipped. Appreciated. I didn't just fuck, nut and run. I took my time to ensure that each and every woman who had the privilege of gracing my bed and consuming my time enjoyed herself to the fullest. It was only fair for the service of distraction that they provided me.

So, yeah. Raven would have remembered me. And that wasn't me being arrogant. It was me being honest.

"Ok," Amber drawled after a few seconds of tense silence. I knew what she was thinking, but before she could voice her concerns, one of the staff members summoned her from the other side of the door, informing her of a phone call.

Once we were left to our own devices, I turned on my most amenably professional smile and climbed to my feet, my hand outstretched. "Good to formally meet you, Ms. West."

She looked down at my hand, but refused to take it, much like her little brother. "I'm sure. And call me Raven."

I nodded, resisting the urge to turn on the charm and woo her panties off. All hope wasn't lost. She may have been glaring at me like I had just skeet-skeeted all over her favorite shirt, but she had offered her first name. People who truly despise you don't give a damn about being on a first name basis.

I pulled my hand back and stuffed it into my pocket casually, like that had been my intention all along. "Nice to meet you, Raven." I made sure to emphasize the V and the N, letting those two letters rest on my tongue for a second longer than necessary. She could hear it too, and cut her eyes into slits in response.

"Come on, Toby. Let's get out of here," she said, turning her attention to her little brother.

With that, the small, quiet boy picked up his book bag and joined his sister at her side. I was positive this would be our last meeting. Whatever beef this girl had with me, surely she would not allow her brother to be subjected to it. And while I would never act unprofessionally in front of a child, I could understand. If she wasn't comfortable with me, there was no way she could be comfortable with me being alone with Toby. So there would probably be some lame excuse as to why he wouldn't be returning to the program, which really was a shame in regards to his social and academic success.

"Well, Toby, it was great hanging out today. You come by and see me anytime, ok?" I wanted him to know that I was here, and my door was always open. Even if he didn't care, I needed him to know that *I* did.

Judging by the smug smile on her face, Raven must've suspected that Toby didn't enjoy his time at HH. But what he did next left her stunned one second, and damn near furious the next.

Toby picked up the pen and pad I had left for him on the side table, scribbled a few words and set down the paper before walking out of the office.

See you tomorrow.

I was still grinning when Raven whirled around to follow him without uttering a word. I'd been given another chance to see them again.

Chapter 5

B Y FIVE-THIRTY, I WAS out my office door and on my way home.

By six, my head was pounding and my dick was aching.

By eight, I was balls deep in the warm, soft, wet confines of my favorite mode of escape.

Tonight, it was Alyssa. Twenty-six. Duke alumna. Kindergarten teacher.

Alyssa was a relatively new face at Dive, my favorite watering hole, and the first stop in my after work routine. Now that Kami was pregnant, and there was no way Blaine was letting her tend bar while his seed grew inside her, she had been coming up with new ideas to expand clientele. One of them was a Happy Hour menu, featuring some fruity mixed drinks, $2 shooters and some cheap eats. It was a hit out the gate, and now Dive was attracting some new patrons, many of them hot, professional women.

Did I mention how fucking fantastic my BFF is?

Alyssa had been in a few times with a couple girlfriends. She always ordered some ridiculously sweet libation with extra cherries. They'd hang out for a couple hours, order appetizers, giggle about their day and leave. She was never accompanied by a man, and there wasn't ring on her finger.

Those variables, coupled with the fact that she was hot in a sexy librarian type of way, put her on my radar.

I watched from my usual spot at the bar between chatting with Blaine and listening to CJ's latest misadventures in dating.

"So let me paint this picture for you," he began, loosening his tie. It was hard to believe that CJ, aka Craig Jacobs, was one of Charlotte's most respected contractors. Apparently, Blaine helped him out with some of his startup costs for his business a few years back, but CJ had turned his dream into a reality all on his own. He was a solid businessman, yet a hopeless barbarian. "I'm sitting at a stoplight, when I turn to see this chick at the bus stop beside me. She's standing there in her basic bitch uniform—UGGs, leggings, and some American Apparel hoodie, sippin' on Starbucks. I would bet my left nut the music blasting in her earbuds was Taylor Swift, but that's beside the point. So I'm lookin' at her, and she's lookin' at me, and it was like we had this psychic connection. Like some fucking telepathic conversation where we didn't even need to use words. I was all *"Get in"* and she was all *"Sure."* Dude, it was totally some Jedi Mind Trick shit."

"Jedi Mind Trick shit?" I laughed. Only CJ.

"Fucking serious. So she gets in, doesn't say a word, and I drive us to the closest motel. Get a room and, well, you know what happens next."

Blaine made a tsking sound and shook his head. "Please tell me you didn't."

"You know I did! I blew her back out! And the only time she made a peep was when she was screaming out for God to come save her from my mighty anaconda!"

Blaine groaned while I doubled over in laughter. CJ was as simple-minded as a box of rocks, but he was always good for a story.

"You do realize there are such things as STD's and un-planned pregnancies, right? Like, you've got to know that you're pretty much playing Russian Roulette with your dick." Blaine raised his brow at his cousin and cringed at the word "dick."

"Aw, cuz, I didn't know you cared. Of course, I know that. That's why on the 8th day, God said, *"Let there be Trojans!"* And little rubbers fell from the sky in a majestic sheet of latex rain."

That shut Blaine up, as he was too busy busting a gut, a tattooed hand covering his mouth.

"You know those aren't 100%, right?" I asked between sucking in gulps of laugh-strangled oxygen.

"What? Bull. Shit."

"No, seriously. I think it's 98% or something like that. And considering the breeds you pick up, you might need to double up before you catch fleas."

I swear, I witnessed every drop of blood drain from CJ's face in about 3.2 seconds. "Excuse me," he muttered before jetting off to the men's room. Blaine and I cracked up even harder than before.

"That was cold, man," he said, popping the top of another

beer and setting it in front of me. On top of being a solidly decent guy, he was a good bartender. Especially since I drank and ate here just about every day for the super low price of *free*. So yeah . . . another reason why I couldn't hate the guy. He was maddeningly unhateable.

"Well, better he learn that now instead of the hard way. Shit, could you imagine if he got some chick knocked up? CJ? A dad? I wouldn't trust him with a cactus, let alone a kid."

Blaine nodded his agreement before drifting over to the other side of the bar to take an order. When he returned, mixing up some type of cocktail that required melon vodka, Midori and a lollipop, I figured I better just come clean with the real intent behind my visit. You know, besides the free beer.

"I had lunch with Kam today," I mentioned casually.

"Oh yeah?" Pour, shake, stir.

"Yeah. She said something about your ex being in town?" I knew I was dead wrong to get involved in their private business, and Kam would probably have my head for betraying her confidence, but I had to know where she stood in all this. I had to know that she was safe, her heart and that precious unborn baby protected. And while I knew that Blaine had been good to her up to this point, an ex-wife could easily change all that.

Blaine looked up from the drink he was making but didn't say a word until he slid it over to the waiting customer. He let the other bartender on duty handle the next few drinks and came to stand right in front of me, leveling his knowing stare at me.

"Yes, she is. And no, nothing has changed. I love Kami, and I love our baby. And Amanda remains exactly where she was—in the past. Kam and our child are my future. Good enough for you?"

"Whoa." I held up both hands in mock surrender, taken aback by his brusque tone. Blaine was one of the coolest, most level-headed guys I'd ever met. But right now, he looked as if he wanted to knock my teeth out. "Look, I'm just looking out for my friend. If she's uncomfortable with a situation, then it is my duty to ensure she's ok."

"Actually, no it's not. It's *my* duty to protect her. You should both know I would never do anything to hurt her. After what happened last year . . ." He cringed at the memory of finding Kami beaten and bloody on the floor of our once-shared apartment. The image still haunted my thoughts daily and always would. You just don't forget the vision of the most precious part of you dying on the ground with a monster hovering over her naked body, lusting over all the ways to defile her. "I can't fathom the thought of her ever experiencing an ounce of pain. I get what you're doing, and I appreciate that you're her best friend, but please . . . let me be her man. Have some faith that I can love her the way that she deserves to be loved."

At that, I couldn't argue a damn thing. He was right. I was overstepping, and I needed to back off. I was man enough to admit it too. "My bad. I guess old habits die hard. We good?" I extended a fist, and waited for him to bump it.

"Yeah," he said, after letting me sit there and stew for a good half minute. "We're good. You're lucky Kam loves you so much. I might have had to toss out the fish tacos Mr. Bradley saved for you."

I could have kissed him right then and there. "Please tell me you aren't just playing with my emotions."

"Naw. Kam insisted after she stopped by after you two had lunch. She told me what you said, and we talked. Thanks for that, by the way."

"I guess we're even," I shrugged.

We had easily shifted back into casual chatter, when Alyssa walked in with two of her girlfriends, minutes later. She wore simple slacks and a lavender, lightweight sweater. Her hair was pulled into a loose bun that only brought my naughty schoolteacher fantasy to life even more. She didn't wear much makeup, which made my mind shift to Raven.

Raven West. *Where the fuck did you come from, and why the fuck are you invading my thoughts?*

I shook it off. Even if she hadn't given me the Elsa treatment and been a cold bitch, she was now officially off limits. Dealing with a student's guardian was just messy, and I actually wanted to help Toby if he'd let me. I couldn't do that by helping myself to his sister.

So tonight's distraction would be Alyssa. She would do just fine.

It took little persuasion to get her to come home with me. And hardly any effort to get her naked on my bed. Turns out, Alyssa was a horny little thing, and not above picking up guys in bars, although she'd insisted she had "never done this sorta thing before."

Riiight. Because she always wore crotchless panties for a roomful of 5-year-olds.

Just as I had predicted, Alyssa was a freak. I barely had my pants undone before she dropped to her knees and wrapped her lips around my dick. I tried to slow her down—early release was not part of the game plan—but she was just so hungry for it. She made the greediest little noises whenever I hit the back of her throat, which was often. Apparently, gagging wasn't an issue for her, and that was definitely a plus.

I stopped her with a gentle hand on the back of her head and eased out of her mouth with a loud *pop*. She looked disappointed at first, but then I helped her to her feet and kissed her swollen lips, stroking her tongue slowly with mine to show her the rhythm I preferred. Rushing would only make our time go by faster, and I desperately needed her to fill the emptiness just a little while longer.

She grasped my shoulders as I kneaded her back while walking her backwards towards the bed. My lips never left hers, and I never stopped touching her. If I did, it would all come rushing back. The memories would creep in and steal me from this moment, sending me into a fit of tremors so bad that I wouldn't be able to do more than curl up in a corner and cry. That had only happened twice before I realized what was happening. I had allowed myself to think about what I was doing, instead of just letting my body focus on physical pleasure. Sex was like a soothing balm to the remembrance of pain. Pain, shame, disgust, humiliation. It helped to quiet them all.

Without warning, she spun around in my arms and kneeled on the bed on all fours, hiking her ass in the air. "Come on, you naughty boy. I want it hard. Make me hurt. Make me scream. Tonight, I want you to fill both my tight, little holes."

I nearly vomited on her and her tight, little holes.

I took a moment to regain my composure, closing my eyes and inhaling through my nose and exhaling out of my mouth for a count of ten. Kami had helped me with some breathing techniques. It helped to tame the rising bile that was singeing my throat.

"Can you turn over?" I managed to ask, my eyes still closed. I could almost imagine her confused expression as she shuffled onto her back. Shit, I didn't want to embarrass her, but I also didn't want to explain why that position was off limits. Just the sight of it . . . it was too much to even imagine.

When I reopened my eyes, she was indeed on her back, but her legs were fused together. Still, she was here, and that meant she wanted me. Being wanted was what I lived for. The feeling of being desired and needed, even if it was superficially, had become a necessity for me.

I approached her slowly, letting my eyes take in her soft, feminine curves. That's what I loved the most about women—their softness, their delicateness. It made them appear breakable, just like me. And it made me appreciate that vulnerability, in hopes that someone could—and would—one day, appreciate mine.

That's why even though I never offered more than a few hours of toe-curling pleasure, I assured each second was spent tending to their sexual desires and making them feel treasured. Just because I was a whore, it didn't make me callous or uncaring. If anything, it made me more aware of my humanity.

I pushed it all away, trading my own hang-ups and idiosyncrasies for the mental numbness that sex could provide and did what I do best: Fuck. I was good at this part—touching, kissing, licking. And when we were both ready—too ravenous with desire to consider my aversions—I drove into her slowly, all the way to the hilt. Until her body completely covered mine and soothed the ache of loneliness with wet warmth. This was the feeling I had been chasing since I was just a child, barely a man. That sweet oblivion that only mindless sex could provide. I was made whole by emptying myself into another, and for the barest of moments, I became separate from my pain and anger. I became the type of man that could look himself in the mirror and not see the horror of his past standing behind him, its razor sharp claws cutting into the skin of his shoulders while it smiled in that sinister way that still made my skin crawl.

I had seen that malevolence in my dreams every day since as long as I could remember. Sometimes it was in the form of a smile, a laugh. Sometimes it wore the face of ecstasy and passion. But it was always terrifying.

I lay in bed, staring up at the ceiling long after Alyssa had passed out in blissful exhaustion. She came twice, once by my tongue, the other with her ankles on my shoulders. She was a screamer, and I kept wondering if Angel would bust in here, wondering if I was fucking or killing the girl. Then, if Alyssa was up for it, she'd join, like she had just this past weekend with Cherri. It wasn't that we wanted each other in that way— oh hell no. We were just better . . . together. It made it even easier to get out of our heads and lost in the movement of our bodies.

It was co-dependent like a motherfucker. And unhealthy. And unconventional. But it was all we knew.

I looked over at Alyssa who was sleeping soundly on her stomach. I had hoped she would be gone by now, being a teacher and all that jazz. But after orgasm #2, I swear she blacked out.

My eyes roamed the milky, soft expanse of her body, drifting over her slight hips and the petite roundness of her backside. I reached over to graze her skin, soaking in her warmth like a leech. God, how I wished this could be enough. I even wished *she* could be enough, or someone like her. Someone sweet and kind and gentle. Someone that didn't know about the ugly scars I bore deep inside me. The ones that had been left by wounds so deep and wide that no amount of intimacy could fill it.

I climbed out of bed and picked up a pair of pajama bottoms from the floor. My room was a mess, as always, but even more so since Kami had moved out. She would have had a fit if she could see it now—littered with dirty clothes, half-empty beer bottles and wine glasses, and condom wrappers. I knew it was disgusting, but it was hard for me to care when the women I slept with didn't care either.

After making a pit stop in the kitchen for a bottle of water, I padded to the other end of the hallway to Angel's room. The door was closed, but I didn't hear any noises that suggested she wasn't alone. I didn't even know if she was home. But I opened it anyway, and entered the darkness, hoping to find refuge.

"Nightmare?" she whispered groggily when I sat on the edge of her bed.

"Can't sleep."

The bed dipped as she shifted over to make room for me without me even having to ask. I climbed in and Angel covered us both with the covers. I laid facing her but not really seeing her against the shades of midnight that filtered through the curtains. She pressed her chest into mine, her breasts covered only by a thin layer of satin, and wrapped her arm around my waist. I imagined her nipples were visible through the scant nightie and could even feel them pebble and harden against my bare skin. It didn't stir any sexual feelings inside me though. I had stopped looking at Angel like that a long time ago. This was solely for comfort. It was a necessity of our survival.

I finally fell asleep sometime around 2 am, clinging onto Angel's tiny frame like she was my lifeline, and I was drowning in a sea of sharks. I had only begun to drift into the deep recesses of my mind when I was thankfully awoken by the sounds of our front door closing around dawn. Alyssa had left, and obviously didn't care to come find me to say goodbye. Guess she did "that sorta thing" more often than she was willing to admit.

"That chick sounds like a dolphin when she comes," Angel murmured, her eyes still closed.

"She kinda looked like one too," I admitted. Alyssa's O-face seriously needed work, but who was I to complain? She came, I came, what more could I ask for?

"Dude, I can still smell her cooch on your rank-ass morning breath. Tell her to lay off the asparagus, for fuck's sake."

I snickered before pulling her closer into my chest, placing her head under my chin. We had slept like that for the remainder of the night—chest to chest, holding each other tight. "Jealous?"

"That I didn't get any pussy last night? Hell yes."

I kissed her crown of blonde locks. "Sucks for you."

"Eh. I'm not into sea creatures anyway. You can keep Flipper."

We lay in each other's arms until the sun was firmly pressed into the cloud-scattered sky. I wasn't ready to get up, and neither was she, but the day beckoned us both. Plus I had something to look forward to—seeing Toby, and ultimately, Raven, again.

Chapter 6

"YOU'RE AWFULLY FUCKING CHIPPER this morning," Angel remarked as she watched me make my daily bowl of oatmeal. I had already hit Planet Fitness on the corner of our street, showered, dressed and was making my morning bowl of oatmeal and fresh fruit. I always offered her some, and she always declined, adding in a few retching sounds to confirm her total repulsion of oatmeal.

"Well, princess, we can't all sleep in until noon and lounge in our pjs all day. Some of us have jobs to get to," I jibed.

"Uh huh," she mused look over the rim of her coffee cup. "But this doesn't have shit to do with your job."

"How so?"

"I don't know," she shrugged, causing the strap of her tiny nightie to slide off her shoulder. "But I'll figure it out."

"Nothing to figure out, Ang. Let it go."

"I know you. Probably better than you know yourself. I just let you get away with shit because I have no right to judge considering my own methods of self-destruction. But I know something is up with you, Dom. And like I said, I'll figure it out."

I was counting on the fact that she wouldn't. Angel was entirely too perceptive. If she got wind of my weird—because that's exactly what it was—draw to Raven, she'd never let me hear the end of it. And she'd meddle her ass off. Shit, she didn't have anything better to do.

Being the daughter of one of the richest, most powerful men in Charlotte had its perks, but when it came to Angel, it was solely monetary. Mr. and Mrs. Cassidy were the embodiment of all things WASP—conservative, republican, narrow-minded and judgmental as hell. This also meant they were against her sexual orientation and refused to admit that they had birthed and raised a gay daughter. Instead, they threw her a few dollars in exchange for her departure from their lives. She didn't get invited to family functions or holidays. Rumor had it, the recent mammoth-size portrait featuring three generations of Cassidy's hanging in the great room of her parents' mansion didn't even include her. It was as if she had been erased from their lives completely. And that literally sickened me.

Angel could have rejected their money, but I almost felt like it was her last and final connection to them. They had to contact her to send those monthly checks and pay her bills, and every so often, they'd even ask how she was. If she refused to accept the money, they'd have no reason to ever speak to her again. She'd just make it easier on them to be done with her for good. So in her own way, she was punishing them. She wasn't allowing them to get rid of her.

My day was much like every day: paperwork, phone calls, and even some groveling for funds towards much-needed programs. There was nothing glamorous about trying to convince people of the benefits of helping the same children that caused them to clutch their purses and lock their car doors whenever they drifted into the more "urban" areas of the city. I didn't get a reprieve until Amber stuck her head in to remind me to eat something before the activity bus arrived. By the time I had dashed to the snack bar, I could hear the sounds of children unloading, their excited chatter drifting in from the front entrance doors. I threw a couple French bread pizzas in the toaster oven and booked it just in time to greet the first wave of students.

"Good to see you today, Bryce," I said, fist-bumping one of our middle school regulars.

"Hey Mr. D," he replied with a bright smile. "Scored a B on my Geometry quiz today."

I clapped him on the back as he passed and gave him a playful ruffle. "My man. Keep it up, B."

"Mr. D! I'm Student of the Month!" a cute little girl in curly pigtails exclaimed.

"Veronica! I'm so proud of you! Make sure you stop by Ms. Amber's office for your free ice cream voucher for McDonald's, ok?"

"What about me, Mr. D?" another student asked. He had been coming to HH for the past few months, but he wasn't as consistent as we liked. We encouraged attendance, and if a student came for 30 days straight, they were rewarded. The same for special achievements at school.

"Darren, you keep coming here and working toward pulling up that that Science grade, and I'll bring in the ice cream sundaes myself."

"Word?"

"Word," I nodded, shaking his hand.

I greeted every child by name, making sure to engage each one of them. *Is that a new haircut? How'd that English test go? Did you catch that basketball game last night? How's your mom's new job? How are the piano lessons?*

For many of these kids, it was one of very few times when they felt someone gave a damn. They weren't being ridiculed or chastised. They weren't being made to feel like they were to blame for the hand they were dealt. They were treated with respect and courtesy, because that was how we wanted them to treat others. We led by example at Helping Hands, and we were firm believers that a little kindness went a long way.

"Toby! Just the man I wanted to see."

As expected, Toby was the last to depart the bus. He appeared much like yesterday—shaggy brown hair, plain, yet clean clothing, blank expression. Still, I refused to let his indifference dissuade me. One of these days, I would say something that he would find interesting, and he would respond. I was sure of it.

Without waiting to see if he was paying attention or following, I turned back towards the kitchen. "I was starving, so I popped a couple pizzas in the oven. Hope you don't mind sharing with me. I made two."

When I went over to the fridge to grab a couple bottles of water, I found that he had indeed followed me. I made sure to school my features and to not crack a smile. I could tell Toby was the type that didn't want to be noticed. If I made a big deal about it, he'd just retreat even more into himself.

After the pizzas were done, I slid them onto plates and set

them down on the table where I had placed the water, along with the notepad and pencil from yesterday. I wanted Toby to know that if he did feel like communicating, the option was there. Luckily, he was open to sitting with me, so that was a start.

"So . . ." I started casually, tearing off a piece of bubbling hot pepperoni and cheese. "Did you happen to catch the game last night? I think Michigan State will totally take the whole tournament. Tom Izzo is like the Yoda of college ball."

Toby watched me as I took a bite of my pizza, unblinking, unreadable as ever. But after I chewed and swallowed, washing it down with a swig of water, he reached over and grasped his, slowly twisting off the top.

"I used to play a little in college, but my school wasn't that great athletically. I had fun though, and that's all it's really about, right?"

I took a pause to dig into my food and to give Toby a chance to respond if he felt like it. He didn't, but he did tear off a piece of pizza and pop it into his mouth. He chewed slowly, his eyes locked on me at all times. This kid didn't trust easily. And that usually meant someone in his life had broken his trust.

Fuck.

I filed it away for later, and picked up our casual, albeit one-sided, conversation. "I guess not being great at sports was ok, considering I was really focused on getting my degree in education. But don't tell anyone I told you this . . . I really wanted to be a theater major," I whispered conspiratorially. "I know, I know. It sounds ultra lame, but I really thought I could make it as an actor. Crazy, right?"

I put some silence between us, scarfing down the rest of my pizza and giving him the chance to do the same with his. He ate every bit and drained his bottle of water with the same gusto. It was a small step, but it was a start. He was warming up to me, which was imperative to helping him.

"So, Toby," I began after we had both finished our meals. "Part of my job is to ensure that you're not only doing well academically, but also socially. And if you're not, I get to figure out how to help you. Not as a teacher or counselor or anything like that. But as a friend. Because friends help each other out, right? Think of me as . . . your fairy godfather. Minus the wings and glitter and wand. I am always on your side, no matter what."

He was silent, of course, but he blinked, an obvious improvement from his usual blank stare. Maybe this was the equivalent of a head nod, or a verbal agreement. Whatever it was, it was better than nothing.

"Another part of my job—the sucky part—is that I have to answer to the big wigs and provide them with monthly reports that reflect progress. So I was hoping you and I could strike up a little deal. Your school counselor informed me that you don't really dig group activities and projects. So here's what I'm proposing: you can do one-on-one tutoring, skip the whole classroom scene, and then afterwards, you're welcome to come hang out in my office until your sister picks you up. And then, maybe like once a week, you drop me a little note, telling me how things are going at school and at home, just to get the boss off my back. Cool?"

Contemplating my words, his eyes narrowed into small slits. Toby's file informed me that he had been eating his lunch and spending recess in the library. He didn't have any friends, and he rarely checked out any books. He just didn't want to be around the other kids. My heart had shattered a little when I read that. I knew what it felt like to be totally isolated from everyone around you. A child didn't choose to be lonely. It was a defense mechanism.

I watched as he took the pencil in his hand, rolling it along his fingertips before pressing it onto the paper.

Deal.

I gave him a nod and a proud smile. He didn't know it, or maybe he did, but he had taken a very courageous step. He was choosing to trust.

I sat in for a few minutes of Toby's Language Arts session before giving him some space to focus on the assignment. When he was done, I found him standing in the doorway to my office. The door was open, so he didn't knock. But he didn't come in either. He just stood there, waiting for me to notice him.

"Come on in and sit," I said waving him in. I motioned to an end table I had cleared off and positioned between the couch and an armchair. On it was a Scrabble board. "I hope you don't mind. I felt like playing and haven't had anyone to play with. You in?"

He dropped his book bag and sat down on the couch, sliding over to face the game board. That was all the answer I needed.

"I'm assuming you know how to play," I said offering him his share of letter tiles. This time, he gave me a single, stiff nod. "Good. I'll try not beat you too badly then."

I was aware of my verbiage, and purposely used the terminology to gauge his reaction to the playful threat of violence. No flinching or diversion of his eyes. That was good. Damn good.

We had played almost entire game when we heard footsteps approach my office. Most of the other kids were in the gym or in the snack bar, and since it was already 5 o'clock, I assumed it could only be one person. Raven.

"Hey, kid," she smiled as she entered. However, when she cut her eyes to me, that smiled was just as quickly erased and replaced with a scowl. I was starting to think that those were the only two facial expressions this chick owned—smile and scowl.

"We're just about done here. Wanna join in?" I asked, despite her hostility.

"No," she snapped. "I have to get to work."

At that, Toby picked up the pad and pencil I'd given him.

No. She has Tuesday nights off.

Busted.

I didn't even try to hide my amusement at Raven's shock and embarrassment when she leaned over to read her brother's words, and I wasn't the only one. A small smile crept its way onto Toby's face although he diverted his eyes down to the board. He knew what he was doing. This kid was on my side! Even he knew his sister was being prickly.

"Fine," Raven huffed, plopping onto the couch beside her brother and crossing her arms across her chest. She wore scrubs again, but these were light pink with little teddy bears on them. I knew she was a nursing student, but I wasn't sure of her specialty.

"Pediatric rotation today?" I asked, tipping my head towards the cutesy pattern.

"Labor and Delivery," she answered flatly, refusing to give me anymore. That was fine. She could ice me out all she wanted. Toby wanted to stay, and it seemed like he would get his way.

"Your move, homie," I said, after tallying up my points for my last move. Toby took a few minutes to contemplate his next word as Raven scooted closer to him to inspect what letters he had left.

"Play those," she whispered. "Triple word score." Toby realized what she meant and sure enough, she was right. Her smug smile was equal parts arrogance and drop-dead gorgeous. Even covered in Pepto-Bismol bears, she was the most stunning woman I had seen in ages, and that was saying something.

Before Raven, every beautiful girl was quickly secretly compared to the one woman I couldn't have: Kami. They were just one of a long line of *buts.*

She's pretty, but she's not as pretty as Kami.

She's smart, but she's not as smart as Kami.

She's kind, but she's not as kind as Kami.

Raven wasn't any of those things, and I was ecstatic. She wasn't just pretty; she was striking in a dangerously edgy way with her nearly black hair, pale skin and vivid blue eyes. She was obviously smart, but it was more than that. She was shrewd and skeptical, which, considering she was the legal guardian of a troubled little boy, was definitely a good thing. And she wasn't nice. Not at all. If I were a different kinda man, I'd say she was a straight up bitch.

But I wasn't. So I didn't.

Instead, I answered her little cutting glares, eye rolls and pursed lips with a teasing smirk, ensuring that she couldn't ever truly believe I was a jerk, even if she wanted to. And yeah, she wanted to. She wanted to hate me, yet I didn't understand why. Come on, *nobody* hated me. I was a good guy—easy on the eyes, respectful, loyal. Even when I shouldn't have been— even when I should have been a total dick to everyone around me—I still chose to strive to be decent. There was enough ugliness in my world. I didn't want to contribute to it.

Whatever the case, my plan seemed to work. It didn't take long before she was actively participating, and—could it be?—enjoying herself. Even Toby had cracked a few toothy grins.

It was half past five when we finally wrapped up our game, with Toby and Raven taking the W. Well shit. And I didn't even let them win. But the loss was totally worth it.

"Hey, kid, I'll meet you at the car in a couple minutes. Go find us a good radio station," Raven said, tossing Toby the car keys. The very second he was out of earshot, she was pinning me with her dubious stare, blue eyes filled with fire.

"What the hell is your deal with my brother?" she spat, fists digging into her shapely hips.

I frowned, caught off guard by her demeanor. We had been having a good time. Her brother was opening up, getting comfortable enough to communicate. I was confused. Had I missed something? "I'm a mentor here at HH. I'm interested in all our students' success."

"But I don't see anyone else in here. Why have you taken a special interest in him?"

"Our center's director thought he'd do better with one-on-

one interaction, and I have to agree. Toby is a special kid, and we just want to see him do well."

"You think I don't know that?" she sneered. "Of course, he's special. That's why, if I find out that you have any interest in him beyond professional—if you even *look* at him in any other way—I will fucking castrate you. That's a promise."

She was out the door and marching towards the exit before I could assure her that if I did—if my worst fears came to fruition, and I became the very same monster that had destroyed my young, fragile body from the inside out—I would castrate myself. And that was a promise too.

Chapter 7

I WAS SIX YEARS old the first time it happened.

At least that was as far back as my memory went.

The doctors said I could have been molested as early as four. The damage was so extensive, my insides so ravaged with scar tissue, that it was hard to pinpoint when the abuse began. So in my mind, it was six. Because that was when I remembered him coming into my room. That was when I remembered screaming and crying so hard that the sides of my lips ripped and bled.

It was a stifling hot night in South Florida. He was drunk off rum. Even then, I knew his drinking meant trouble for me. My uncle was kind and charismatic normally. A beloved member of the community. A devoted brother to his late brother and his young wife. A caring, loving uncle and caregiver to an orphaned toddler. But when he drank, he became frightening. The way he watched me as I colored at the dining table or played with my trucks on the floor. I felt his eyes on me as I watched my favorite cartoon. And even worse, his touch

. . . the way his hands felt on my tiny body during bath time. Fingertips grazing my spine from my neck to the top of my backside. The extra attention he paid to washing between my legs. I told him I was a big boy—I could do it myself. But he was so insistent on proving that he was an attentive caregiver. He wanted to make sure it was done right.

It was wrong. I knew it was, even then. He was a liar and a thief. He stole my innocence and told me it was done out of love.

He had to hold me down. I still remember the weight of his palms on the backs of my wrists and the sweat between our skin. I cried so hard for so long that my pillow was soaked with tears and blood from my cracked lips. At some point, I must've vomited too. It was hard to fully grasp what was being done to my body.

I lay on a mattress saturated with my blood, urine, feces and his fluids for two days after. I was afraid to get up. It hurt all over, and I had no control of my bathroom functions. My insides had been pulverized into pulp, and I was sure I needed to go to the hospital. But I had no one to turn to. No one to talk to. But him.

He came in to carry me to the bath. I was too exhausted and sore to fight him. I was frightened and I was sick. I had been naked and covered in filth and sweat for days, and with my open wounds going untreated, I surely had some type of infection.

He washed the dried blood from my thighs and shampooed my hair. He touched me gently, reverently. And after a long time, he told me how much he loved me and how proud he was to be my uncle.

He said I was a good boy.

That was all I had strived to be. After my parents had died, I was so afraid of losing someone else that I always tried my best to be good. I was quiet, respectful, helpful. I kept my head down and did as I was told. Sometimes my uncle would reward my good behavior with candy and toys, so I quickly learned that being good also benefitted me.

This was his reward. This was his prize for taking me in and caring for me.

That was the first time I remember wishing that I would have died on that stained mattress. Wishing I had had the courage to bury my head in that tear-streaked pillow and smothered myself to death. At least I would've been with Mama and Papa again.

Tonight, it was Lauren.

Aerobics instructor at Planet Fitness. Vegan. Very flexible.

She and I had flirted before in the cardio room. She said I should check out her class. I told her only if it was a private session.

Tonight I got my wish.

After Raven stormed out of my office, wisps of black hair becoming unraveled from her messy bun from the sheer force of her stride, I couldn't clear my head of all the putrid bullshit that put me back in that place . . . that place where I was a helpless little boy crying out for a mama and papa that would never, ever hear him again.

I didn't want to go to Dive. Kam would see it on my

face, and chances were good that Angel would be there too. I couldn't escape those two. They knew . . . they knew how it was for me when the memories took hold.

I wasn't ready to be alone either, so I decided to grab my gear and pound out my frustrations on the treadmill. Eminem was blasting in my headphones, spitting venom over vibrating bass lines and digitized drumbeats. I had just hit mile 3 when Lauren approached, resting her forearm on the handle on my machine and striking a pose. She wore tiny spandex cropped pants and a sports bra. The laces of her sneakers matched the hot pink pattern on her scant top.

I removed my headphones to be polite. I didn't feel like being bothered, but I also didn't want her to think I wasn't interested. I was. Or at least I could be.

"Hey, I've been thinking about that private class you had mentioned," she smiled, her lips looking much too glossed to have been working out. Her sun-streaked hair was in a messy knot on top of her head, which instantly made me think of Raven's mane being pulled up in the same way. I shook it off. Our last conversation left a bad taste in my mouth, and *shit,* just thinking about her triggered my saliva in preparation for vomit.

I hit Stop on the treadmill and went for my water bottle before I got sick all over this poor girl. "Oh yeah?" I asked breathlessly. I wiped the sweat from my brow with a towel and returned her flirtatious grin, despite the bile roiling in my gut like a whirlpool. "Draw any conclusions?"

"I did actually. The studio is free if you're still interested."

I told her I'd meet her in there, and dashed to the locker room to wash my face. I didn't bother to shower or any shit like that. This girl knew what she was getting, and part of me thought she liked it that way.

I was right.

A few stretches and breathing techniques later, I had her back stretched along a yoga ball, her sneakers locked together above my bare ass and her hands fisting my sweat-drenched hair. Thank God, I never left home without condoms. This actually wasn't my first gym romp. You'd be surprised how many chicks dig sweaty, funky sex.

I didn't shower until I got home. Public showers around other men was completely out of the question for me. It was hell for me in high school, but I made do.

When I was finally able to stand under the hot spray, letting the water wash away sticky layers of sweat, sex and shame, I gave into the ache in my chest and released the sob that had been stuck there since the moment Raven had fled my office with a piece of my dignity. I let myself cry for the little boy that endured years of agony and abuse because he thought that was the price of love. I cried for all the nights he was pressed into his twin mattress, that monster's rum-tinged, hot breath fanning over his tear-streaked cheeks, telling him what a good boy he was. I cried for every doubt he had about himself and what he was as a man thereafter, feeling like his masculinity had been tarnished. And I cried for that man whose heart and body had been broken beyond repair, who had longed for someone to see all those horrid cracks and fissures and not run in repulsion, but instead, help him to repair the damage.

As I slid onto the tiled floor, scalding hot water beating down on my back until it was raw, I found that I was crying for Toby too, for fear that someone had hurt him in the most reprehensible way, stealing his voice and all the goodness in his young world.

Chapter 8

I DID MY BEST to do right by Toby and uphold my end of our bargain, but I was still rattled by Raven's warning. Maybe she saw something in me that I had been trying to deny. Maybe she could tell I was meant to be a statistic—a clinical fact in cases like mine. I had spent most of my life trying to prove I was nothing like Hector Trevino, but maybe I was. Maybe his sickness had infected me. Maybe that sordid depravity was contagious.

I could tell Toby knew something was up. He kept watching me with those sharp, brown eyes, his stare as piercing as his sister's. After a few minutes of awkward silence during a mindless game of Connect Four, he picked up the pencil and pad.

She's like that with everyone.

"Everyone?" I asked, a small sense of relief washing over me. Maybe it wasn't me after all.

He shrugged before picking up the pencil again.

She doesn't trust people. Especially men.

"Why do you think that is?"

Another shrug, but this time he didn't write more. Interesting. Could I have been reading this all wrong? Could Raven actually be the victim?

I honestly couldn't imagine Raven being *anyone's* victim. The girl was just too fiery and tough. I almost pitied any guy that crossed her. She probably had a tin bucket of testicles stashed away in her trunk that she took to the driving range to practice her swing. Fore!

Heartbreak had hardened many a woman, but it didn't explain her deep-seated hatred for *me,* a guy she didn't even know. Sure, I may have been a little touchy during our first meeting, but once she made it clear it wasn't welcomed, I backed off. For me, *No* meant *Hell No.*

We didn't talk about Raven again after that, and she hardly spoke two words to me until Friday. And that was only because she had to.

I got the call late morning, and was already grabbing my coat before I could hear the whole story through the receiver. The school was only a ten-minute drive from Helping Hands, but I was pretty sure I made it in five, traffic laws be damned.

"What happened?" I huffed out, winded from the jog from the parking lot.

The middle school's vice principal, Carol Jenkins, shook her head solemnly and exhaled. She and I had worked closely in the past on a few cases involving troubled students. She knew I was serious about my kids.

"Looks like some boys cornered him in the bathroom. He tried to give as good as he got, but they must've overpowered him. He's in with the nurse."

"Boys? How many?"

"No clue," she shrugged. "He won't tell us who it was, and the kid who walked in on them didn't get a good look. Either that or he's afraid of the ramifications. We have our suspicions, and we've got the staff looking for any kids who look like they've been fighting. We'll find them, Dominic. And when we do, they will be punished harshly, I can promise you that. Let me take you in to see him."

"Thanks, Carol," I nodded, as I followed her down the hall to the tiny office.

Toby was sitting on a cot, an ice pack over his eye, looking pale and disheveled. His lip was also cut and bleeding. He looked up when I entered, and for a split second, he seemed . . . hopeful. Like he was almost happy I had come.

"Hey, Pacquiao. Heard about what happened. How you feeling?"

He shrugged, one side of his swollen mouth turning up into a sad half-smile.

"He'll have a pretty good shiner," the nurse reported, kneeling down in front of him to bandage his knuckles. The kid got a few good licks in. Good for him. "Busted lip and a few bruises. I'm sure his injuries are superficial, but just watch for any discoloration and pain around his ribs. He should be fine in a few days."

"Will do. Have you contacted his sister?"

"We called and left a message. When we weren't able to contact her immediately, I figured you'd want to know," the vice principal explained before pulling me to the side.

I kept my eyes on Toby as the nurse cleaned the cut on his lip with some antiseptic. He flinched at the sting but didn't make a sound. Shit. My heart broke for him. There's no telling what those punks would have done to him if someone hadn't walked in. And with him unwilling to talk, we would never know what had actually transpired before they ran off. I made a mental note to talk to some of our students that also attended school here. Maybe they knew who was behind the attack, or could at least point us in the right direction. Maybe even watch Toby's back during school hours.

"I appreciate it, Carol. Listen, if you hear anything at all regarding him being bullied or harassed, you have my number."

"I do," she nodded before returning back to the nurse and Toby. I was watching from a distance, and letting them do their jobs, when Raven rushed in, her wind-whipped hair a nest of onyx on top of her head. Her cheeks were flushed to a bright pink, and her blue eyes were wide with worry.

"Oh my God, I'm so sorry. I came as soon as I got the message," she prattled off before kneeling in front of her brother, inspecting his cuts and scrapes with the gentlest of touches. She was so frantic that she didn't even notice me there. Come to think of it, she didn't really acknowledge anyone directly. Her main focus was Toby. She was as concerned as any parent would be if their child were hurt.

"Not a problem, Ms. West. Mr. Trevino was just minutes down the road and came as soon as he heard."

At that, she went all Exorcist on us, her head snapping back in an almost inhuman way. "What?"

"We called him when we couldn't immediately get in touch with you. He works closely with several of our students here."

I could see Raven struggle with that realization. She wanted to go full-on bitch mode and list all the reasons why I had no business being here for her brother, caring for the kid just like she did. Maybe she wasn't used to people having a genuine interest in helping him, or something. Because I swear, the thought that she wasn't alone—*they* weren't alone—really fucked with her.

She quickly schooled her features, releasing her anger through flared nostrils, before mumbling, "Thank you." I don't know if it was meant for me or Mrs. Jenkins, but I nodded in acquiesce anyway. I'd take any improvement from the eye rolls and death glares.

"Hey, Carol, if he's good to go, think Toby could just take the day? You can email me the rest of the day's assignments, and we'll get them turned in next week." Raven looked shocked that I had spoken up on their behalf, but she didn't stop me. I doubt she wanted to send her little brother back to class in his condition.

"Sure, I think that's a great idea. I'll send them over." Then Mrs. Jenkins went over to lend a few more encouraging words to Toby and a few promising ones to Raven before exiting the room, taking the nurse with her to write an official report. That just left the three of us.

"Hungry?"

Raven cut her eyes at me and barked out a stiff no—of course—but even with his purpling eye covered in an ice pack and his lip twice its size, Toby nodded yes.

"Good. I know just the place for lunch. My treat." This was one of those rare occasions when No actually meant Hell Yes.

"Wait a minute. We're not going anywhere with you." She rose to her feet, her hands already perched onto her hips and that scowl fixed onto her face.

"Ok," I shrugged with nonchalance. "Well, I'm starved and it *is* lunchtime. So if anyone's hungry, and would like to eat the best burger in Queen City, they should probably follow me. I'll just be on my way . . . driving the black Charger." I turned toward the exit, but not before I saw Toby stand and tug on his sister's sleeve.

"What?" she whispered. After a short pause and a reluctant sigh, I heard her reply, "Ok, fine."

#Winning.

"Hey, Trevino," Raven called out, annoyance in her voice. "Wait up."

I waited for them to climb safely into their car, which surprisingly was an old Camaro in pretty stellar condition. The red paint job had seen better days, but the body was intact. I wouldn't be surprised if Raven was into classic cars. And here I was, trying to impress her with my recent modeled Charger with all the bells and whistles. I probably sounded like a straight-up wanker.

"A bar?" she frowned looking up at Dive's marquee. She was still halfway inside her car, refusing to get out, although Toby had already joined me on the sidewalk. "You brought us to a bar?"

"And *grill*," I said, pointing to the signage. "Come on. It's cool, trust me."

"*Trust you.* Hmph," she muttered. But she still got out of the car and shut the door with more force than was necessary, even for the older vehicle.

"Yo, Dom!" CJ called out as soon as we entered. I swear, for a guy that supposedly had a steady cash flow, there was no way he could have a job. He was here every afternoon and late into the night. I got that he was Blaine's cousin and Mick— the former owner's—son, but shit. How the hell did he run a business when he was always boozing at a bar and picking up random broads at bus stops?

We did the guy half-hand slap, half-hug thing before CJ set his sights on Raven, wearing a wolfish grin. "Well, well, well, what do we have here? Don't I know you from some- where?"

"No," Raven snapped, dousing those two letters in enough venom to incapacitate a bull. At least I knew I wasn't the sole recipient of her spite.

"I'm sure I do." Just then, CJ got a view of Toby, partially shielded behind his sister with his head down. "Damn, Dirty. You never told me you were a family man."

Oh shit. Before Raven could step forward and decapitate the poor bastard Game of Thrones style, I wedged myself be- tween them, blocking his view. I was protective . . . of both Toby and Raven . . . and I didn't like what he was insinuating, even if it was harmless. And I damn sure didn't appreciate the way his eyes roamed her body, no doubt imagining what was under her scrubs.

"Shut it down."

"I'm just saying . . ."

"You're not saying shit," I replied, low enough that Toby wouldn't hear, but loud enough that CJ could hear the threat in my voice. "Now shut it. The. Fuck. Down."

I was still staring him down, taking things from playful

to very fucking serious when Blaine came in from the back room, carrying a large box of bottled imports. "Whoa, whoa," he said, setting down the box. "Everything good?"

I looked over at Blaine, the constant voice of reason, the level-headed guy with the patience of a saint, even though he looked more like a sinner with the ink and piercings. I could see the concern on his face, and it immediately made me remember myself and present company. Shit. I was losing my head.

"Yeah, we're good," I nodded, backing off from CJ and shaking off the tension of the moment. "We're just here for lunch. We'll take one of the booths."

I led Raven and Toby farther into Dive, and we slid into our seats just in time to see Blaine smack CJ upside the head as he shrugged his shoulders, struggling to explain himself. I laughed out loud. Luckily, Toby and Raven were seated across from me and didn't catch the exchange.

"What?" Raven asked, her eyes narrowed in suspicion.

"Nothing. Just . . . honestly, he's harmless. Dense, but harmless. Sorry you had to see that."

She brushed off my apology with a shrug and picked up a laminated menu, shielding her face. "It's fine. I deal with guys much worse . . . as you know."

Ouch.

"Yeah, uh, sorry about that too."

When Lidia, one of the waitresses, came over to greet us and take our order, I was thankful for the reprieve from the awkward silence. Trying to talk to Raven was like running full speed into a brick wall over and over again. Her tenacity was unshakable. It made me wonder why the hell I kept trying to break through that stubborn wall of pursed, pink lips, narrowed, blue eyes and clipped, cold responses. Call me persistent. Or maybe insane. Yeah, probably just insane.

"Hey, there, Dom. What can I get y'all?" Lidia smiled, her drawl like a sip of southern sweet tea. Girls in the South had a kind of sweetness that made your teeth hurt. Obviously, Raven was not from around here.

I ordered the special—pulled pork with Mr. Bradley's special Carolina BBQ sauce—and Toby took my suggestion of Dive's famous burger. Raven ordered a chicken sandwich, and even managed to smile when she did it.

Luckily, the food was fast, and I didn't have to keep trying to strike up a conversation that apparently wasn't going to happen.

"Hey, guys," Blaine said in greeting, approaching our table. "Sorry if my cousin caused you any trouble. I hope he didn't ruin your lunch. I'm Blaine, by the way." He looked down at Raven and Toby and flashed a smile. And I swear to God, Raven damn near swooned in her seat. Un-fucking-believable!

"No, not at all," she grinned back, her voice perfectly polite. "I'm Raven, and this is my brother, Toby."

"Good to meet you both. Glad you guys dropped by. Everything good with your meals? How's that burger treating you, man?"

Despite the extra adornments, Blaine was the epitome of class. He didn't even flinch at Toby's bruised face or question me about who they were. He had a way of making everyone around him feel welcomed and accepted. I really hated how much I couldn't hate the guy. But there was no way he could have known that Toby didn't talk. And the protector in me wanted to save him from any undue embarrassment.

"It's fine," I snapped before I realized how completely out of line I must've sounded. "I mean, it's great. Thanks, B. Um, Kam around?"

Blaine shook off my rudeness and answered with a shake of his head. "Appointment. Should be back soon."

Ah. So Kami really was seeing Dr. Cole regularly. It obviously wasn't an OB appointment. No way Blaine was missing one of those.

After Blaine had returned to his station behind the bar, and I had returned to my lunch—feeling like a jackass—I looked up to find that Raven was staring at me. Not with contempt or disgust, but just . . . staring.

"You come here a lot, don't you?"

"Yeah," I shrugged. "It's my Cheers, I guess." Goddamn, that made me sound lonely as hell.

"That guy . . . before . . . he called you Dirty. Why?"

"Uh, nickname. Long story." Not a long story, actually. But I wasn't about to tell her that I had acquired it in high school, along with my reputation for being a young Hugh Hefner. Girls just seemed to flock to me. It wasn't my fault, honest.

"And who's Kam?" Damn. First she doesn't want to talk to me, and now it's 20 questions? Ok. If she wanted to play, I'd play too.

"Best friend."

"*You* actually have friends?"

"Of course. Don't you?"

That question seemed to give her pause, as if she had to think about it long and hard. What person had to think about whether or not they had friends? Shit, between me, Angel and Kami, we were more nuts than Almond Joy, and we still managed to find each other in this big, wide, crazy world.

She shook her head and diverted those magnetic eyes to her food that had been left to grow cold. "I have a job and school. I don't have time for friends."

I wanted to say that was bullshit, but I settled for, "The world is a scary place. Especially when you have to brave it alone."

She looked at me then, dropping the poker face and allowing me see her hand, if only for a moment. "I'm not alone. I have my brother."

I saw her courage and raised her some honesty. "Yeah, I know that. But who has you?"

Chapter 9

Raven

WHO HAS ME?

Shit. I didn't even know how to answer that question.

Truth be told, no one did, and no one had for a very long time. And I not only preferred it that way, I had designed my isolation specifically to keep nosy ass people like Dominic Trevino from delving into my life. Yet and still, he managed to find me. Four billion people in this damn world, and *he* found *me*.

Coming back to Charlotte was a mistake. This wasn't my home anymore, and if it hadn't been for Toby, I would have never returned to the one place that served as the gravesite for every one of my demons. You don't return to the scene of the crime. You run from that shit. You run and you never turn back.

I glanced over at my kid brother, who was pretending to be overly interested in his food. I knew he was listening to every word, probably even siding with this arrogant prick across the table. I could tell he actually liked the guy, which threw a monkey wrench in my quest to completely ice him out. Shit. It wasn't like I could just remove Toby from Helping Hands after our caseworker "suggested" the program. But that didn't mean I had to deal with the guy. Yet, somehow, here we were. Having lunch like one big, happy, fucking family. The man-whore, the mute and the misanthrope. It was like a bad sitcom on the CW.

Honestly, I didn't want to hate him, or anyone else for that matter. I hated playing the role of the bitch; I was tired of shutting out the world. And a long time ago, I was a starry-eyed, naive and optimistic young woman with her whole life ahead of her.

But that all changed in one night. One night that served as the first tumbling domino in a long line of tragedies that completely shattered our world. And the guy that sat across from me, gazing at me with heavy lashed, hazel eyes swirled with green, he was the nudge that tipped that domino, sending our fate into motion.

He just didn't remember it.

Of course he didn't. Fucking narcissistic sluts rarely did keep tally of the lives they'd ruined.

I hated the way he looked at me. I hated that he was so nice to us, and so good with Toby. I wanted to believe he was an evil, despicable person down to his core. Because if he was in fact devoid of all redeeming qualities, it'd make it easier to see past the gorgeous exterior. It'd ensure that I wouldn't feel fucking butterflies flapping around in my gut whenever he was near. Dammit.

The first night I saw him again—sitting at that table at The Pink Kitty, those hooded eyes sliding over glitter-dusted skin and teased hair extensions—I told myself I could do this. I could play it cool long enough to get close to him, play to his wanton desires, and when I had him right where I needed him, I'd do to him what he did to me.

I'd fucking end him.

That was before one very important variable changed all that. Toby.

I wouldn't let him get hurt in all this. He had already been through enough. Selectively mute children needed support and understanding. And after the hell he'd witnessed, he needed stability. He didn't need another crazy ass broad turning his already ravaged life upside down. I was all he had. Hell, he was all *I* had. And I had to do right by him or I could lose him for good.

"Well?" Dominic urged, the intensity in his stare turning my insides into goo. I hate that he had that hold over me. I felt possessed by him, the demon wriggling its way inside my soul and stealing my resistance.

I couldn't say a word in response to his question. I couldn't tell him that I lay awake almost every night, staring at the cracks embedded in the ceiling of my tiny, shoebox apartment until I felt as if it were closing in. Caging me in my own denial and regret, and making me a prisoner of consequence.

So no. No one had me. I was alone, just as he had left me.

"Hey kid, you just about done there?" I turned to ask Toby. He had polished off his burger and most of his fries, as well as two rounds of sweet tea. I didn't even give him a chance to nod or shrug or whatever. I stuffed a hand into my purse, slapped down a twenty and slid out of the booth. "Come on, Toby. Time to go."

He looked disappointed, but he wiped his face and hands and got up anyway. I felt like an asshole, but I couldn't let this . . . this poser . . . continue to pretend to care for one second longer. People like him were incapable of feeling for anyone outside of themselves, no matter how many charity cases they took on.

"Hey, wait up!" I heard Dominic call out once we got outside and were trekking to the car across the lot. I didn't want to do this here, but he just wasn't getting the message. Leave. Us. Alone.

"Why don't you get a good station warmed up for us," I grinned tightly down at Toby, handing him the keys. That was our thing—channel surfing in the car. There weren't many ways for us to communicate, so we did it through music. And since my car was old school, yet legendary, so were the music stations.

The moment he was safely in the passenger seat and occupied with his task, I turned my gaze on Dominic, who was trying to hand back the twenty dollar bill. My face was so tight with rage that it hurt, and my hands were shaking as angry adrenaline pumped through my veins.

"Listen here, jackass. I don't know what your angle is here or why you seem so invested in "helping" us," I spat, demonstrating the air-quotes with my trembling fingers. "But you can drop the act now. I know what the fuck you're about, and it's downright sick that you're walking around here like a fraud . . . like you actually care about Toby. We don't want your fucking help, you understand me? And we damn sure don't want your friendship. So you can take your fancy suits, and your flashy ass car, and the fake smiles, and shove them up your ass. We're fine."

I should have left it at that—I had definitely gotten my point across. But emotion had taken hold, and I couldn't stop the ugly truth from tumbling out, taking with it my fears and insecurities. "You don't know shit about us—you have no idea what it's like. You get to go home everyday to a plush, cushy life with some false sense of satisfaction, feeling like you've done good by the poor, mute kid and his sister. Fuck that, and fuck your charity. Save it for someone who cares."

He looked shocked . . . hurt . . . like I had just zapped him with a taser. Maybe even a bit humiliated that I had pulled his number and called him out on his bullshit. But that look of horror only stayed frozen on his face for a split second before the veil dropped, shielding any weakness that may have been exposed. Because the only thing those enigmatic features displayed after that was fury, rage, and pure disgust.

He opened his mouth to reply, but quickly turned on his heel, mumbling, "Fuck it," as he swiftly strode to his car. But the very second I exhaled, releasing all the frustration . . . the hurt . . . he was right back in front of me, close enough to give me a start, yet far enough not to seem threatening.

"What the fuck do you know about my life?" he spat, his voice so low and menacing that it was only for my ears. "You don't know shit about what I go home to. So no . . . *fuck you.* Fuck you for making snap judgments about shit you have no goddamn clue about. You want to be so selfish to deny that boy the care that he needs? Because you have some personal vendetta against me that I don't even know about? Fine. I'm done. But before you ruin that kid's life with your hatred, think long and hard about what you're doing. You wanna shut out the world and be a bitch, go right on ahead. But don't drag Toby down into your misery. He deserves better than that."

With that, he whipped around and didn't stop until he was inside his car and peeling out of the lot, tires screeching, leaving me with my twenty dollar bill at my feet.

He'd heard me. He'd heard the years of pain and anger in my voice, and it had worked. Dominic Trevino would officially be out of my life. Again.

Chapter 10

Dom

I VIOLATED EVERY TRAFFIC law known to man trying to get to Helping Hands. But when I looked up from the view of road through the frame of my windshield, I realized I hadn't made it back to work. I hadn't even made it home. I was at The Pink Kitty.

It was if my body had known what my soul needed to mend itself from the verbal assault that had left me open and bleeding. Sex was that healing balm for me. And this was exactly the place where I could find it.

None of the dancers here were prostitutes, and I never paid to get laid. Ever. They fucked me because they wanted me. And I fucked them because I needed them. It was an even trade.

Contrary to popular belief, I didn't stick my dick in just anything, and other than Cherri, had only been intimate with two other girls there: Skylar, a hot sophomore at UNC Charlotte, stripping her way through college, and Velvet, a tattooed, purple-haired vixen from England who fucked like a porn star and cursed like a sailor.

Right now, I needed Velvet. If anyone could make me forget the last twenty minutes, Raven's razor-sharp words and myself, it was her.

My legs carried me inside, despite the numbness I felt. I didn't want to be here, but I needed to be. And once I had the soft silkiness and warmth of a woman's skin against me, I'd feel a helluva lot better. Luckily, Velvet was there for a day shift, working the lunch crowd in her usual getup of velvet and chains. Today she wore a cut-out thonged romper that left little to the imagination. And that was fine by me. I was tired of thinking anyway.

"Hey love," she smiled as I approached. Her lips were painted a deep, dark eggplant purple that almost looked black. I'd have the color smeared all over me within the hour, most of it in places invisible to the public.

I didn't waste any time. I didn't have it in me to go through the motions and pretend I was here for anything other than sex. I leaned in close to her ear, letting my lips brush her earlobe in that sensual way I knew would get her hot, and whispered, "Back room in 10." Then I quickly made my way to the bar to slam a shot of tequila.

She was there when I arrived, lounging on a plush loveseat with her heeled boots propped up on the arm. She looked at me with sin gleaming in her heavily lined eyes and gave me a slow, Cheshire grin. "Someone's awfully anxious today."

I was already loosening my tie as I stalked towards her

and said, "Clothes off, boots on and get on your knees."

Velvet didn't waste a second. She slipped out of her one-piece in a swift movement and sank to the floor. The moment I felt her take me into her warm mouth, it was like a thousand pounds had been lifted from my shoulders.

A long time ago, long before I should have, I learned to separate the physical from the emotional and mental. I told myself that just because my young body had been stolen from me and manipulated in ways that would make even the toughest man cry out in agony, I didn't have to feel it. Not deep down inside. I didn't have to accept what was being done to me. So I pretended to be somewhere else. I pretended to *be* someone else. I let my mind drift to thoughts of my parents, imagining what they may have looked like, dreaming about happy smiles and warm hugs and kisses on my cherub-like cheeks. I painted pictures of family vacations at Disney World and barbeques in the backyard. I told myself that we would have a dog named Buddy. Mama would tie bandanas around his neck, and Papa and I would take him for walks and play Frisbee with him at the park.

I had built an imaginary fortress, and in it, nothing could touch me. I was safe. I was happy. And I was loved. That was what I told myself, and that was what I held onto every day since to survive.

As I grew older, and was no longer held captive by the physical pain, I was left to face the emotional hurt that no one could see. I was like a pariah to the family that had taken me in. We were related, but they didn't know me, and what they did know about me was deviant and disgusting. Too awful to talk about. So I suffered silently in my mind until it became necessary to tell myself lies.

Lies like the ones I was telling myself right now.

I want this. I need this.

I'm totally normal.

There's nothing wrong with me.

Being a man means having sex with as many women as possible.

These women desire me because they need me. They love me.

They love me.

She loves me.

It was the only way I could keep doing this. The only way the shame and disgust and self-hatred didn't keep chip-chip-chipping away at the fragments of that broken boy. The boy that had grown up to be a shattered man. The man that couldn't be mended.

Velvet sucked me until I was on the brink of release and for a quick moment, I thought about just getting it over with. But I needed more. I needed that physical connection. I yearned for her touch, her kiss, her smell. It reminded me that I was not like him. I was not what he had hoped I would be. It stated that just because I had been violated, that didn't make me . . . it didn't make different. It didn't make me *gay.* I didn't want that. I wanted *this.*

Spreading those shapely, toned thighs and filling her up until I pulsed in her womb validated me. Every stroke was a confirmation, and the deeper I went, the more whole I felt. But the moment it was over, the moment I pulled out of her, my latex-sheathed cock wet with her gratification, the doubt began to claw its way back in. Telling me that I was dirty—*stained.*

Used. Useless.

She smiled lazily at me, the dark kohl outlining her eyes smudged along the apple of her cheek. I brushed it tenderly with the pad of my thumb and told her she was beautiful.

"Oh, Dom. You're such a sweet gent. Too bloody sweet for this shit," she giggled, looking soft and girlish. I liked her better that way, untarnished by the hardness of life.

"You think so?"

"I know so. Good guys like you shouldn't be fucking strippers in the middle of the day. I mean, I'm not complaining—I can still *feel* you inside me, for crying out loud—but, I don't know. You deserve better."

I winced at her words, and how much I longed for them to be true. She was just feeding me more lies, and I was ingesting them like candy.

Except this one. This one I knew would never be true. Even if it was the one I wished for the most.

"Nah, I don't. They don't call me Dirty for nothing."

Chapter 11

Raven

I'D FUCKED UP. I knew I had. And it was hurting the one person that I couldn't fail.

I knew going off on Dominic would cause a ripple effect. I pissed him off, he pissed me off, and in turn, we would disturb the tiny bit of peace that Toby had found in working with him.

Toby had seen everything, had probably even heard everything. And considering that he hardly looked at me after I got into the car, he agreed with Dominic. He admired the guy. I don't know why, but he had made a genuine connection with him. He actually enjoyed hanging out with him after school, and playing board games. Which was huge, because Toby didn't like anything. I hadn't seen him find pleasure in regular everyday activities for as long as I'd had him in my care. And before that . . . I don't know. I wasn't in his life then. And while part of me wished I had been, I was grateful I escaped the mental anguish that came with being birthed by Adeline West.

I called her Adel because she told me she was too young and too beautiful to be someone's mother. And she was too young and beautiful. Just as she wasn't much of a mother. People called her a free spirit, and free spirits couldn't be contained. My grandparents couldn't, so when she was just fifteen, she flew away from the nest of her childhood home. She literally lived by her own rules, refusing to be bound by laws or social etiquette. Meaning that for most of my young years, I was as wild and free as she was.

I remember her laughing a lot and smiling a lot. I remember singing at the top of our lungs during car rides in her Camaro. My mom was the most badass person in the entire world to me, and I wanted to be just like her. I wanted to be ruled by passion and creativity, and not by other people's perceptions of what was right and decent.

We lived like gypsies for a while, wandering the world in search of beauty, until love grounded us. Gene Christian was the complete polar opposite of Adel—patient, hardworking, level-headed—and he was completely smitten with her. I'd have liked to say that he wooed her, but I think it was the other way around. They both fell fast and hard, and soon our dynamic duo became a trio, and Adel got married. She was happy, so I was happy. And Gene was good to me, providing me with the father figure I had never had. The father figure I never realized I needed.

Gene brought much needed structure to our lives. I couldn't play hooky from school to go swimming at the lake with Adel on hot days. I couldn't have ice cream for dinner or brownies for breakfast. And I actually had a bedtime. I was confused at first, maybe even a bit resistant. But then I realized what a difference those rules made in my overall wellbeing, and I was grateful for his intrusion.

I felt the same way when Toby came along. He was a tiny little thing—barely six pounds—but he was easily the cutest baby I had ever seen. Where I took after my mom with my dark locks and ice blue eyes, Toby looked like his dad. His hair was light brown, as were his eyes. And he seemed to hold a warm tan all year round. My skin was pale, and I was lucky just to pick up a little sun on my cheeks without scorching.

Adel was in love with him instantly, but she still didn't have a maternal bone in her body. She still wanted to sleep all day, and stay up late at night listening to records as she poured over photos in her makeshift black room. She was a self-taught photographer, an artist, and I was enamored by her talent. Even though I was left to the task of caring for a newborn, she was still majestic to me, as most mothers are to their children. We don't know any better at that age.

We lived happily for years, and for some time, Gene was able to tame Adel. He had found a way to tether her to reality long enough to give us a somewhat normal life.

That normalcy lasted until my freshman year in high school. Then it all fell to pieces like the torn remnants of an old photograph.

When Gene left Adel, it was like he took a piece of her soul with her, and that fun-loving, fancy-free woman we had known ceased to exist. On the other side of that carefree attitude was a darkness so deep and vast that even the love of her children could not fill it. She became completely consumed by her grief, as if Gene was all that had ever mattered in her world. It was like we were just accessories, and without him, nothing fit. And even though she blamed me for Gene's departure—rightfully so—it didn't explain why she took her pain and anger out on Toby. Maybe it was because he looked like his father. Or maybe because down to her core, past all the beauty and flightiness, she was a miserable bitch.

And just as I had wished as a child, I was becoming just like her.

I walked into The Pink Kitty Friday night, with a bad attitude and cramps. I was not to be fucked with. I hated working there as it was, but after having words with Dominic, serving drinks to desperate pervs and frat boys seemed even less appealing. Still, the tips were good, especially on the weekend, and we needed the money. A year ago, I only had myself to think about, and could scrape by on part-time photography gigs like weddings, graduations and births. Now, I didn't even have time to take a selfie with my POS phone, let alone pick up my camera to capture something worthwhile.

Passion didn't pay the bills. Art didn't put food on our table. And dreams didn't take care of my kid brother.

So here I was, gearing up to prance around in short shorts that barely sheathed my ass-cheeks and a tank top so tight that you could see the outline of my nipples. Wedge sneakers on my feet because I refused to strut around in platform heels like some streetwalker. What kinda tacky shit was that anyway?

Most of the girls were cool, with the exception of a few chicks that I knew were trash. I could smell it on them—the desperation . . . the jealousy. Mean girls in glittery thongs and edible body butter. They looked down on me like they were superior in some way, like taking their clothes off for a roomful of strangers made them goddesses. I laughed at them and treated them like the clowns that they were. Maybe that was why they hated me so much.

I walked into the dressing room to stow my purse and change into my booty shorts, because quite frankly, I'd rather go outside butt naked than be caught dead in them. It was packed, and it seemed like every girl was working tonight. Great. So not only would I be busting my hump slinging cocktails, I'd also have to deal with some of TPK's resident cunt nuggets. One of them being little Miss Cherri. She looked sweet and innocent on the outside, but the bitch was a slut in sheep's clothing. And I didn't just think that just because I saw her being overly friendly with Dom that one night. She really was a tramp, and I was pretty sure she was turning tricks on the property.

"Ugh. What a waste of a perfectly good pair of jubblies," a familiar British accent sounded behind me. I turned around to a jarring flash of purple hair that belonged to Velvet, my closest friend at The Pink Kitty, before she flopped into the vanity seat beside me. I hadn't been working there long, but Velvet instantly welcomed me with open arms and had insisted we become friends. So we did.

I followed her gaze over the door where Cherri had just arrived. She was a featured dancer which, in her eyes, made her Mariah Carey of the pole. Classy.

"Awesome," I remarked, rolling my eyes.

"She grates my fucking nerves, that one. Good thing I got

laid today. I actually don't feel like stabbing the slag."

"Laid? Oh, do tell." That got my attention and I spun around, my expression begging for more. Shit, my sex life was nonexistent, so I lived vicariously through Velvet who was always willing to share a juicy story.

"Ah, just a friend. Nice guy, actually. Sexy as all hell and fucks like a rock star, good God. I think he fucked me so good, I passed out at one point. And that big, thick knob of his tastes like you're smoking a clove cigarette, I bullshit you not."

"The fuck . . . ?" I managed to spit out before laughing my ass off. Only Velvet would use such a colorful description.

"Seriously! Fucking divine. I just wish he wasn't such a bloody nice, suit-and-tie wanker. A few tatts, maybe a cock piercing, and I could work with him. But he's as straight and narrow as they come. He'd be perfect for you though," she smiled conspiratorially, propping her thigh-high patent leather boots on the vanity counter.

"Um, no thanks. I don't do sloppy seconds," I remarked as I focused on applying eyeliner in the mirror. I rarely wore much makeup during the day, but it was necessary here. I wasn't as talented as Velvet and the rest of the girls, but I knew how to put on eyeliner, mascara, lipstick and a little blush. That was all I could pick up, considering my mother had never taught me.

"Oh, don't be such a fucking prude. It's not like I want to date the guy. But you could."

I just shook my head. Velvet was my friend, yes, but she didn't know about Toby. Nobody did, and I planned to keep it that way. So I couldn't just tell her that I was too busy to date because I was raising a selectively mute preteen.

"Well, suit yourself. You could use a good shagging." She groaned as she climbed to her feet, sore from her day shift. Or maybe it was from the sex. "Ok, I'm completely knackered, love. Think about what I said." Then she pinched my ass and left to go home for the evening.

I sighed heavily as I inspected myself in the mirror. My large baby blues seemed even bigger outlined in black, and my lips looked full and plump painted in red. I would never be bold enough to wear this color outside these walls, but in here, any and everything was game.

As I was tying an apron around my waist, I brushed past Cherri as she was changing into her first getup of the evening—a pair of high-wasted shorts that exposed her butt cheeks and a teeny tiny triangle bikini top adorned with cherries.

"Excuse you," she sneered, in her nice-nasty tone. Men thought it was adorable. Women could hear the fakeness in it with every saccharine-laced syllable.

"Sorry," I mumbled, not meaning it.

"Of course you are. I swear, you'd think a *waitress* would be more coordinated. But I guess anyone off the street could hold a tray of drinks." She looked me up and down, her shiny, glossed pout pursed in distaste. "Or maybe not."

I paused. Counted to ten. Took a deep breath. Anything to keep from snatching this bitch by her red weave and smashing her face into the lockers. I couldn't afford to get fired, and that would surely happen if I disfigured TPK's cash cow. Plus, we had a strict, zero tolerance policy when it came to violence or substance abuse.

Still, the urge to throttle her ass was almost as strong as my need for employment. Pre-Toby, she would had been picking her teeth off the floor. Post-Toby, I had to just deal with it and walk away.

If he could live with Adeline West at her lowest of lows, I could certainly deal with a prissy bitch wearing clear plastic platform heels that she bought at *ho-sale* from Stripper Warehouse.

Do it for Toby, I told myself. *Do what she wouldn't have done.*

Even if that included making amends with Dominic Trevino.

Chapter 12

~~Dom~~ Dirty

IT HAD BEEN ONE of those weekends. Drinking at Dive until the wee hours, snagging a chick at last call, waking up and feeling like shit on top of shit, spread on shit. Warmed over.

By Sunday, my liver felt like a fucking raisin, and every bone in my body ached with exhaustion. Last night had been . . . crazy. I wasn't even sure how I got home. I just know that when I woke up, there was a redhead in my bed, and a brunette on my cock. The redhead was Cherri. The brunette was Alyssa, the elementary school teacher that had adopted the concept of sharing is caring. Fine by me.

I let her suck me off, then I watched through hooded eyes as the girls kissed, their fingers moving between each other's legs. When they were hot and ready, I positioned myself between Cherri's thighs while Alyssa straddled her face. Then we became one, me fucking Cherri, and her fucking Alyssa. It was blissful, erotic, and almost enough to make me stop thinking about Raven. Almost.

Even as I came, I saw her face pinched in that little scowl that was just too cute for me to take seriously. I hated myself for thinking of her fondly after what she had said to me . . . after what she had stirred inside me. It wasn't the rejection that hurt. It was the fact that she actually felt those things about me. She really thought I was some phony, narcissistic asshole that didn't give a rat's ass about Toby or her. And that could not have been further from the truth.

I silently left the room to clean up, taking my time so the girls could slip out with whatever shred of dignity they had left. Unfortunately, they didn't accept the gift, and made themselves at home. I followed the trail of female chatter and laughter, dinging of pots and pans, and the clamor of silverware to the kitchen where I found Alyssa and Cherri cooking. *Cooking.* In *my* kitchen. Wearing *my* clothes.

No. Just . . . No.

"What's going on here?" I asked, my voice carrying over their vibrant conversation.

Cherri spoke up first, twirling on bare feet with a spatula in her hand. "Breakfast, baby," she said, strutting towards me. She raked her fingers over my bare chest and leaned in close. "Hope you're hungry."

"No."

"No? You're not hungry?" She looked disappointed, but I didn't care.

"No, I'm not. And no, you're not fixing breakfast."

She reeled back as if I'd slapped her. "Excuse me?"

"This!" I exclaimed, motioning towards the sizzling skillet and the plate of fresh, fluffy pancakes. "This is over. I don't want breakfast. I want you both to leave."

"But we thought . . ." Alyssa's voice was just a tremor, much softer than her raucous screams in the bedroom.

"Don't think," I deadpanned. "Just leave. Leave now."

I knew I had hurt them—I could see it smudged on their faces along with last night's mascara—but I couldn't care. Caring got me nowhere—that much was obvious.

"Ouch. Rough night?" Angel asked, leaning in the doorframe of the kitchen in nothing more than a long t-shirt. She had to have heard everything. The girls weren't exactly quiet about their grievances as they got dressed.

The front door slammed, rattling the entire apartment. I could still feel quivers in my gut. Or was that guilt?

I shrugged. "Awkward morning."

She sipped coffee from her new favorite mug, it stating:

I'm not always a bitch.

Just kidding.

Go fuck yourself.

I had given it to her this past Christmas, and apparently, it was love at first sight. Novelty coffee mugs were my go-to gift. Between the three of us—well, two of us now—we probably owned over twenty of them. I gave Kami one that was fashioned like a prescription pill bottle, which was more ironic than funny. She was a good sport about it though.

"You're totally bugging out, dude. I told you something was up."

"Whatever." I could feel her eyes on me—and hear the question in her statement—as I turned away to make myself a cup of coffee in the mug that was fashioned as a handgun. Fitting. Angel could tell something was up. The problem with having friends that were your family was that they knew you entirely too well.

"Seriously. There's something you're not telling me. And it isn't that you've been fucking the bootleg Sister Wives either. I can smell it on you . . . you okay?"

I turned and leaned against the counter, waiting for my coffee to brew. "Can we not do this right now? I just got called every kind of prick and asshole in existence, and a few I'm sure they made up just for shits and giggles. I really don't remember paging Dr. Phil."

"Fine, fine. But this emo boy shit has got to stop. God, I feel like I'm rooming with a teenage girl right after she found out that kid left One Direction. What's his name?"

"Zayn."

"Right, Zayn. And I'm going to pretend that you didn't just know his name, because I'd really like to remember you having balls between your legs. I mean, I love vagina. But you'd make a really ugly, hairy girl. Quick—go chug a beer and scratch your nuts."

"You're pretty obsessed with my boys, you know. Could you be switching teams? I mean, I'd be willing to help you test it out. I'm that good of a friend." My eyebrows danced suggestively, causing Angel to make a face.

"Ewww, no thank you. After what you just did with Ginger and Mary Ann? I'd rather bone the Skipper."

We laughed together, and it felt good, serving as a dose of the therapy I so desperately needed. I had been self-medicating for so long that I had become numb to it all. And I wasn't talking about meds.

"Hey, you have plans today?" she asked suddenly, her big blues dancing with excitement.

I shrugged. "Nope. Laundry."

"Ok, stick around." Just as quickly as she'd showed up, she disappeared into her room.

A few hours later, I was taking my second load out of the dryer, and had just finished washing my car. I skipped the gym—I couldn't move even if I wanted to, and I really wanted to avoid bumping into Lauren, or any other chick I had slept with. Just as I was done folding my whites, I heard the front door open, and the rustle of shopping bags.

"Hello?"

I tossed the roll of socks in my hand, and darted out to the hall. Kami stood there, her arms draped with bags, her face glowing like the sun, and her smile bright enough to light the darkest night.

"What are you doing here? And why didn't you call me? You know you shouldn't be carrying all this stuff," I chastised, taking the bags from her and heading towards the kitchen. "Go sit down and put your feet up."

Kami rolled her eyes, completely disregarding my orders and followed behind me. "Angel said I was needed, so here I am. Oh, and quit your worrying. I'm pregnant, not paraplegic." However, she let me put the bags on the table and unload them. Kami looked beautiful, as always, but tired. Her belly was round and protruding, but the rest of her had stayed slim. I had to worry if she was stressing. She tended to lose weight when she was overwhelmed in her life, and with Amanda back in town, I knew she wasn't comfortable.

"Everything good?" *Translation: I'm going to try to respect boundaries and all that other shit, but . . . How are things with Blaine?*

She started rummaging through the bags, pulling out various pints of ice cream, chocolate chips, whipped cream and chocolate syrup. "Good. As good as can be expected."

She was lying to me. "And that means . . . ?"

Kami sighed, pausing in front of the freezer with a pint in each hand. "It means that his ex is a desperate, ruthless bitch who wants him back, and is willing to use not only her body, but a freaking child to get what she wants." She yanked open the freezer drawer, nearly pulling it off with the force of her aggression. "Can you believe that she's trying to say her son—a kid he's never even met—looks up to him as his dad? This child she conceived *while they were married,* that has no idea that Blaine even existed until now, all of a sudden considers *him* as his dad? It is *total fucking bullshit!*"

"Damn." I replied shaking my head. I went over to her, took the ice cream out of her hands before she Hulk-smashed them, and led her to a seat. "Who cares what that crazy loon is saying. Blaine isn't buying it, is he?"

"No," she sighed. "At least I don't think so. He doesn't want to hurt the kid, but they keep popping up—the bar, his uncle's house, *our* house. It's like, enough is enough. When is he going to set her straight and send her packing?"

Standing behind her, I rubbed the tension from her shoulders while she prattled on about Blaine's ex, Amanda. I had only caught a glimpse of the girl, who was pretty enough, but in a more obvious way. She still couldn't hold a candle to Kami.

According to Angel, she was everything Kam was not—out-going, boisterous and overly sexual. And apparently, Angel had given the girl a little advice too. *"Watch it, heifer. You fuck with her, you fuck with me. And don't let the cute face fool you. I will cut a bitch."*

But as it seemed, Amanda hadn't taken the warning, and made it her mission to try to make Kam's life hell. I get that Blaine was trying to be diplomatic about the whole thing, but let's face it—some broads didn't respond to decency and reason. And any chick that would knowingly get herself knocked up while married to another man was devoid of both.

Bottom line: You can't argue with crazy.

"I hate her, Dom. I know that's a strong word, but I do. I hate her." Even though her voice was just a broken whisper, it was enough for Angel to catch as she entered the kitchen.

"Who do we hate?" she said, coming over to kiss Kami's cheek and rub her round belly like it would bring her luck.

"Amanda," I answered for her.

"Oh God. Not that trick again. Dude, seriously, say the word, and I will break my size six stiletto heel in her silicone ass."

I raised a brow at Angel's colorful vernacular and chuckled. The girl was five-foot-nothing and about as threatening as a little pink pixie. But she was dead serious. She would kill for Kami. We both would.

Kam considered her offer for a hot minute before shaking her head. "No. that's not necessary. Tempting, but not necessary."

"What happened to the kid's father?" I asked.

"Gone. Long gone. Back in the day, he and Blaine came to

blows over something unrelated, or so it seemed. Blaine ended up putting the guy in a coma, which led to him . . . having to go away for a while. After he recovered, the guy just disappeared."

"Shit. That's right." I had heard the story before. Amanda used to date that kid—Clark was his name, I think. The guy had a serious temper, and had put his hands on her. Of course, Blaine being the good Samaritan that he is, had defended her honor. But Amanda is as dumb as she is pretty and ended up cheating on B with the same motherfucker that whooped her ass. And after that . . . well, let's just say Blaine was no stranger to the Mecklenburg County jail.

"So after all this time, what would make her come back here?" Angel asked.

"I don't know. She wants something—money probably. Word must've gotten back to her that Blaine has plenty of it."

We decided to put a pin in the Amanda mystery and finish unloading the food, along with enough ice cream and toppings to satisfy an entire sorority with PMS. Kami also picked up one of our favorites—Chipotle. Frozen sweets, big ass burritos . . . she was not playing around.

"Oh my gaaaawd. I love Chipotle," Angel mocked in the most annoying, nasally voice known to man. She did the bit, mimicking the YouTube sensation, every time we indulged in mounds of grilled chicken, black beans and guacamole wrapped in mammoth-sized tortillas. *"Chipotle is mah liiiife."*

I picked up a monstrous, foil-wrapped roll and smiled down at Kami. "Remember these in college? Broke as fuck and hungover. Shit, one of these would last us all day!"

We grabbed our burritos and took them to the living room

to sit cross-legged on the carpet. It was still rough to even be in this space after finding Kami here, nearly dead, less than a year ago. Before she got out of the hospital, we ripped up the carpeting and changed all the furniture and décor. It looked like an entirely different room, but the memory still lingered in the atmosphere. Shit, I couldn't even get the smell of blood out of the walls for weeks. But Kami insisted that we not allow it to have any more power than it had already claimed. She didn't want to give *him* the satisfaction.

"I brought all your favorites," she said, digging through a canvas tote between bites of burrito. "*Transporter* 1 through 56. All the *Fast and Furious* movies, rest in peace, Paul Walker. All 27 *Die Hard*s. Everything Arnold pre-Governator. Take your pick."

"Wait a minute. Chipotle, ice cream and action movies," I mused through a mouthful of cilantro, rice and beans. "What the hell are you two up to?"

As if it were rehearsed, both girls shrugged their little shoulders innocently and said, "Oh nothing." They were both shit actors. Cute as hell, but they weren't fooling anyone.

"Seriously. Did someone die? Are you moving away? Shit, did they cancel *Scandal?*"

"No," Kami assured, touching a hand to my cheek to calm me. "The Gladiators will be back for another season, I swear."

"Then why the hell are you guys acting so . . . nice. Especially *you,*" I glared accusingly at Angel, my eyes narrowed in suspicion. "We've sat here for nearly five minutes, and you haven't compared my dick to a rotten tree trunk or said I smell like gonorrhea-scented Axe body spray. Something's up, and I don't like it."

"Oh, God, you can be such a vagina, I swear," she huffed, rolling her eyes. "Can't I be nice for a fucking change?"

"No."

"Well, maybe I want to now, asshole."

I wasn't buying it. There wasn't enough bite in the "asshole." No conviction. "Thirty seconds to tell me what's up, or I'm marching into your room and sending your favorite dildo down the disposal."

"Oh, please. Give it a rest. You wouldn't dare. You don't have the guts."

"Twenty seconds."

"You're such a hater, you know that? You're probably insanely jealous of that dildo, considering that it makes your dick look like a tiny, tan Tic-Tac."

"Ten seconds."

"You motherfucker. If you touch Tyrone, you are dead. You hear me? I will beat you to fucking death with that big horse dick!"

"Enough already!" Kami interjected, just as I began to rise to my feet. Angel looked like she was on the verge of angry tears. She was really attached to Tyrone. I'd heard her praise it by name more than a few late nights.

I sat back down and picked up my burrito. "Then spill it."

Kami looked at Angel for confirmation, then back to me, her expression stricken with concern. "Angel said you've been having nightmares again. Talking in your sleep . . . screaming." She swallowed then chewed her bottom lip, something she often did when she was pained or conflicted. "Crying."

Shit.

I hadn't told anyone about their reoccurrence. I had always been a rough sleeper. It was impossible to ever close my eyes again without expecting to be woken up in the worst way. And while it was common for the evils of my past to intrude on my dreams, the nightmares had gotten progressively worse. It usually happened when I was stressed or upset about something. But I honestly couldn't think of anything in my life that had changed except . . .

Raven. And Toby.

But that wouldn't be a problem anymore.

"She's been coming in your room at night. Holding you while you sleep and leaving before you wake up. She thought maybe some downtime—just the three of us—would be good for you."

I looked at Angel. Her face was still screwed up, yet her scowl had softened a bit. "On the few nights that you're alone, of course," she mumbled, casting her glance down to her hands knotted in her lap. The girl had a heart as vast and deep as Lake Norman. She just didn't let anyone see it.

I took a deep breath before setting down my food and crawling over to her side of the table. And before she could protest, I wrapped her in my arms and squeezed until I could feel her heart pounding against my chest.

"I love you, muff diver," I muttered before kissing her hair.

"Love you too, McSlurry."

"Awwww," we heard Kami sniffle beside us. "These goddamn hormones. I don't care. I love you both." And with that, she wrapped her tiny arms around both of us, remaining the glue that held us all together.

A few tears and three big ass burritos later, we were

watching something with Bruce Willis that included explo-sions, gunfire and him in a dirty tank top. So we pretty much could have been watching any Bruce Willis movie. A huge tub of popcorn sat on Kami's lap in the middle—although it was dangerously close to the edge and battling her protruding bel-ly—and we were passing around a bowl of ice cream with all the trimmings.

"I meant to ask you," she began, scooping up a dollop of triple fudge ice cream with a piece of popcorn. "What's this about you being in Dive with a woman and her son?"

"Yeah, what's up with that? You get hitched and have a kid without telling us?"

Crap. I'd done well with avoiding their questions. Dive was too crowded for the third degree, and luckily, Angel was busy most evenings. I knew I couldn't keep Raven and Toby a secret forever, and honestly, I didn't want to. I just didn't know how to verbally explain what I was feeling. Not without sounding like a complete idiot.

"The boy is a kid from the center. Selectively mute. Tough upbringing. The girl is his sister, who's also his legal guardian. The mom OD'd last May."

"Oh, that's awful," Kam remarked.

"It is, for sure," Angel agreed. "And I can see why you'd be protective. But it doesn't explain what you were doing with them, especially when you're so adamant about keeping work and your personal life separate. Plus according to CJ, you got all alpha male on him and slapped your dick on the bar when he was just joking around. What's up with that?"

I shook my head and diverted my attention to the TV screen, although I couldn't see a thing. It was ridiculous that

I was still thinking about her. What kinda self-respecting man put himself out there for a chick that clearly wasn't interested? Was I developing some sick masochistic tendency?

Hell no.

"Nothing is up," I muttered, the half-truth sour on my tongue. "She's made it very clear that she wants me to stay away from her and her brother. She's been nothing but rude and nasty towards me since the day we met. I'm passing their case along to another mentor tomorrow morning."

"I'm so sorry, sweetie," Kami whispered, giving my thigh a squeeze.

"Still doesn't explain why you pissed on CJ's leg."

I cut my eyes at Angel, knowing exactly what she was doing. That trollop was annoyingly perceptive.

"She hates me. End of story."

"But you don't hate her." She wasn't even trying to mask her amusement at my discontent.

"No." I sighed and scrubbed a hand over my face. "I don't. And it doesn't help that I've grown attached to the kid. I worry about him. He's not . . . he's not like other boys. And yeah, she's a bitch to me, but still, for some reason, I'm attracted to her. Not even because she's gorgeous. I'm attracted to . . . shit. I don't even know. Are you happy now?"

"Not yet." Angel reached over to grab a handful of popcorn, tossing a few pieces in her mouth. "Maybe it's because she's probably the one person you want but can't have."

"Or maybe it's because she's the one person you need," Kami offered with a small smile.

"I don't know," I shrugged. "I can't push it further. I can't put myself out there like that. Not anymore. Not if I want to avoid getting hurt."

Again, Kami squeezed my thigh, as if relaying a secret. "I understand you want to guard your heart, and I would too. But maybe . . . maybe that's exactly what she's doing too. Pushing you away to keep from getting hurt. When people do things like that, it's because they've felt real pain. The type of pain that slices down to the bone. The kind not even time can erase. And they're afraid of feeling it again."

I let her words hang in there like fragrant smoke, contemplating the reasons why Raven would feel the need to shield herself from me. I'd always expected that there had been more to her story—to their story. But even after checking with their caseworker, I couldn't turn up any indication of abuse. Still, I knew something—or someone—had changed her. No one was born a cynical, distrusting shrew. They were forced that way by experience.

Chapter 13

Raven

IF IT WERE POSSIBLE for a mute kid to give you the silent treatment, that was exactly what I received from Toby all weekend.

So by Monday, I knew that I had to swallow my pride, pull on my big girl panties, and make shit right. Which was the complete opposite of my plan when it came to dealing with Dominic Trevino.

I had a late morning break between classes, so I jumped in my car and headed over to Helping Hands. I sat in the parking lot a good five minutes, giving myself a mental pep talk. I had to admit that it wasn't that I just didn't want to see him. A part of me was a little embarrassed. I'd acted irrationally, and I'd said things I shouldn't have said. And even if he did deserve it—and he did—it wasn't the time or the place. Bitch or not, I do have a lick of sense.

I stared at myself in the mirror, feeling as haggard as I looked. My hair was in a messy bun, tendrils of dark hair spilling every which way, and I looked tired. Luckily, I had my meager little makeup kit with me that I used for work nights. By the time I finished slapping on some mascara and lipgloss and had smoothed my hair into a neat ponytail, I felt marginally better about the task at hand.

His office door was half open—as it always was—but I couldn't see him through the crack. I knocked anyway. I wanted to at least attempt to be on my best behavior.

"Come in," he answered from inside. I took a deep breath and pushed open the door to find him at his desk, eyes diverted to a stack of files in front of him. He was so engrossed in whatever he was reading that he hadn't realized I was there.

I shuffled from foot to foot nervously to avoid locking up with nerves. I didn't even know why I was so freaked out about being here in his office, but the thought that we were somewhat alone . . . together . . . it just brought it all back.

The pain.

The rejection.

The anger.

The lust.

There once was a time when I wanted Dominic Trevino more than anything on this earth. I saw him in my dreams at night, and woke up with the sun to see him in the morning. And he couldn't even remember my fucking face.

I get it. I was pathetic then. But that didn't excuse his total disregard for others. If I had been one of those skanks that wore eight pounds of makeup and low-rise jeans with my thong hanging out, would he have remembered me? Or if I spread my thighs at the drop of a dime or offered to blow him in the bathroom, would I have been worthy enough for him to know my name?

No. Of course not.

But even as I stood before him, fidgeting with anxiety, I couldn't find the strength to truly hate him. He was so beautiful, even after all this time. And the way his presence filled the tiny room, suffocating me with a mix of his intoxicating scent and heady pheromones, I found myself even more drawn to him. I was that pathetic girl again, and if anything, it made me hate myself.

As if just remembering that he had a visitor, he looked up, pinning me with those dark-lashed, hazel-green eyes. He seemed shocked at first, but the light in his expression quickly dimmed. He narrowed his gaze, and his mouth—oh God that mouth—puckered into a frown.

"Can I help you?" But it didn't sound like a question. Unless that question was, *"What the fuck do you want?"*

"We need to talk."

His brows raised in mock amusement. "Oh really? I thought we did in the parking lot, when you accused me of being a narcissist and a phony. Did you forget something? Need to accuse me of being a puppy murderer too?"

"Dom . . ." The word was out before I could stop it. Only his friends and loved ones called him that. And I was neither. Right? "Look, about the other day . . ."

He lifted a hand, cutting me off from saying any more and climbed to his feet. "Don't bother. I've heard enough. You'll be happy to know that I've set Toby up with another mentor here, and I will do my best to stay away from him as much as possible. I've also heard from the school regarding the attack on Friday. They have a few leads and have questioned students, but I'm sure you already know that. I let them know that they shouldn't contact me in the future with anything involving Toby, seeing as you've denied my help. However, his new mentor will follow up on anything further, and will contact you. Anything else?"

Whatever I had meant to say before coming in here quickly dissolved on my tongue, leaving the bitter aftertaste of embarrassment. He was still angry at me. My words had cut him deeper than I thought. And in turn, he was lashing out.

But not only that, he was leaving Toby. He didn't realize it, but he was. And that kid had been acquainted with abandonment for far too long.

"He needs you."

"What?" he sneered, still fuming.

"Toby . . . you can't leave him. He needs you."

Dom shook his head, but I could see that my admission had cooled him. "Apparently, he doesn't. You said so yourself."

"I was wrong." There. I said it. Without the use of a curse or scowl, I might add.

"You were wrong?" He half snorted, half laughed and shook his head. His expression was . . . odd, to say the least. As if it hadn't dawned on him that he was right all along, and that he really wasn't all the hateful things I had spewed at him in my rage. "You were wrong."

"I was. I shouldn't have said those things to you." I took a step forward, so I was just a few feet away from the front of his desk. I was sincere, and I wanted him to see it. And if it took me showing some humility and vulnerability to get him to keep working with Toby, then so be it. "It was completely out of line to speak to you like that and accuse you of those horrible things. I don't think that about you, and neither does Toby. He likes you, and you need to know that's not easy for him. So please . . . you can hate me all you want. You can think I'm the biggest bitch this side of the Mason-Dixon. But please don't let my brother suffer for my mistake. He's suffered enough."

I sucked in a breath and waited for his reaction. Would he laugh? Would he humiliate me further by telling me to get out?

"Dammit," he muttered before running a hand through his jet-black hair.

Breath held, heart racing, I watched as he came around his desk, closing the distance between us in just a few long strides. He still moved like a man who had full control of his body. As if he were comfortable in his skin. I envied that.

Dominic stopped directly in front of me, leaving just inches between the tips of our shoes. It was closer than what was socially acceptable, but I didn't step back. I didn't retreat. Not then, and not now.

"I could never hate you, Raven. Believe me, I tried."

His words were confusing, but his face wore a mask of resignation. As if he had given up—or given in—to whatever friction crackled between us. On one hand, it seemed like animosity. But on the other, there was sexual tension so thick you could slice it with a knife. I'd always felt it when in his company. And maybe Dom was feeling it too, after all this time.

"Knock, knock, handsome!" a feminine, melodic voice trilled from behind us. I spun around just in time to see a beautiful brunette step past the threshold of the door. She looked at

Dom, then me, then back to Dom. And as realization dawned on her, her mouth dropped into an *O* and her almond-shaped eyes grew twice in size. "Oh, uh . . . ? Oh!"

"Kami," Dom said, stepping around me as if I were nothing more than a pothole in his path. Embarrassed, my gaze dropped from the gorgeous woman's stunned expression, and that's when I realized . . .

She was pregnant.

Pregnant.

And considering the way Dom rushed to her side and slipped an arm around her waist protectively . . . lovingly . . . it was his baby.

Oh my God. Of course. *Of course,* he would have a stunningly exotic girlfriend. And, *of course,* she would be pregnant with his child. And, *of course,* I would be standing here, looking like a fucking idiot in duck-printed scrubs, thinking that there were remnants of the past still lingering between Dom and me.

I heard him say, "Kami this is Raven. And Raven, this is—" But I didn't let him get any further.

"Yeah. Got it," I mumbled through a tightly clenched jaw. I was hurt. I was humiliated. I was pissed at myself for doing this shit once again! What the fuck is wrong with me? What the fuck is wrong with *him?* Why be so adamant about being around me if he had a girlfriend and a baby on the way this entire time? Oh, shit, could they actually be married? Ugh! That lying, cheating sack of shit!

I collected what was left of my fractured pride and brushed past them both, not allowing my legs to stop moving until I was revving the engine of my car.

Fuck Dominic Trevino. And I didn't mean that in the way I wanted merely two minutes ago.

Chapter 14

Dom

"WHAT WAS THAT ABOUT?" Kami asked, still watching the door just as I was.

"I have no idea." And I didn't. I was just about to introduce Raven to Kam, maybe even invite her to join our standing Monday lunch date. I thought the two would really hit it off. Apparently not.

"She seems . . ." I knew what she was thinking. *Bitchy. Rude. Stuck up.* " . . . pretty." Good ol' Kam. Never one to make a snap judgment.

"Yeah. She's usually much . . ." Well, shit. I couldn't say *nicer.* Raven was never nice. Tolerant, yes. Decent, ok. But nice? " . . . more . . . polite?" Even I didn't sound convinced.

"Don't you think you should go after her? You may be able to catch her if you run."

Me? Run after a chick? My name attached to that action

didn't even make sense.

"When have you ever known me to run after a woman?"

"Well, I've never seen you this intrigued by one you weren't sleeping with either. Funny how that works, huh?" she smirked.

Funny as fuck.

"Nah," I said, shaking my head. "Just let her go."

If only it were that easy.

Today's lunch special was BBQ brisket, and Mr. Bradley did not disappoint. We sat at the bar, shooting the shit with Blaine and CJ and listed potential names for Baby Jacobs, who was due for an appearance in only a couple short months. The proud parents had chosen to be surprised with the rest of us over the baby's sex, so we had to be prepared for whenever he or she arrived.

"Dude, you totally have to give your kid a badass name, especially if it's a boy," CJ said between unceremoniously shoving French fries into his mouth. "I'm talking Falcon or Hawk. Or how about Bullet?"

We all just stared, waiting for him to break into guffaws and say, *"Just kidding!"* But he was dead ass serious.

"We're having a baby," Blaine deadpanned. "Not a super-hero."

"How do *you* know?" CJ retorted with a straight face.

Blaine returned his unflinching stare for a good ten seconds before turning to the rest of us and announcing, "Well, that settles it. CJ is officially out of the running for god-parent."

"Thank God," Kami mumbled beside me before swiping

the pickle spear off my plate. She had already eaten hers and the three extra Mr. Bradley had added to her plate.

"If it's a boy, how about the name Luke?" Blaine offered as he fulfilled a drink order brought over by Lidia.

Kami cringed. "Luke? As in Luke Skywalker? All I can imagine is Star Wars."

"Then how about Wyatt? Or Liam?"

She made another face, expressing her disapproval at Blaine's suggestions. "I don't know."

"Well, is there a name you *do* like?" he asked, exasperation in his tone.

"Well . . . I like the name Blaine," Kam said meekly, her smile sweet and sheepish. "What if we named him after you?"

The pride on B's face shone like rainbow rays of prismatic sunlight. "Blaine Junior," he mused, testing it out. "Yeah, I like that too."

"We can call him BJ for short!" his crude cousin added with boisterous laughter. Leave it up to CJ to turn baby names into something dirty. I was starting to believe that the guy genuinely lacked an *Off* switch.

"Um, make that Blaine-the-second," Kami corrected over CJ's howls. Of course, he was the only one laughing at his dumb joke.

Moments later, Angel strolled through the doors of Dive, her face somber and her eyes wet with watered down mascara. She leaned in to kiss both me and Kami on the cheek before sliding into the stool beside me. I reached over and took her hand, telling her that I was here for her, whatever the problem may be, but I wouldn't press. And I damn sure wouldn't ask her to rehash whatever shit was on her brain in a bar. I didn't have to. The three of us were bonded so deeply, that those social nuances weren't necessary. She knew I would be waiting to listen when she was ready. And if she needed me to be a punching bag, I could do that too.

"Hey, I was thinking," Kami said, switching everyone's focus off Angel's evident pain. "I want us to start getting together for dinner every week. We can take turns hosting and cooking. So since it's my idea, how about dinner this Sunday? I'll cook!"

As soon as the words were out of her mouth, she was bombarded by appreciative hoots and hollers and even a few requests. Kami was half Filipina, and the girl could cook her ass off. Not just Asian food either. She was just a natural in the kitchen. A few weeks ago, she had even suggested a special once-a-week that would feature her famous pancit, adobo and lumpia. But of course, Blaine wouldn't allow it right now. He wanted her off her feet as much as possible.

"Great! So it's settled. Dinner this Sunday."

"Aw, aren't y'all sweet. Looks like my invite must've gotten lost in the mail."

Damn.

And we almost made it through an entire meal.

We turned around to face Amanda, each of us displaying our irritation without remorse. She seemed not to see it, or maybe she just didn't care. I had decided on the latter. Any person that delusional and self-absorbed didn't give a damn about aggravating others.

"But I have plans anyway," she explained, as if someone had asked her a fucking question. "I ran into Kenneth Walters today. Remember him from high school, Blaine baby?

Anyway, he's a successful lawyer now, driving around in a Maserati, and he looks amazing. He asked me to join him on a Sunday drive down to this little vineyard he frequents. The weather is supposed to be beautiful, and you know I love to ride with the top down."

Barf.

"Good for you," Blaine stated flatly, not meaning any of it.

"I told him it may not be a good idea, considering you and him weren't the best of friends, and given our relationship—"

"There is no relationship," he corrected, his tone clipped.

Amanda waved it off with a chuckle before twisting a lock of hair between her fingers. She wanted to believe it was a flirty move, but it was actually a sign of insecurity. "You know what I mean. Anyway, he assured me that you wouldn't mind, considering that he was once very, *very* good friends with Miss Kami here. Isn't that cute."

The smugness in her over-tanned face was the icing on the shit-filled cake that she had just served Kam. I was seething mad, and considering the heat I felt from both Angel and Kami on either side of me, I knew that shit was about to go down.

Blaine wasn't taking the bait. "And your point?"

"Oh, just thought that was interesting, is all. Someone like him with someone like her." She flipped her hair on the word *her,* which looked every bit like a dismissal.

"Someone like her?" Angel sneered, her voice eerily calm. Oh fuck. I knew exactly what that meant. And considering she was already in a mood, this would not end well for poor, personality-stunted Amanda. "What the fuck do you mean, *someone like her?* Someone kind? Beautiful? Compassionate? Because you are fucking right that some pretentious dick-knuckle like Kenneth "Minute Man" Walters has no fucking business with a girl as amazing as Kami Duvall. Just ask *Blaine baby* over here. Obviously, *he* likes it. And that's why he's putting a ring on it."

Amanda reeled back like Angel had just slapped the taste out of her mouth. *"What?"*

"What?" Kami gasped, just as stunned.

My eyes darted from her to Angel, who had her hand clasped over her mouth, and then to Blaine, who was frozen in place, his eyes as wide as his mouth.

"Daaaaaamn!" CJ howled, slapping his hand on the bar. It served as the war cry that set all hell loose.

"You didn't hear that!" Angel trilled at the same time Kami said, "I didn't hear that!"

Amanda demanded an explanation for Angel's heinous claim, as if someone here actually gave a fuck enough to even remember she was still standing here. CJ continued to laugh his ass off. And I turned to a pale white Blaine to apologize on Angel's behalf.

I felt horrible. This was not how he wanted that news to come out. He had been waiting for the right time, and that time could not occur as long as Amanda was still sniffing around, trying to proposition him at every turn. She had tried it with me the first time I saw her, hoping to get him jealous, but I quickly shut her down, letting her know where my loyalties lie.

"Dammit," Blaine snapped, before throwing a dishtowel at CJ to shut him up. "You cover the bar." When he looked at Kami next, his gaze softened immediately. He extended his palm to her. "And you . . . come with me."

Tentatively, Kami rose to her feet and slowly walked to the half door on the side of the bar. Blaine met her there and ushered her to the back room. They needed privacy, and as much as I wanted to stick around to find out if Blaine would officially pop the question, I needed to get WikiLeaks Cassidy out of here before she got another bout of verbal diarrhea. I pulled out a few bills and slapped them on the counter.

"CJ, tell her I'll call her later." I didn't have to specify *her.*

Then I slid off the stool and went to stand before Amanda, a mocking grin on my face. "Your open case with social services . . . interesting. I happen to be tight with most of the staff over there. Be careful. All it takes is a phone call . . ."

I didn't even wait to witness the horror. I just grabbed Angel and got the hell out of there.

"Open case? Social services?" she asked as soon as we burst through the door.

I shook my head. "I was bluffing." Just as I had bluffed with Raven. I had never passed Toby on to another mentor. But she didn't need to know that. "But considering she didn't refute, it tells me that she has one. Hopefully that'll be the motivation she needs to quit coming around."

"Genius, Trevino," Angel mused, wrapping an arm around my shoulders. "You're a fucking genius."

"And you're a fucking Chatty Cathy. Seriously, Ang?"

"I know, I know," she groaned, smacking her forehead. "Shit, I wasn't even thinking. I fucked up."

"You did. But your ass-chewing is going to have to wait. Some of us have jobs to get to." I leaned over and pressed my lips to the soft skin of her cheek, tasting the salty remains of tears. "We'll talk tonight, but I have an errand to run after work. Think you can meet me?"

"Sure. Where?"

I ignored her question and simply said, "Bring singles."

Judging by the wicked gleam in her eye, no further explanation was necessary.

Chapter 15

Raven

YOU'D THINK MOFOS HAD better things to do on a Monday night than be holed up in a strip club. But nope. They were here—which was why I was here—balancing a tray of drinks while wearing something I'd probably wear to the beach. And to top it all off, I was still reeling from the news of Dominic being very taken by his very pregnant girlfriend/wife/significant other/what-the-fuck-ever. So as usual, I was in a mood. But at least Toby was back to not hating me, so that was a plus. Actually, it was the only thing that was keeping me going at this point, and the reason why I put up with this bullshit job.

I never wanted to work in a strip club, but being a student by day and raising a kid meant that my options were limited. And say what you want, but pervy guys were good tippers. So I did what I had to do to pay the bills, even if it did make me feel like I had bathed in the sweat, spooge and shimmery body oil every night.

"Hey, love. What's up?" Velvet greeted me, as I loaded my tray with beers for a table full of guys in suits. They looked nice enough on the outside but had been way inappropriate. I had had to slap a few hands already.

"Nothing much," I sighed before nodding at the table in question. "Dickhead alert."

Velvet turned around to catch one of them pretending to deep throat an invisible cock. His friends cracked up like it was comedic genius and not something baby pricks did in middle school. She shook her head and looked back at me with a frown. "Did you tell Tiny?" Tiny was one of our bouncers, and at 6'7 and pushing 300 pounds, he was anything but tiny.

"Nah. They're just assholes. Hopefully, they'll drink their bottled piss and go home to their wives soon."

"Well, if they keep bothering you, don't put up with that shit. You know Tiny will have them shitting themselves in a heartbeat. It's been a while since he's had a good barney."

I smiled and shook my head. "You Brits and your verbiage."

"Well, *this* Brit is going to set you up this weekend. You need a date, love. I love you, but you get pissier and pissier every day."

"Not this again," I groaned, hoisting the tray on my shoulder. "I am not going out on a date with a guy you've slept with. That is just skeevy as hell."

"It's not like that! Honest!"

I rolled my eyes and peered over at the table of guys who stared back expectantly, thirsty for both the beer and the opportunity to harass me some more. "Look, we'll talk about this later. The longer I stand here and stall, the more those idiots will ogle me from across the club."

"Ok. But we *will* talk about it." Then she pecked me on the cheek before slinking towards the exit, hips swinging.

I braced myself before scurrying over to the table, eager to get it over with. As I expected, the guys started in on me as soon as I got in earshot. I didn't get it—they had a whole club-full of naked, available tits to stare at. Tits that *wanted* their attention. So why were they ogling mine? I mean, they were pretty decent tits, but they were nothing like the huge racks on display.

"About time, sweetheart. I was getting so thirsty, my tongue had gone dry. Wanna feel?" one especially slurry douchenozzle shouted over the pulsing rhythms of Rihanna.

His equally fuck nut friend looked me up and down, licking his chops. "Aw, Kenneth. She looks like the type that would know how to wet it for you. Aren't you, darlin'?"

I ignored it. They wanted me to react. It would have served as entertainment for them. Instead, I simply distributed their beers, a tight, manufactured smile on my face. As I was leaning forward to place a bottle in front one of the morons, I felt a hand sneak up my bare thigh. Instantly, I flinched, and the bottle slipped out of my hand and toppled over onto the table, its foamy contents splashing onto the lap of the jerk off who had called me *Darlin'* in that mocking, southern drawl.

"Fucking hell! Watch it!"

"I'm so sorry," I said, trying to bite back a smile, as I sopped up the mess with the extra napkins stuffed in my apron. "Here. Let me go get a towel."

I took my sweet ass time getting back to them, even taking a detour to check on my other tables. When I arrived, I could feel the drunken agitation in their stares, crawling all over me with a mix of both hate and lust. They hated me because I had purposely made them wait, and they knew it. Yet, that did nothing to cloud their lust.

"Took you long enough," Mr. Wet Crotch snapped, snatching the towel from me to dry his soiled pants. I couldn't contain my sly grin. It was hard enough to keep from laughing in his sour-pussed face. He would have been handsome if it weren't for his personality and the fact that he was rotten to his core. I could tell he was one of those men that felt he was superior to everyone, and a person's worth was determined by their paycheck. So to him, I was nothing, not even worth the simplest of courtesies.

"Something funny?" he grumbled. His words were icy daggers, but his eyes still took me in and devoured me like the sweetest sin. He was drunk, but not drunk enough not to know what he was doing, which was trying to intentionally make me uncomfortable. Men like him thrived on the fear and discord of others.

"Not at all," I answered, unwilling to give him the satisfaction of looking him in the eye as I worked to dry the table.

"No. You do. You think ruining a four hundred dollar suit is funny, don't you?"

"No. I find it hilarious that you feel the need to tell me how much that ugly ass suit costs. Do you carry the receipt around with you?" I couldn't help it. I couldn't stop the next words from leaving my tongue. I was possessed by anger at his arrogance and annoyance at being mentally undressed as he tried to chastise me like an errant child. I had no problem with assholes. But the pretentious, entitled ones? I had a zero tolerance policy when it came to that specific brand.

His boys cracked up at his expense, and he was less than thrilled at being the butt of my joke. Something told me that he had been the butt of many jokes with that attitude, mostly behind his back.

"You think you're funny, don't you? You think you're a fucking comedian." He turned to the guy next to him and gave him a nudge. "Hey, Kenny, would you look at that? Standup comedy with our lap dances. The bitches here are multi-talented."

I flinched at the derogatory name, not because I had never been called a bitch before, and not because I didn't believe I was one. But because this fucker did not earn the right—the privilege—of calling me that. He didn't know shit about me. And truth be told, he hadn't seen the bitch in me. Not yet.

"Multi-talented, yes. Bitches, no. But considering your IQ would seem to match your dick size," I gestured at his beer-soaked crotch, "I can see how that would be hard for you to discern. Don't worry. I'll color you a nice picture later so you can understand. Ok, sweetie?"

Raucous laughter, accompanied by a few knee slaps, shook the small, rickety table where they sat. I knew I was playing with fire; this guy was about to blow a gasket. But it felt to good to let off a little steam. I had plenty of it, and I was just getting started.

"You have a smart mouth. A pretty, smart, disrespectful mouth. But you look like you need something to fill it. I'd be happy to shut you up, darlin.'"

"No, thanks. I just ate. But I'll let you know if I need a toothpick."

Satisfied, I spun around to get back to my other more amenable customers, when a hand shot out and gripped my wrist, spinning me around. "No so fast. You gave me the comedy bit. Now I want the rest." He tried to pull me into his lap, his rough grip tightening around my wrist, his nails cutting into my skin. His other hand grabbed hold of my waist.

I struggled, telling him to back the fuck off, but before I could align myself with his balls and crush them like grapes with my knee, I was being tugged out of his grasp and whipped behind a steel-hard back and iron shoulders. And then there was the crunch of bone grating against bone and the wet slice of flesh. I smelled blood immediately, but it didn't freak me out. Even aside from being a CNA, I'd seen Tiny crack many a skull during my short time here. Naked chicks and liquor seemed to bring the worst out in people.

But this was not Tiny. I knew it the minute he touched me and electric fire shot up my arm, leaving a lasting burn that settled deep within tissue and muscle, quietly kindling. The man in front of me was undoubtedly muscular and broad, although a bit shorter. And he wasn't bald with piercings up and down his ear lobes. And, instead of Tiny's usual tight tee, he wore a grey suit, much like the one I had seen earlier today.

"Hands off, motherfucker," Dom seethed, the ire in his voice pretty damn scary. Scarier than I had ever heard it. I thought I had seen him angry; I thought I had felt the brunt of his wrath. I was wrong.

"Easy, now," one of the jackholes—Kenny, his friend called him—said, his palms up in surrender. "Hey, Dom, you know me. This was just a misunderstanding."

"The only misunderstanding I see is your punk-ass friend not understanding what the word *No* means." He bent in closer to the man that was now sprawled out in his seat, blood gushing from his nose. "Touch her, or anyone else in this club again, and you'll be choking on your own fucking teeth. Do you understand that? Is that easy enough for you to comprehend?"

But the asshole wasn't done. Instead of apologizing or merely staying silent to keep blood from dripping inside his mouth, he spewed, "Fuck you, man! Do you know who the fuck I am? You couldn't even shine my shoes, you fucking wet back!"

Oh shit.

Did he just . . . ? No, he did not just go there.

Pressed against his back, I could feel every tight tendon prepare to strike. But just as Dom launched his body at that sick fuck, Tiny was knocking me out of the way and pulling him back. I bumped into a cute blonde in head-to-toe pink, who looked just as vicious and ready to brawl as Dom. She didn't even register me or my stumble, just kept spitting insults and threats, her small fists balled in front of her. I should've known she'd be with him. She didn't recognize me, thank God. She looked different from the last time I saw her, but that wasn't saying much. I did too. Angel had always been scrappy, and I was positive that if it came to (more) blows, she would be fighting right along beside him.

Tiny somehow got Dom out of the bar—kicking and screaming for him to let him go, no doubt—and me and the blonde followed closely behind them.

"What the hell is going on out here?" Sal, the general manager, shouted as we burst through the front entrance doors. The sun was setting, casting a warm amber haze on everything around us. I'd always loved the effect—nature's sepia through the lens of the heart. But right now, I couldn't afford to enjoy. Not when chaos clouded the splendor of the sky.

Everyone answered at once, Dom telling him that I was being harassed, his blonde companion coming to his defense, Tiny telling what little he saw—Dom attacking the prick, and me trying to give my account. It was a clusterfuck of epic proportions, only made worse when Cherri came rushing out, dramatic as ever, scurrying to Dom's side.

"Oh my God, I came as soon as I heard," she trilled, cradling his face in her hands. "What happened, baby?"

At that point, I just shut up. There was no mistaking that there was something intimate between Dom and Cherri. *Baby?* And not even the usual connotation she used for customers. She really meant it. She really *felt* it.

How vast was this dude's stable? I didn't know, but I knew for a fact that I wouldn't be a part of it.

"All right, enough!" Sal demanded, silencing the fray. He turned to Dominic and leveled his stare with him, scrubbing a hand on the back of his neck. "Dom, I want you to tell me why you just attacked a customer without provocation. And make it fast."

He told Sal about walking into the club with Angel. They had just come through the doors when that asshole caught a case of butthurt, and decided to grab me. He damn near flew to the other end of the club to get to me and rip me out of that jerk's grasp. And that was it. Just one punch to get him off me, and a warning not to try that shit again.

Sal's face softened with understanding as he listened, but by the end of the story, he was heated again. He turned to Tiny, and I swear that beast of a man was reduced to three feet by the Joe Pesci doppleganger. "And where the hell were you, while some animal was feeling up one of our girls?"

"Uh, um . . . bathroom, sir." Was I seeing this right? Tiny was . . . scared? I guess the rumors were true about how well-connected Sal's family was.

"Bathroom, huh?" He shook his head and heaved a sigh, pinching the bridge of his nose. "Thank you, Dom. I owe you one. Rest assured, that asshole will be dealt with," he said, extending a hand to shake his hand. Then he turned his hard, squinty stare on Tiny. "We'll deal with this. For now, come with me, so I can clean up this steaming pile of shit."

The second Tiny and Sal were gone, Cherri was fused to Dom like the front of his suit was lined with fly tape. "Oh my God, did he hurt you at all? Are you ok?"

He wore something that could only be defined as a cringe-smile. "I'm fine. Raven is the one you should be worried about."

When his gaze touched me, the discomfort in his expression receded, and he looked almost . . . fearful. Not of me, but maybe for me. I don't know what I read in those hazel-green eyes, but it touched me.

I lived in that moment for only a breath before Cherri was looking me up and down, sucking her teeth in disdain. "She looks okay to me. That guy probably did her a favor," she scoffed, turning her attention back to Dom. "Why are you and Angel here? Looking for me?" The lust in her gaze was so blatant, I thought the poor boy's clothes would melt off under her stare.

He nodded before looking over at Angel, who gave him an encouraging smile.

"Actually, yes. We need to talk."

Then all eyes were on me, watching, waiting expectantly. That was my cue to get back inside and leave them alone. That was the evidence I needed to remind me that I wasn't wanted. He hadn't come to see me. He had come to see Cherri.

"Thanks . . . for that," I mumbled before turning toward the entrance doors. They were only a few yards away, but they seemed like miles. I couldn't escape fast enough.

"Hey Raven," I heard Dom call out behind me.

I stopped and looked over my shoulder tentatively. "Yeah?"

A good five seconds ticked by as I watched him struggle with his words. "Be careful."

Something told me that those two words meant more to him than I would ever truly know.

Chapter 16

Dom

IFLEXED MY BRUISED knuckles for the 80th time today, not only to work out the soreness caused by my fist crushing that sick fuck's nasal cavity, but to ensure I didn't forget the horror I felt when I saw Raven fighting him off her. In my mind, time stood still, locked in a frozen cesspool of disgust and dread. But in reality, it all happened before my brain even had time to process it. I just reacted. And while it brought the foulest of feelings right to the surface, I was glad I was there. God only knows what would have happened if I hadn't been there.

Work was torturous, my only reprieve provided by Toby's arrival after his tutoring session. We played an oldie but goodie: Connect Four. He really seemed to enjoy board games, so I had made it a point to pick up some new ones, sticking to the ones that didn't require verbal communication. I never wanted him to feel alienated by his muteness. He had his reasons for not talking, and putting him in a position that made him feel cornered, would only further isolate him.

Today, I asked about school and shared my favorite movies with him. He listened, nodded, and even smiled at one point. Surprisingly, he picked up his pencil and pad and listed all the movies he hadn't seen, but wanted to.

"Oh, man. You haven't seen Rocky?"

He shook his head and shrugged.

"We might have to fix that. Rocky is a bonafide classic!" I went on to quote one of my favorite parts animatedly. "*Aaaaadriiiiiaaaaan!* Rocky!"

That time, Toby almost laughed. I could see he wanted to, but it was almost as if he had forgotten how. My heart sank. This kid—this little boy—probably hadn't laughed in so long, that it had become foreign to him. No child deserves that. No one should have to live in the prison of their despair. Even inmates received time in the sunlight.

I wanted to ask him if his sister was okay, but I figured she hadn't told him what had happened. I wasn't naïve to the fact that Raven probably had guys groping her left and right. It still didn't make it any easier to witness.

When 5pm rolled around, Toby gathered his things and began making his way to the door.

"Hey, shouldn't you wait for your sister?"

He shook his head, and leaned over to scribble, "She told me to meet her in the front."

I frowned and he added, "It's fine. Must mean she's starting to trust both of us."

I thought about that. Yeah. Maybe. Maybe her reasons for

coming inside last week was to ensure he was in good hands, which is what any decent guardian would do. I was happy to earn her trust, but I had been looking forward to seeing her. I wanted to make sure she wasn't afraid of me. Yeah, I had gotten a bit intense last night, and I didn't take acts of violence lightly. Or maybe she was angry. Maybe that man's hands were welcome on her body, and I had screwed things up for her.

I walked Toby to the door and kept a safe distance away, as I watched him jump into his sister's beat-up Camaro. She ruffled his hair and smiled at him, the gesture so completely unguarded . . . warm even. I had never seen her like that and, if possible, she seemed even more beautiful to me—ugly scrubs, messy hair and all.

After they disappeared down the road and out of my sight, I suddenly felt lonely. I knew they didn't have much, but they had each other. They were a family. And no amount of raunchy hook ups would ever compare to that bond. That was why I had gone to The Pink Kitty last night—to break things off with Cherri. But first I apologized for kicking her out the morning after our romp with Alyssa. I hated when people were upset with me. I couldn't help it. Hurting people unintentionally was something I could never learn to be passive about, especially towards women. It was like something inside me didn't just want to please people, it wanted people to love me. It was ridiculous, but it was true. And if I didn't make things right, the guilt would drown me.

Like most evenings, I headed to Dive for a few beers before heading home. I scanned the Happy Hour crowd in hopes of seeing Alyssa—she also deserved an apology—but she wasn't there. I wouldn't be surprised if she never showed her face again. And that was shitty, considering it was because of me.

"Well, if it isn't the stripper vigilante," CJ started in as soon as I grabbed my spot at the bar. "So do you apprehend people with garters and blind them with glitter glue? Is your costume a bedazzled thong and nipple tassel launchers?"

"Ha Ha. Hilarious." Angel and her big mouth. I was more than thankful when Blaine came over with an ice-cold beer for me without me even having to ask.

"You know I'm just screwin' with ya, man," CJ laughed, slapping me on the back. "More than anything, I'm pissed you didn't invite us along!"

"Keep me out of it," Blaine commented. "Strip clubs are the last place I need to be."

I raised my beer in salute, giving Blaine the respect he deserved. He was a good guy through and through.

"*Shit,* that's the *first* place I need to be! Better than hanging out with lame fuckers all the time. Maybe we should make Ladies Night clothing optional. Even do like an amateur stripper contest. Boy, this place would make a damn killing!"

Blaine looked at his cousin like he had the word MORON stamped on his forehead. "Yeah. Let me just run that by Kami."

"Run what by Kami?"

Speak of the devil, Kami appeared from out of the crowd, followed by Angel, the pair stopping to stand beside us. Kam waited expectantly, her green eyes darting to our guilt-ridden faces.

"Uh . . . um," Blaine stammered.

"Blaine wanted to ask you if we could do an amateur stripper night and make Ladies Night clothing optional," CJ prattled off before anyone had the chance to stop him. That awkward second of silence following his tirade was deafening, everyone completely motionless in mock horror.

"What?" That one word from Kami's lips was cool and calm. A contrast to Angel's, "Oh, hell no!"

"Wait, I didn't say that," Blaine insisted, raising his inked hands. "That was CJ's dumb ass."

CJ was firm in his resolve, and even had the balls to shake his head with the same face of disappointment that both girls wore. "You said you would run it by her. Don't try to pin that shit on me, dude."

I was doubled over in laughter, too overcome with hilarity to intervene and set the record straight. Plus I was kinda enjoying the fact that Mr. Perfect wasn't looking so perfect right now. I was being petty. Sue me.

"So this is what you want? And somewhere in your distorted mind, you thought I would be okay with this?" Kami questioned.

Blaine leaned across the bar, and leveled his sincere stare with hers, blocking out Angel's accusatory curses, CJ's phony concern, and my deep belly laughter. "Babe, seriously. Does that sound like something I would want? Or does it have CJ's stupidity stamped all over it? There is nothing a stripper could do for me. There is no other woman on this earth that could drive me crazy and make me feel like the luckiest man alive all in the same breath. You know that."

She took a minute to consider his words before looking at me to verification. I shook my head and tipped it to Blaine, putting him out of his misery. "Wasn't him. All CJ."

Right on cue, as if it were choreographed, both Kami

and Angel smacked CJ upside the head, as we had witnessed Blaine do a million times whenever his cousin was acting like an even bigger dumbass than usual. He hardly even flinched. He was probably numb to the assault.

"Oh come on! You know it'd be popular. Am I right, Angel? I know you can appreciate a room full of tits."

Angel shook her head at him, but replied, "I can. But not everyone should be walking around naked. Could you imagine Mick?"

We all cringed and shivered at the mental image of CJ's dad sporting a beer gut, three inches of body hair, and nothing else.

"Blech," CJ grimaced. "Good point."

I hung out for another hour or so before I had exhausted every excuse to stay. I was fidgety, on edge and unfocused. My friends kept trying to pull me into their conversations, but I was too preoccupied to engage. I didn't want to be there, but I didn't want to go home. And the only place I wanted to be, I assumed I wasn't welcomed.

I couldn't take it anymore. I couldn't keep denying where my heart and mind were. I was just going through the motions for my friends at this point. And that wasn't being fair to me or them. I knew what I wanted was stupid, reckless, and could potentially get me fired, but I just had to try. I wouldn't be able to sleep tonight if I didn't, and that was hard enough as it was.

"Hey, I'll catch you guys later," I said suddenly, sliding off the barstool.

"Where are you going?" Angel frowned. Everyone I cared about was already here, and if I had a "date," I wouldn't need to deal with her until much later. Plus she knew I was trying to slow down and get my head together.

"Something I need to do."

She looked perplexed, but let the issue drop, just as I had done for her the day before, and looked to Kami who nodded her head. We all had a lot to discuss—Angel's tears yesterday . . . Kami's impending doom, I mean, nuptials. But this wasn't the time or the place.

"Be careful," is all she said, mimicking the very same words I'd offered to Raven last night. Little did she know that I wasn't warning her against men in the club. I was warning her against me. Hell, maybe I was warning myself.

Chapter 17

Raven

I DIDN'T GET A lot of free time to spend with Toby, so when I did, I tried to make it count. My days off were devoted to him and to trying to instill some normalcy in his life. So on Tuesdays, I cooked. It wasn't anything grand, and honestly, I wasn't great at it, but it was something he liked helping me with, and something I enjoyed.

There wasn't much Toby and I could bond over. We hadn't had the same upbringing, and for that, I harbored a lot of guilt. Nobody knew how bad it had become after I had left. Nobody could have known that our mother would self-destruct after Gene left. But that didn't ease the feelings of regret and sorrow for my little brother. I'd always feel responsible for what she'd done, yet selfishly glad that she hadn't done it to me.

"Pass me the oregano, kid," I instructed, stirring the pot of marinara simmering on the stove. It was jarred sauce, but we always spruced it up with our own special touches. To-night we had sat at my crappy little dining room table and rolled the craziest looking meatballs in existence. Some were big, some were small. Some were shaped into our initials that would probably look like turds once they were cooked. But we did it together, and we had fun. Toby smiled, and that was all that mattered.

"You know what this needs? Hot sauce!"

Toby nodded enthusiastically and grabbed the bottle of Texas Pete. We ate it with everything, I swear. On scrambled eggs, in tomato soup that we dipped grilled cheese in, atop the crunchy potato chip layer of tuna casserole . . . One time I had dared him to put it on his ice cream. After much coaxing, he did, but quickly spit it out, scraping the cold, spicy goop of his tongue with a spoon.

"So I heard from your vice principal today," I remarked casually. I didn't want to put him on defense and cause him to shut down. "She said they're positive they've found those punks that cornered you. So if you were worried or anything . . . you don't have to be anymore. They're handling it."

He shrugged and focused on tearing lettuce for the sal-ad. It wasn't much of a response, but it confirmed that he had heard me. I'd take what I could get.

I had just taken the meatballs out of the oven and popped in a cookie sheet of garlic bread when there was a knock at the door. Simultaneously, we frowned, the shared dimple be-tween our brows deepening, and looked at the closed door. We weren't expecting company, and it wasn't as if either one of us had a social life. Factor in the less than desirable neigh-borhood, and I was already reaching for the aluminum bat that was situated against the coat rack with the umbrellas, and Toby was moving toward the back of the apartment.

I looked out the peephole, but it was too dark to see much more than a shadowy figure. The hall light was out again. Usually, I didn't get home from work until after 2 in the morning. Making my way to the door was like walking on a minefield wearing a blindfold every night.

"Who is it?" I called out, letting my voice drop a few octaves as if it would make me seem more intimidating. I sounded ridiculous, and had probably just relayed that we were alone to whoever was on the other side of the door.

"Um, uh . . ." a muffled male voice stammered. "Dominic . . . Dominic Trevino?"

Dominic? What the . . . ?

I clicked open the locks and tentatively cracked open the door. There he was, sheathed in shadows and twilight that spilled in from the hall's single, dingy window. He wore a white, button-up shirt with the sleeves pushed up to his elbows, and black slacks. His hair was black silk styled in its usual *un-styled* way. He wore a pensive expression, as if he were still trying to understand what had brought him to my doorstep. I was sporting something similar. "What are you doing here? Is something wrong?"

He shoved his hands in his pockets nervously, the light spilling from my apartment highlighting the frustration on his brow. "No, nothing's wrong. I just . . ."

I had the feeling that there was no simple answer for why he was here. That even if he knew it somewhere subconsciously, it wasn't possible for him to verbalize it. Maybe it was the same impulse that had made me spew my guts in his office yesterday. Whatever the case may have been, I saved us both the awkwardness and invited him in.

Toby was already at the door, looking at Dom with expectation and wonder. And . . . joy. It was like his best friend had just come over for a sleepover. And that made me both relieved and sad for him.

"Hey, my man," he said, greeting Toby with a fist bump, which he happily returned. Then he was looking at me with guarded eyes. "Sorry to drop in on you like this. I just . . . I wanted to see that you were ok."

I crossed my arms in front of my chest and squinted at him. "How did you get my address?"

"Your file . . . shoot, I hope you don't mind. I didn't mean to overstep."

I heaved out an irritated sigh through tight lips. "Well, you did. Is there something you need?" Having him in my space was too real for me. In public, I could keep him at arm's length. I could turn and walk away, even flip him the bird, if need be. But he was here . . . in my home. And suddenly, the place seemed even tinier, and my furnishings even shabbier. Judging by the way he dressed and the car he drove, he probably didn't come to this side of town often. So it made sense for him to spit out what must've been so dire that it couldn't wait until tomorrow, and get back to where he came from.

"I, uh, wanted to check on you. We didn't get the chance to talk once—"

"Once I was dismissed because you were there to see Cherri."

He looked stunned at the bite in my words, and I was more than embarrassed for coming off as a jealous (non) girlfriend, but I didn't back down. I gave him an expectant smirk, daring him to lie about last night, yet secretly praying that he'd say it wasn't true. That he didn't give Cherri more ammunition to deem me weak and hopeless. That he wouldn't confirm that he had zero interest in me. I mean, I wouldn't care anyway. He had a girlfriend. Girl*friends,* for Christ's sake. I just wanted him to want me for the sole pleasure of being able to shoot him down.

I watched a million shades of discomfort and regret flash across his face before Toby put him out of his misery and handed him a note scribbled on one of the dozens of notepads we kept around the apartment.

Can you stay for dinner?
"Oh, um, sorry, man. I don't think . . ."

Toby snatched the notepad out of Dom's hands before he could think of a good reason and quickly started writing another one. He tore it off and handed it to him, his pen ready to shoot down any further excuses.

Do you like spaghetti?
"Sure, I do. It's just . . ."
Have you eaten dinner already?
"No. Not yet."
Then stay. Please.

Dominic looked to me for help, but I had none to offer him. Toby wanted this. Maybe he needed this. It had been hard for him to bond with anyone, and God only knew how lonely he had been before our mother died. I couldn't deny him this one wish, especially since he never asked for anything.

"Fine," I huffed. "Dinner's almost ready. You two can set the table while I finish up. I'm about to burn the rolls."

Dom nodded his thanks. It seemed like he was just as adamant about making the kid happy.

As I pulled the bread out of the oven, I watched with stunned eyes as Toby grabbed Dominic's hand and pulled him toward the drawer where kept the silverware. He rarely touched anybody, even me. The first few times I tried to hug him, he clammed up and his body went rigid. I had made it a point not to invade his space since then. But here he was, casually touching this guy that he barely knew. Shit, Dominic was a stranger to him! I didn't know whether to be suspicious or grateful that he had finally bonded with someone.

I decided to let go of my skepticism just for one night. Tomorrow I could be a nagging harpy. Tonight, I would be what Toby deserved.

"Four plates?" Dom questioned, looking at the dishes in Toby's hands. He looked around warily. "Are you expecting someone else?"

I shook my head. "No. The fourth is for Mrs. Ralston in the unit next door. She keeps an eye on Toby while I'm at work. In return, I cook for her a couple nights a week and help her around her apartment. Toby can take care of himself, and he has . . . before. But she's an elderly widow, and I think she just enjoys the company."

He nodded at my unintentionally long explanation and watched in silence as I made Mrs. Ralston's plate. Then Toby got her key from the hook and took it over to her while I watched him.

"He's a great kid. Thanks for letting me stay," Dom whispered, sending a shiver down my spine. I hadn't noticed how close he was to me. He was also watching Toby, leaving a mere hairsbreadth of space between us. I could sneeze and be in his arms.

"Yeah, he is. So I appreciate that you're decent to him. I'm sure this is the last place you want to be."

Dom snorted a chuckle, causing the hardness of his chest to press against my back. Oh dear Lord. "Actually, I couldn't imagine being anywhere else."

I turned to look at him over my shoulder, searching his face for any sign that I had misheard those words. But he just stared back, those hazel-green eyes completely clear and sober. As if he actually *meant* it.

The closing of Mrs. Ralston's door brought us both back to reality, and Dom quickly stepped aside, giving Toby room to reenter, and putting a full three feet of space between us. I hated that I noticed. I hated that it bugged me even more.

"Ok, let's eat," I announced, brushing past him to tend to the pot of spaghetti. No more doe-eyed looks. No more talk about his reasons for being here. I needed to keep my hands busy and my focus on hating him. Or pretending to hate him.

The three of us sat down at the rickety, old table that I'd scored at a yard sale, and dug in. After a few minutes of silent chewing, Dom made a sound in his throat and said, "This is really good, Raven."

"Thanks. Old family recipe." I shot Toby a wink, and he replied with a small smile. Huh. He was on a roll.

"Really?" Dom mused, twirling a bite around his fork. "I didn't know your family's name was Ragu."

"Prego. Get it right."

We shared a chuckle, shifting the mood into something much less suffocating. I could do this. I could be casual. No sweat.

"It's Spaghetti Tuesday. Toby and I always make spaghetti on Tuesdays."

"Why spaghetti?" he replied, stabbing a deformed meatball. He didn't seem to mind.

"Never got into Taco Tuesday. Hate tacos."

"You hate tacos?" he grumbled around a mouthful of ground meat and sauce. He quickly grabbed his soda to wash it down, and tried again. "You hate tacos? How can anybody hate tacos?"

I shrugged. "I just do."

"Like, is there a specific type of taco you hate? Or you hate them all?"

I shrugged again. "I don't know. I just hate the whole meat and veggies and condiments thrown inside a tortilla mechanism. It's like handheld chaos."

"Dear God, woman," he said shaking his head. "It's like you aren't even human. Soon you're going to tell me that you go around kicking kittens for sport."

"You never know. The night's still young," I jibed, smiling genuinely. Oh yeah. I could totally do this. I was *killing* casual.

We finished our plates, Dom quizzing me on all the stuff I liked versus all the stuff I hated. Then he would ask Toby his opinion on things, who watched us with rapt attention, so intrigued by the exchange that one would think he was viewing a tennis match. After he and Dom cleared the table—Dom's idea—I told Toby to go get his shower and get ready for bed. This left me alone with Dominic Trevino, the one person I *shouldn't* be alone with.

"These are great," he said studying the framed prints situated on almost every flat surface and wall. He picked up one of my favorites—a black and white picture of a homeless man huddled in the corner of a storefront, sharing his meager meal with his dog. He was covered in grime, his clothing mere shreds. Yet he was giving what little he had for the sake of love and companionship. I envied that.

"Local photographer?"

"Yup," I answered, grinning. Oh God, I was grinning.

"Really? Who? This artist has an incredible eye."

"Me."

The look of utter disbelief and admiration on his face was one I wished I could capture and hang on my wall. "Seriously? You're a photographer?"

"I wouldn't say that," I said, moving beside him to get a better look at the photo in his hands. "I used to wish to be one a long time ago. But life has a funny way of happening."

"That's crazy. My best friend says that. *Life happens.*"

"It does."

He nodded, but his expression turned somber. "Sometimes I wish it would happen less."

"But isn't that what we wish for? To live in the moment? To seize the unknown? If everything happened as we planned, our experiences wouldn't define us. We wouldn't know how to embrace the good, because we would never know the bad. We would never be able to accept true happiness, because pain would be foreign. And I want to know happiness one day. Don't you?"

I didn't know how we came here. How we found ourselves at this juncture, sharing a piece of honesty just as that homeless man shared his sandwich. Dom had revealed just a shard of himself to me, and, in return, I did the same. Now we were even. Now we were connected.

Needing the space and the time to think, I excused myself to check on Toby, who was already in his tiny, twin bed. The ghost of a smile remained on his face as he closed his eyes and turned on his side. He'd had a happy day. He would wake up tomorrow morning, and the sun would shine a little brighter, and his cereal would taste a little better. And maybe, he would begin to believe that life, in general, could be better.

When I returned to our small living room, I allowed myself a moment to watch Dom gaze at the photo that meant the most to me. I had kept it all this time, and no matter what it represented, I refused to see anything but beauty and innocence.

"Cute kids," he remarked when I stepped beside him. "Who are they?"

"Me and the kid." I had a devastating haircut with a severe bang and wore fuchsia overalls. Toby was just a plump, roly poly bundle of baby, his gummy grin almost too cute to stand. I kept it to remind us both that he was happy once, and to give him hope that he could be happy again.

"Who shot the picture?" I knew the question was coming. I had armed myself with the answer the moment I saw him looking at the photo. That way, it wouldn't hurt as much.

"My mother."

There. One more little thread of truth. I just wasn't sure if I was done giving them away, offering these fragments of me that would eventually reveal who I was and ruin everything.

Tonight, I can be free. I told myself. *Tomorrow . . . back*

153

in the cage I go.

"You mind if I show you something?"

I was already grabbing my camera bag before he could respond.

Chapter 18

Dom

THOUGHT FOR SURE that Raven would slam the door in my face when I showed up uninvited. No sane person would do that, especially one that wanted to remain employed. But I guess it was true when it came to matters of the heart. They made you dumb as fuck. Dumb and happy.

"Where are we going?" I asked, as she locked the front door, securing Toby safely inside. She said she wanted to show me something, but I didn't expect us to leave.

"You'll see."

I followed her down the dark hallway and to the decrepit elevator. I had taken the stairs to her place—no way was I going to trust that dinosaur—but she didn't bat an eyelash at the steel box of death. So, neither would I.

We rode up to the top, me trying my damnedest to avoid gripping the filthy railing or wondering what the hell that sticky substance was on the floor. Then there was a short stair-way and a door that led to the roof. The moment we stepped onto the gravel, I paused.

"You didn't bring me up here so you could push me off, right?" My expression was dubious; my heart was hammering out of my chest.

"No, silly," she replied, waving me off. "If I wanted to kill you, I'd take you down to the basement. Fifty-five gallon drum, some sodium hydroxide. Much cleaner."

I was still frozen in the doorway when she busted out laughing. "Dude! Seriously, I will not kill you! Come on!"

I followed her on shaky legs as she picked a spot for us to sit near the ledge. That explained the blanket she had stashed under her arm before we left. For a second, my mind was headed straight to the gutter. Hell, maybe it still was.

"Look," she gasped, breathing in the breathtaking view of Charlotte's bright city lights against the indigo backdrop. Mountains of glass and steel and concrete that had been erect-ed in an urban jungle, twinkled like fallen stars. From here, ev-erything looked bigger, scarier, yet exhilaration surged inside me. It was odd, seeing the city like this. I knew these streets like the back of my hand. Yet, from here, I felt like a stranger.

I hadn't noticed that Raven was taking pictures, until I heard the whir of her camera. I watched her work, mesmerized at the way she moved along the ledge, eager to catch it all, encasing this moment together in immortality. She was happy like this—I could see it. It was a side of her that I had never known existed.

"I've probably got a million photos from this vantage point, but every one seems different." Then she turned to me and snapped a picture before I could object. "See? Now you're mine."

She flinched right after she said it, but just went back to capturing the city lights. I didn't want her to take it back either.

"If you had 24 hours to live, what would you do?" she asked, her back facing me.

"I don't know." I didn't. That was the honest-to-God truth. "I never thought about it."

"Then think about it."

I did as she instructed, but kept coming back to the same conclusion. "Uh, honestly? Have sex . . . ?"

I could almost visualize her rolling her eyes. "Ugh. Lame. And extremely cliché." She turned around and came back to the blanket to stuff her camera back in her bag. Then she returned to the ledge. "I would try to rent a small plane and see as many places as I could before I kicked the bucket."

"Who would pilot it?"

"Me, of course."

"You fly planes?"

"No. But I will . . . one day. Maybe. There's just too much world to see."

In an act of sheer lunacy, she carefully stepped onto the ledge, balancing herself with arms outstretched.

"Whoa. Get down from there." I was on my feet in a flash, slowly moving toward her as to not spook her. "Seriously, that's dangerous."

"Danger is my middle name," she retorted, smiling.

"For real. The cement on that doesn't look stable." Another inch. Shit, what was this girl thinking?

"Nonsense. I've done this a dozen times. I'm good, promise."

"Alone? Are you crazy?" I let out a frustrated groan. "But what if you fall?"

""*Oh, but my darling, what if I fly?*"" She looked at me, conviction and serenity burning in those big, blue eyes, her version of the popular Erin Hanson quote still lingering on her tongue. I could only stare back and long to taste that freedom . . . that fire.

Something passed between us then—an unspoken truce, yes—but something more. Something bigger than the both of us.

I reached for her, and she took my hand, letting me pull her into the safety net of my arms. I only had the pleasure of holding onto her—this feral, beautiful creature—for just a moment, before she was already spinning away, jet-black hair dancing in the night breeze.

Then something both mortifying and unfortunate happened. I tripped. Over my own two feet, taking her down with me as an innocent bystander.

She let out a squeal as I reached out for aid and accidently grabbed her breast in the process. The gravel bit into our skin when we hit the rooftop floor, although I tried to absorb most of the impact with my back. We had somehow ended up chest to chest, face to face, like we'd been transported into one of those cliché chick flicks Kam and Angel liked to watch. But there was nothing staged or scripted about what was happening between us. The way she looked into my eyes—those blue depths flaring with some unnamed emotion—it was inevitably real. I felt every bit of it as if I was reenacting the story of my life.

I didn't think. I didn't pause to consider the ramifications of crossing that invisible threshold. I leaned forward and kissed her, acting in a haze of lust and adrenaline. I pulled her body closer to mine, pressed mine into hers. Tried to taste and feel every bit of her. My hands roamed the soft expanse of her curves, kneaded the mound of her ass and teasing the skin at the edge of her sweatshirt. Just that little patch of skin had me growing in my slacks, and I surged upwards, wanting her to feel it. Wanting her to feel what she did to me. She made a garbled noise in the back of her throat, which only spurred me on. I wanted to make her moan. I wanted to make her scream. I didn't care if we were on the rooftop, exposed to prying eyes. I wanted the stars to watch in envy as I made her mine.

It only felt like mere seconds had passed when her warmth and weight were stolen from me. Ravenous, I reached for her, drawing her back to me, but she jerked away with a scream.

"What are you doing?" she gasped, scrambling from her place against my chest.

"I thought . . ." I thought she wanted it. I thought she wanted *me*. I was sure she did.

"You thought you had permission to kiss me? To *touch* me? What the fuck were you trying to do?"

Permission? Oh God . . . Did she think I was pushing—*forcing*—myself on her?

"No, of course not," I explained, jumping to my feet.

"How dare you touch me like that. Who the hell do you think you are?" Raven hugged her body tight, almost dissolving into her loose sweatshirt. "You don't get to do that to me. You don't get to hurt me. I don't want . . ."

She didn't finish her thought, but I knew what came next.

She didn't want me. My kiss, my touch, had been unwelcome. I was an intruder . . . a trespasser to her body. And that realization pierced deep inside me, straight to my center. I felt dizzy, the blood whooshing inside my head so loudly that the noise of the city below us became muffled. She was saying something . . . asking me something . . . but I couldn't hear her. I couldn't look at her. I was too overcome with my own revulsion.

"I . . . I'm sorry," I stammered, my voice hoarse. I was going to pass out if I didn't get out of here. And if I did . . . she wouldn't understand. She couldn't possibly be able to comprehend the level of self-hatred I harbored. Or the pain of rejection that brought every insecurity, every fear, right to the surface.

I swallowed around the knot in my throat and began to stagger past her, struggling to escape the darkness of dread that had begun to eclipse my vision. "I have to go. I have to go," I kept repeating, desperate to put some distance between us.

"Wait! You don't have to . . . ."

"I have to go."

I didn't look back. I didn't say goodbye. I just forced myself down flight after flight of stairs, frantically trying to get away. I hadn't meant to offend her, but I had.

Oh, God. Had I hurt her? Had something so small and insignificant as a kiss been a gross violation?

The moment I reached my car, I locked the doors and tried to disappear inside myself, hoping the shame couldn't touch what it could not see.

Chapter 19

Raven

I STOOD THERE ON the rooftop for at least five good minutes before moving again. Before breathing again.

I couldn't tell you what had happened. First, we were talking, laughing, playing around, and then I was on top of him, and he was kissing me. *Groping* me. And I just . . . snapped. I had been in that very situation before, and I knew what it felt like to be wanted by Dominic Trevino. Just as I knew what it felt like to be abandoned by him. Left vulnerable, bare and alone. It was true—there was nothing like being touched by him. The only thing that was comparable to that level of insanity was being rejected by him.

I knew he was gone, so I took my time getting back to my apartment. I could still smell his scent hanging in the air, could see his thumbprint tattooed on the glass picture frame of one of the photos. While I'd had my reservations about allowing him in my humble space before, now everything seemed shabbier, and the lights seemed dimmer. It went back to being just walls and paint and junk.

I didn't see him the next afternoon when I picked up Toby from Helping Hands, or the afternoon after that. Apparently, Dominic hadn't shown up for work, which made something twist in my gut, and Toby was worried that he may have been sick. I didn't know what to tell him, considering that wasn't really the case. I couldn't—wouldn't—reveal what had transpired between us. I couldn't go there without telling my truth, and that was out of the question. My anger and hatred had covered me like a security blanket for the past seven years, and taking it off would leave me naked and exposed. Again.

Thursday night at The Pink Kitty was unusually slow, affording me too much time to think. The only bright side was the fact that Velvet was working the evening shift. I hadn't seen her since Monday, and since Sal had sent me home early after the "incident" to diffuse the situation, I hadn't had the chance to talk to her about what went down. Word was, the toolbag had threatened to sue the club, stating I had led him on, even asked him for it, when he was unjustly attacked by some thug. Sal didn't believe a word of it, but also didn't want the heat surrounding the establishment, so he took care of it. Neither one of us was sure what *took care of it* meant, but we hoped the jackass wouldn't come around anymore.

"Shit, I wish I could've been here, love. I would've throttled the bloody wanker on his pasty arse," she said, twirling a violet lock around her finger. Tonight she wore a black and purple plaid skirt, a white shirt that covered her arms but not much else, and black-framed reading glasses. She was playing the role of preppy goth girl and slaying it.

"It's fine, don't worry about it," I replied, waving it off before rushing off to deliver an order. When I returned, she was still at the bar. I dropped off the ticket in my hand and started loading my tray again.

"However, I heard you met my friend," she beamed, placing a whiskey sour on my tray.

"Your friend?"

"Yeah. Remember . . . my mate with the golden cock. The one that makes me all quivery inside. The guy that shagged me so good, I very nearly fainted."

"I got the point, V."

"Well, he saved me the awkward introduction, apparently."

"How so?"

I turned to tend to my tables, and she was right on my heels. "Your rescuer, you twit! Was that purely coincidence, or do you know him from somewhere?"

I paused so abruptly that she ended up running into my back, causing the drinks to slosh all over my tray. "What did you say?"

"Dominic? Better known as Dirty Dom? He's the guy I was telling you about. Don't you know him?"

Dirty Dom? Dom was fucking Velvet too?

I couldn't believe what I was hearing. How the hell could a guy who had more lovers/girlfriends/fuck buddies stashed around than Hugh Hefner, have had time to eat crappy spaghetti and meatballs at my crappy table, and allow me to carry on about my silly hobby on the rooftop of my crappy apartment building? Obviously, his hope was to make me just another bunny on the ranch, but that didn't explain his reaction. He was remorseful for kissing me—fearful even. Seeing the look of horror on his face actually had made me feel sorry for the guy. So it didn't make sense that he was so . . . generous . . . with his body in one breath, yet so sensitive with his heart the next. A guy as promiscuous as he wouldn't give a damn about kissing someone like me.

"No. I don't know him." I said, resuming my walk to a tableful of thirsty, faceless customers. "I don't know him at all."

Chapter 20

Dom

I was just shy of thirteen the first time I experimented with my sexuality.

Naturally, I'd always had questions about who I was . . . what I was . . . but I had no one to guide me through the confusion. And honestly, I didn't want anyone. I couldn't relay the terror, the shame, to another living soul.

The state had taken me out of my uncle's house after he'd been arrested, and I'd been placed in a group home until they could find a reliable family member to take me in. It was positively hellish, but it was an upgrade from going to sleep in my own blood and filth every night.

I was smaller than I should've been at that age after years of malnourishment. It wasn't that my uncle wouldn't feed me. I was just too sick with fear and revulsion to keep food down, sometimes for weeks at a time. On the outside, everything seemed normal. I had clean clothes, a roof over my head, and I went to school. But the truth was, I was being held captive by a rapist that I happened to love, as sick as it was.

Many of the boys at the home taunted me or ignored me all together. However, there was one boy . . . Matthew. He didn't just talk to me; he was nice to me. The other boys called him a sissy . . . a fag, they said. I didn't know to care. I was just glad that one person didn't see me as a pariah.

Matthew was sixteen and had more privileges than me. He went out every evening and sometimes didn't come home until very late. I asked him what he was doing when he left. He told me he was seeing friends. I asked him if I could come too, but he told me that these *friends* were older, and wanted to hang out with him alone.

Some nights, Matthew came home with treats for me— candy, soda, cookies. Sometimes even wine coolers. They tasted sweet and made me feel more mature when I drank them, so I asked Matthew to bring me more. I asked him where he got all this stuff—he didn't have a job, yet always had money. He told me he got it from friends.

It was late one night, and everyone had already gone to bed. Matthew snuck in with a six-pack of hard lemonade and a bag of Swedish Fish. We shared them both, tenting a blanket over our heads and whispering under the light of his cell phone, another gift from a friend.

"You ever kissed a girl?" Matthew asked when we were two Mike's in.

I didn't know where that question came from. We never talked about girls, although I would have expected it, considering his age. I just shook my head, telling him the truth.

"You want to?"

I shrugged. Did I? I should, right? But I didn't know if I *could*.

"You ever have sex before?"

I stayed silent at first. I knew there had been rumors about what had landed me here. Since I was a minor, my case was kept quiet. However, nothing was ever really a secret. And even though my file was supposed to be sealed, I didn't doubt that there had been chatter amongst the adults who were supposedly helping me.

I nodded. I don't know why I was honest about it. All I knew was that Matthew was my only friend, and I didn't want him to be mad at me. I didn't want to disappoint him.

"With a girl?" he added on. I knew he knew the answer, so I didn't bother responding this time.

"Did you like it?"

A sick, sinking feeling roiled through my gut. I assumed it was the alcohol, but I didn't stop drinking it. I would need all the help I could get with this line of questioning.

"It's ok if you did. I won't tell."

I wanted him to stop talking. I wanted to tell him to get off my top bunk and go to his bed below. But, I stayed quiet, just as I was taught. Speaking up made people angry. I couldn't stand when people were unhappy with me.

I don't remember what happened afterward that had motivated Matthew to kiss me, but he did. His lips were firm and warm, his breath hot and sweet with a tang of citrus. I stayed perfectly still, and when his tongue swept the roof of my mouth and began to move, I didn't reciprocate. But I didn't push him away either.

I had thought that it would feel natural when it happened. I thought it would be the moment that would define me and give a name to what I was. But it didn't. It simply . . . numbed me. All my emotions had shut down, and only my body was present. No feelings of warmth and acceptance stirred in my chest. No ravenous hunger overcame me, causing me to give over to my desires. I just sat there and let him do what he pleased. Wasn't that what I was supposed to do?

After Matthew pulled his lips away, he smiled at me, satisfied with himself. Then he told me he wanted to give me a massage. Since we were sitting knee to knee, I didn't understand how he expected that to happen. But when his long, thin hands began to knead my thighs, I realized that he didn't want my back. He wanted my front.

His hands were firm, and his touch was confident, like maybe he had experience . . . massaging people. I was wound so tight and rigid that it was a surprise that his fingers didn't ache. He just kept kneading, slowly moving upward. And when his hands reached the tops of my thighs, he stopped.

"I have to pull down your shorts to massage the rest," he said.

I was perfectly still, perfectly silent, as he pulled my pajama shorts down. I was compliant. That was what all good boys were.

When he wrapped his hand around me, I expected to feel . . . something. Whether it be joy or desire or disgust, I wanted my body to make the choice for me so my heart and mind didn't have to. It was easier that way. But instead, I felt nothing. And looking down at my limp penis in Matthew's palm, he could tell.

That only made Matthew more determined. I hadn't objected, so surely I was willing. But why wasn't I aroused?

He massaged and caressed me, twisting his wrist, going fast, going slow. I knew he was getting annoyed with me, so I tried not to look at him. Instead, I closed my eyes, and thought of the Dominic Trevino that still lived in a parallel universe with his mama and papa. He was in 7th grade, just like me. But that Dominic made straight As. And he was class president. And a star athlete. Everyone knew him and loved him. He'd walk down the halls of his middle school, and classmates would shout out, "Hey, Dom!" and "Good game, superstar!" and "School dance this Friday night . . . Can't wait to see you!" He was popular, smart and beloved by all. Especially his parents, who were his biggest supporters in everything he did.

Mindlessly, I let myself look down, and realized that I wasn't flaccid in Matthew's hand anymore. I wasn't numb anymore. Yes, my mind had managed to block it out and trade my reality for a fantasy, but my body could feel him. It was responding to what he was doing to me, and Matthew was overjoyed.

No.

No, I don't want to feel it.

I don't want to like it.

This feels wrong.

Wrong and disgusting.

But it also feels okay. And it doesn't hurt.

It doesn't hurt, so that means I like it.

But I don't want to like it.

I didn't speak up. I wanted to, but I didn't. So maybe that meant I wanted it.

Maybe it meant that this was okay.

That his hands and his mouth and his skin were okay . . .

I jerked awake in a pool of my own sweat. I was panting, shivering, and I wasn't alone in my bed.

"Shhh, shhh. It's ok. I'm here. I'm right here with you." Her familiar scent washed over me, and I felt her small arms around my frame, squeezing with all her might. "I've got you, baby. I'm here. It wasn't real. It was just a dream . . . just a dream."

Angel was soothing me, holding me close to her body and absorbing my pain. My face was wet and salty, but it was not with sweat. I had been crying. Just like she said I'd been doing for the past week or so.

I nestled into her bosom and just let her hold me until I had calmed myself enough to speak. I didn't like this weakness; I didn't relish the fact that I needed her to take care of me. That had been my job. And now . . . now I was that little boy, willing to do any and everything just to feel loved.

Angel rubbed my back until the movement lulled me to sleep again. This time, I didn't dream, and when I woke up, it was well past the time I was due in for work.

I jumped up like my bed was on fire. "I already called. You have the flu," Angel rasped, her voice heavy with exhaustion. She was lying beside me, but I could tell she had been up for some time. A big mug of what I suspected was coffee was on my nightstand. There were only three bold, black letters printed on the mug—U, N, T. However, the handle was also painted black, fashioned into a C. If that was indicative of the type of day that was ahead of us, I was in deep shit.

"This is the third day I've missed this week. I have to go in." I ran a hand through my sweat-dampened hair. The moment I lifted my arm, I realized how achy I was. Maybe I did have the flu. That would have been much easier to explain than the real reason I had been avoiding work, or the entire world for that matter.

Angel sat up, shaking her head. "Amber insists you take another day and come back refreshed next week. She doesn't want to risk getting the kids sick."

Of course. Always about the kids and their well-being, as it should have been. Too bad I hadn't just kept it just about the kids. Nope. I had to go and fall for Toby's sister. And she didn't want me. She had rejected me. Not only that though. She was *repulsed* by me.

And all that only solidified what I had felt inside for years. I was disgusting. I was flawed. I was ruined. A girl who worked in a strip club to raise her mute kid brother and lived in one of Charlotte's sketchiest neighborhoods, looked at me like I was scum. Like I was a monster.

Angel was right. I was still too raw with doubt and self-loathing to try to inspire those young minds. How could I anyway? I was no role model. Even without the dark cloud of my past looming over me, they shouldn't aspire to be some self-absorbed prick that would pretty much fuck anything with two holes. Who the hell did I think I was to even think I could be some type of mentor to young men? At nearly 25 years of age, I didn't even have my own shit together.

"Kami is already on her way over," Angel stated, breaking

me from my reverie. "Take a long, hot shower. She's bringing breakfast."

I shook my head. "Why do you always have her on food runs?"

Angel mimicked my gesture with a shrug. "She insists. She said she misses taking care of us. And now that Blaine won't let her work behind the bar, she's bored and feels like she has no purpose. Plus, let's face it . . . we like to eat."

She was right. We did always seem to bond over food. Emotional eaters to the core. And if it helped Kami come to grips with slowing down, then who was I to stop her?

I did as I was told and spent a good twenty minutes under the hot spray of the shower. I reeked of dried sweat and two-day-old funk, and my hair was greasy and matted. Angel had given me my space when I asked. She was used to my highs and lows, but she had never seen me this bad before. Calling Kami ensured I couldn't avoid my problems—my feelings—any longer. It was two against one, and I had a feeling they were prepared for battle.

After I had slipped on a pair of loose sweatpants and towel-dried my hair, I padded out to the kitchen, where Kami and Angel were unpacking Styrofoam trays of food and small bottles of OJ. The aroma wafting from those containers had my mouth watering, and my stomach growled so loudly that I almost blushed with embarrassment.

"Mr. Bradley did me a solid and whipped up something special for us," she smiled before leaning forward to peck me on the cheek. "He knows how much you love a good southern meal, so we've got homemade biscuits and sausage gravy, eggs, grits, country ham steaks and fried green tomatoes. Dig in!"

Everything looked as delicious as it smelled, and considering that I hadn't eaten more than a few handfuls of dried cereal and a bag of Chex Mix in the past couple days, I was more than grateful for the unexpected gift from both Kami and Mr. Bradley. Their thoughtfulness was overwhelming, and for a second, I felt undeniably full.

We sat down cross-legged on the carpet like we always did, the TV on but muted. It seemed like it'd been weeks since we saw each other instead of days, and I was glad to listen to the girls prattle on about their recent adventures. Besides, we had a lot to talk about.

"And then I told that bitch . . ." Angel trilled, waving around a forkful of scrambled eggs animatedly, "if you don't shut your damn mouth, I will come through the fucking phone and slap you so hard that your teeth will knock together. And that heifer acted like she didn't even hear me! Can you believe that?"

"Angel . . . it was an automated message," I deadpanned. "She didn't hear you. Because *she* is a machine."

"I don't give a damn! I told her my credit card was not closed. It's a fucking black card. You can't close a black card."

I shrugged. "Maybe there was a glitch?" In reality, I was concerned for her. Not because she was cussing out a computer-generated voice over the phone, but because her card had been closed. The card her parents had been paying for. The parents who had ostracized her for being gay. Maybe they were cutting her off for good.

"Glitch my ass," she grumbled before digging back into her breakfast. She talked a good game, but deep inside, Angel was as soft and sensitive as they come. I wondered if she was as worried as I was. And if she was, in fact, being cut off, what did that mean for her? Was this their way of ceasing all communication and making her disappear?

"Anyway," Kami began, successfully changing the subject. Thank God for that girl. "Something interesting happened today during my OB appointment."

"You had an appointment?" I questioned, around a mouthful of fried green tomato. Mr. Bradley was a beast in the kitchen. After going from an Army cook for thirty years to a culinary god who could probably land a job at any fine establishment, I truly admired his loyalty and perseverance.

"Just a routine one, no big deal," she waved. "Anyway, like I was saying, something interesting happened."

"And that is?"

"I saw your friend again. Raven, right?"

If the stunned, slightly pained, expression on my face didn't explain what I felt, surely my jumbled words did. "You saw . . . what? What do you mean? How? Where?"

"At the hospital. She was assisting my nurse. You didn't tell me she was a nursing student. Makes sense, considering the scrubs that one day in your office."

I hadn't told them much of anything, really. But some things were better left unsaid. Like the fact that I had tried to kiss her, only to grossly offend her.

"Yeah," I shrugged. "Did she recognize you?"

"I think so. I mean, obviously, she didn't want to say anything since she was working, and Blaine was there. But before we left, I stopped her in the hall."

"And?"

"And, I said hi."

"And that's it?" Why was she being so reticent? She had to have known I was chomping at the bit for answers.

"And I asked her how she was. Honestly, she was a bit standoffish. Like she didn't understand why I was speaking to her, or she was surprised I was. And once she realized I was trying to be nice, she kinda looked . . . surprised. I don't know. You didn't tell her I was a cold-hearted bitch or anything like that, did you?"

"Me?" I snorted and shook my head. "No. Trust me, if I did, she'd probably welcome you with open arms. Maybe even teach you a secret handshake."

Kami lifted a speculating brow. "Yikes. Jaded much?"

"Sorry," I muttered. "Look, I really don't want to talk about her right now. Can we talk about something else? Like, oh I don't know, your freakin' engagement?"

Now it was Kami's turn to squirm with discomfort. Even Angel gave a co-signing *Mmm Hmmm*.

"Engaged? Who said I was engaged? Don't you think I would have told you guys something like that? And do you see a ring on my finger?" She wiggled her fingers in front of her face to emphasize her point.

"So you told him no?" Angel asked, reaching over to steal a chunk of Kami's country ham off her plate.

"No. I had nothing to say *no* to. He didn't ask."

Angel and I gave her a skeptical look. She was bullshitting. Everyone knew Blaine was insanely in love with Kam and couldn't wait to give her his last name.

"We both agreed it wasn't the right time," she tacked on. "And when it is, we want it to be on our terms. Not because someone spilled the beans and we're obligated to."

Angel dropped her gaze to her plate, reliving the regret of ruining Kam and Blaine's special moment. She had apologized a hundred times, and they both forgave her, of course. But she still felt bad. So did I, for telling her.

She also hadn't told us what happened that day when she came into Dive in tears, and now I had to wonder if it had something to do with her parents. Or the straight, married *friend* she had been spending all her time with.

I lifted a hand and brushed her cheek, causing her to look at me. "Speaking of that day . . . what happened? You were upset about something. Talk."

She shook her head, but spoke anyway. "It's just . . . Gia. She keeps telling me what a massive dick her husband is, and how it'd be so much easier if she could just leave. And how she wishes she *was* gay, because she loves me, and I'm her best friend, and it'd be so much better, and *blah blah blah.* I'm just so sick of hearing all the ways she wishes she could be with me, yet won't. She keeps going back to him."

Shit. She told me she wouldn't get involved with a married woman. She knew Gia was married *and* straight—two things that Angel couldn't and shouldn't fuck with.

"Have you two . . . ?" Kami asked, her voice soft and comforting.

Angel shook her head. "We kissed once. We were both drunk, and she said she had never kissed a girl before. So . . . you know." She let out a pained sigh, prompting both me and Kam to reach out to touch her.

"You don't need to be anyone's experiment, Angel," I told her and meant it. "You are not some chick's guinea pig, you hear me? If she can't see what an incredible human being you are, then fuck her. Leave her to be with her shitty ass husband. That's not your concern. And if she cared anything about you, she'd stop *making* it your concern."

"I know," she nodded through a tight smile. I really hoped that she did.

We finished off our plates, and Angel popped a bottle of champagne to make mimosas for her and me, hoping to lighten the mood. Kam looked into her pathetic little glass of juice. "God, I can't wait to have this baby. I miss tequila. And sushi. And sleeping on my stomach."

"And sex?" I asked, wriggling my brows.

"Why would I miss that?" she blushed. "I think we do it more now than ever. Hormones . . . they're something else."

"Ew!" Angel squealed. "Doesn't his dick hit the baby? Is little Baby B going to be born with a huge dent in his head?"

"No!" Kami chuckled, leaning back onto a mound of throw pillows. We were all stuffed and sleepy. "The baby doesn't feel it at all. Actually, my doctor suggested that we keep doing it. It'll help when it's time for delivery."

"But isn't that weird?" I asked, genuinely curious. "I mean, I get that pregnancy is a beautiful part of life and all that, but your belly is right there . . . And the baby can hear you . . . you know." For all of my whorish ways, talking to Kami about sex was just something I couldn't do. She was delicate to me. A sweet, delicate flower. Angel was another thing. I could pull my pants down, show her a mole on my balls and ask, *"Does that look weird to you?"* and she'd drop to her knees and thoroughly inspect it.

Of course, even this made Kami's face turn beet red, even

though she was accustomed to the plethora of freaky shit that had gone down under this roof. "Actually . . . it's better. And before it was . . . you know . . . amazing. But now . . . *oh my.*"

"Really?" It was surprising to admit that I had never done the baby bump thing. I thought I had pretty much covered the entire spectrum when it came to women. Hell, I'd slept with a lesbian.

"Really," she deadpanned with sincerity.

Somehow, the three of us ended up falling asleep right there on the floor, and when I came to, Kami was gone and Angel was getting dressed for AngelDust's performance tonight at Dive. AD had become local celebrities, and the place was standing room only when the all-girl band took the stage on Friday and Saturday nights. I was proud of them. Every one of those girls put their all into the music, especially Angel. It was the one thing that brought her pride and purpose, and it showed.

"I'd think you'd be sick of sleeping, considering that's all you've done for three days. You gonna make it tonight?" Angel asked, slinging her guitar case over a shoulder.

I sat up and stretched the soreness out of my joints. How long had I been sleeping? "Yeah. What time is it?"

"Almost 5. Better hurry before CJ tells everyone you contracted Ebola and starts up a GoFundMe to raise money for your medical expenses."

I chuckled and shook my head. He would totally do something like that.

"All right. I'll meet you there."

Just before Angel hit the front entrance, she paused and

shot over her shoulder, "Don't think you're off the hook about Raven. We *will* talk about it."

I nodded in response, anything to get her to leave the subject alone, even if only for tonight. I just needed to get through tonight.

Chapter 21

Raven

IT WAS FRIDAY NIGHT, and the unthinkable had happened. I had the night off.

I always worked Fridays, so I hadn't thought to check the schedule. But there it was, in black and white. Other than tomorrow night, it looked like I was off for the rest of the weekend, which meant I would be losing some major tips.

I went to Sal's office to question him about it, wondering if there was something going on that I didn't know about. He fed me some bullshit about the other waitresses asking for more hours, so he wanted to be fair—which meant whatever waitress he was screwing got the extra hours. I was pissed. I needed that money. My tips paid for our groceries, gas and utilities. I could have applied for assistance, but I refused. I did have my dignity, and as long as I was able-bodied, I would support us.

Velvet was just getting off shift when she spotted me in the hall, still seething. "What crawled up your arse, love? You look positively miffed."

"Sal cut my hours," I huffed, shaking my head in disbelief.

"Ah, yes. He's shagging that blonde one . . . Britney. Don't worry. He'll tell her to bugger off soon enough, and will be looking for a new hole to stick his tiny todger in."

"Well, he better not look here," I grumbled, crossing my arms over my chest.

She slipped her arm around my shoulders and led us to the dressing room. "Oh, he wouldn't dream of it! But look on the bright side, love. We're both young, beautiful and single on a Friday night. And you look like you need to get completely pissed. We're going out!"

I groaned. "Out? What do you mean by *out*? I'm not dressed for a club," I explained, looking down at my ripped skinny jeans, black ribbed tank and wedge sneakers. At least my hair and makeup were done for work.

"Tosh! You're perfect. Besides, I hate bloody clubs. Bad enough I have to work in one. I just need to stop by my flat to wash the stripper grime off me."

"I don't know . . ."

"Come on. I'll even drive. I want to see you let loose for a change."

I had to admit, I was tempted. I hadn't had a night out since moving back here to take care of Toby. Pre-Toby Raven partied all the time between coasting through classes. Post-Toby Raven had to transfer schools and move from everything and everyone she knew, to start all over again. Which meant no social life.

And as infuriating as it was, I kept hearing Dom's voice in my head. Maybe he was right. Maybe I was purposely shutting out the world, sabotaging any chance of a real connection with another human being. Velvet was cool, but we had never hung out, despite all the times she'd asked. I always had an excuse, that excuse being Toby. But right about now, Toby was over at Mrs. Ralston's, probably engaged in an intense game of Gin Rummy. I wasn't expected back for hours, and it wasn't as if they'd begrudge me one night to myself. Hell, Mrs. Ralston had been trying to set me up with her grandson from Raleigh for months. She'd probably be delighted.

I was out of excuses. I honestly had no reason to *not* want this for myself. Besides, it was just one night. How much harm could it do?

"Ok. Fine," I resigned. "Let's do it."

Velvet's apartment was in a hip, artsy area of Plaza Midwood, and it fit her perfectly. I knew she had to be dropping some major coin to rent the lavish space, which spoke volumes of her loyal tippers at The Pink Kitty. No wonder she chose the lunch shift. She was making a killing!

"I'll just be a minute. Make yourself at home!" she said before dashing into the shower to wash away the edible body glitter and sweat.

While she got ready, I took the liberty of grabbing a glass of water and checking out her digs. She liked art—oil paintings mostly—and was pretty well read. She had everything from Anthony Doerr to Tina Fey and Anne Rice. Even a few authors I'd never heard of. I picked up an orange paperback and read the synopsis. It sounded pretty good. Actually, whoever this Kate Sedgwick character was, I envied her optimism. I could use a dose of it myself.

"Oh, that's one of my favorites. You should read it," Velvet said from the hallway, still wet and wrapped in a towel. Her hair was in a turban on top of her head, and her face was bare. She looked absolutely stunning without the dark makeup she usually wore.

I looked back down at the book so she wouldn't think I was gawking at her. "*Bright Side,* huh? Trying to tell me something?"

"Not at all. Just thought we all could use a little perspective. I won't be much longer, love. Promise!" Then she was scurrying to her room. I guess constant wardrobe changes made her a pro at dressing quickly.

In fifteen minutes flat, Velvet emerged fully dressed in leather leggings, a slouchy white tee, a leather jacket and black heeled booties. Her violet hair was blow-dried, and her minimal makeup was flawless. She wasn't Velvet the stripper. She was *her.*

"Wow, I just realized that I don't even know your real name," I said shaking my head. It was stupid to refer to her as some alias.

"Victoria," she smiled. And she was. This was my friend, Victoria. "What's yours?"

"Raven." I inwardly cringed. It was mostly true, and that would have to do for now.

"Oh. I just assumed it was as stage name. Most of the waitresses use them too. And considering the dark hair and pale skin . . . well, you know."

"Nope," I smiled, glad she had bought. "Just Raven."

Before jumping in her drop-top Mini Cooper, I went to my car to grab a zip-up hoody and lock up. Not that anyone in this neighborhood would even bat an eye at my old girl, but she was a good car, and had been good to me. Some things didn't go out of style. They just needed a little renovating.

"So where are we going?" I asked, reapplying my lipstick in the visor mirror.

"This cool little place I've been dying to check out. I pass by it all the time, and it's always packed on the weekends. Plus, one of my uni mates told me they've got live music."

"Uni? You're in college?"

Velvet—I mean, Victoria—chuckled and shook her head. "Not anymore. I came to the U.S. to attend university, but after graduation, I just had no desire to go into law. So I started dancing. Good money . . . good hours . . . why not?"

Wow. So she could have been in law school right now, or maybe even a lawyer, but she chose not to? I envied her freedom to choose. I envied the fact that she even had choices.

"Here we are. Ace! A parking spot!" she said, pulling her tiny car into the space. She was right—it was packed. And with the marquee lit up, it looked completely different since the last time I had been here.

"Dive? You want to go to *Dive?*"

"You've been here?"

Crap. I couldn't answer that truthfully without giving away the fact that I knew Dom, the guy she was sleeping with. But I didn't want to lie either. "Once. For lunch."

"Oh. Well, I heard this place completely transforms at night. Come on!"

Victoria was buzzing with energy and excitement as she

hopped out of her car and practically skipped onto the sidewalk. Me, not so much. The place looked decent, and there was a line to get in, so I assumed it would be a good time. But I didn't want to risk seeing Dom. However, according to Toby, he was out sick with the flu, so I highly doubted that he'd be in a place like this.

It didn't take long to get inside, and once we did, we were on the hunt for seats. It was packed, yet not so much that you couldn't walk around without getting stepped on or saying "Excuse me" a hundred times. A few guys had taken one look at Victoria and offered seats at their tables. She turned them down every time, telling them it was a girl's night. When they looked over at me expectantly, I just shrugged and kept walking.

After a good bit of walking, we lucked out and scored a tall round-top near the bar just as an older couple was leaving. The place was getting considerably more crowded by the minute, so I assumed the live music would be starting soon. We flagged down a waitress and ordered drinks and a couple of appetizers for dinner before she got completely swamped. I made sure to be extra polite to her. I knew the struggle.

"So, what do you think?" Victoria asked, as she dipped a loaded potato skin in some avocado ranch. Those things were dangerous. I'd already had three and was thinking about ordering more. Actually, everything was delicious. The sirloin sliders and mac and cheese fritters would have me doing three extra miles around my neighborhood tomorrow.

"It's nice," I replied. "Cool spot, I guess. Great food."

"And one of the best pomegranate margaritas I've ever had. How's your mojito?"

"Great," I replied, holding it up before taking a sip. I wondered if she would freak if I told her that the bartender was just as yummy as the drinks. I had caught a glimpse of him through the break in the crowd around the bar, but it was enough to verify that he was working tonight. Good Lord, that man was sexy. I could totally see Victoria salivating over all his tattoos and piercings. Too bad he was taken. After seeing Dom's lunch buddy at the hospital this morning, it confirmed that he was *not* the father. And I didn't even need Maury for that one.

We ordered another round of drinks, just in time for the lights to turn down, causing the whole room to erupt with cheers and move closer to the stage. I could see shadows of people moving into place on stage, but it was too dark to make them out. However, the guy who hopped on stage with a beer in his hand and grabbed the mic was impossible to miss.

"Welcome hot coeds, MILFs and cougars. Fuck you, dickheads, douchebags and posers. I'm CJ, and I wanna welcome you to Dive, the best fucking bar on the planet! And why are we the best bar? Other than this sexy hunk of man that stands before you? Well, we also have the baddest fucking band in Charlotte, rocking your fucking tits off tonight! Give it up for AngelDust!"

The crowd went ballistic once more, and didn't calm until the drummer's count. Then, I nearly choked on my strawberry basil mojito. Holy shit, it was Angel. And she was singing and playing guitar. And she was *good.* Hell, she was amazing. The entire band was.

"Bloody brill! An all-girl band! And they're fantastic!" Victoria was already grooving in her seat to the fast paced song, and I knew it wouldn't be long before she would be dragging me onto the dance floor. I sucked down my second drink for the extra liquid courage. I had to admit, it was hard *not* to move to the infectious beat.

Victoria somehow caught the waitress and placed an order. I was way too caught up in the shock of seeing Angel and the music to hear what it was. But when two shots appeared in front of us a bit later, I knew that Victoria was dead serious about getting me *pissed,* as she called it.

"Drink up, love! I'm ready to get out there!"

I picked up a shot glass and sniffed. Oh Lord. Tequila. I'd be calling upon the porcelain gods later tonight, for sure.

I waited for her to take her glass, but she just shook her head. "All for you. Cheers!"

My eyes flared with shock. Holy crap. *Two* shots? But then I thought about it. I used to drink much more Pre-Toby. And dammit, I deserved just one night off to have fun. Maybe it was the mojitos talking or the music rattling my skull, but I wanted to be free tonight. I'd worry about hangovers and work and growing up tomorrow. Tonight was just for me. And even though that made me feel guilty as hell, I just swallowed it down with the tequila.

Two shots later, we were on the dance floor, fist pumping in time to the rhythm and bopping our heads as we hopped around laughing. Seeing her like this, being goofy and carefree, it was hard to believe Victoria took her clothes off for a living. There was no choreography, no gyrating, no hair flipping. She was happy to just be here, having fun with me.

When a particular song started—obviously a fan favorite—I took a moment to watch Angel. She was beautiful up there—charismatic, engaging, alluring. But more than that, it was like she was singing right to me. I mean, obviously she didn't even know I was one of dozens in the crowd, but the lyrics . . . they spoke to my soul. They were everything I had been feeling translated into song. Trapped. Lonely. Afraid.

I needed a break after that one, so we made our way back to the bar area. Someone had snagged our table, so we decided to just hit up the bar. I was feeling no pain, but decided to have another drink, and Victoria didn't object. Especially when she got a load of what I assumed was the head bartender.

"What can I get you ladies?" he asked, his tattooed hands and deep brown eyes focused on grabbing bottles and mixing drinks effortlessly. When neither of us answered, too breathless by his mere presence, he looked up. And froze.

Crap. I'd been made. I'd totally forgotten. Like the song goes, *blame it on the a-a-a-a-a-alcohol.*

"Hey," I said nervously. Oh shit. Would he tell Dom that he'd seen me?

"Hey," he responded with the same apprehension.

"Heeeyyy!" Victoria trilled through giggles. "We'll take two shots of tequila, handsome."

Then the bartender, Blaine as I remembered, did something that had our panties melting down our legs. He smiled. Then said, "My specialty." Then had the audacity to follow that with a wink. How dare he be so fucking hot! *The nerve!*

"Can I touch him?" Victoria whimpered as soon as he walked off to grab our shots.

"I wish. He's got a girlfriend. And a baby on the way," I pouted.

"Oh, bollocks. He would."

We shared girlish giggles and gabbed on about whatever

came to mind. It had been so long since I'd had a girlfriend. I had missed this camaraderie, having forgotten what it felt like to be young and boundless.

After he dropped off our shots, Blaine told us they were on the house, then quickly moved to the other end of the bar, bypassing several people hoping to order. Most of them were women, so they didn't seem to mind much. The view from behind was just as enjoyable.

Once again, Victoria pushed the shots towards me, and I didn't put up a fight. My tongue had just tasted the lip of the second shot and was tipping it back when a dark shadow fell over us, blocking my view of the stage and causing Victoria to gasp. I paused mid-sip and looked up.

The moment he looked at Victoria—or Velvet as he knew her—then pinned his glare on me, I thought I might get sick. It was only my pride that kept my stomach from heaving.

"What the hell are you doing here?" he seethed through a clenched jaw.

Shit. So much for girl's night.

Chapter 22

Dom

I WAS PISSED. AND scared. But mostly pissed.

Here I was, trying to enjoy my Friday night by putting all that shit with Raven behind me, and she had the audacity to insert herself into my space. I had accepted that she hated me, and probably would have for what I had done to her on that rooftop. But it would never amount to how much I hated myself. Still, I just need a night off from the self-loathing. Just a small escape from my guilt. But could I even do that? No! She had to come to *my* favorite place. Where *my* friends were. Even with *my* occasional hook up! It was like she wanted to flaunt her repulsion of me. She wanted me to be reminded of what I'd done.

"What the hell are you doing here?"

The question was harsh on my tongue, but I was tired of being nice. When I was, she pushed me away. When I was a dick, she apologized and begged me to stay (in Toby's life). It was some sick, twisted game of cat and mouse, and I was tired of playing.

"Well?"

She looked stunned, as did Velvet. But what did she expect? She knew Blaine worked here. She had to have known he would tell me she was here. Hell, if I hadn't had my back to the crowd all night, too busy wallowing, I would have probably seen her myself. But I didn't feel like being social. And I damn sure didn't want to risk running into anyone I'd slept with. I wasn't in the mood.

"Um, I, uh . . ." she stammered. She had the nerve to look surprised to see me. "Hey, um. I'm just . . ."

Velvet practically pushed her aside in an act of defense and stepped into my face. Since when did they become best-fucking-friends? "We're here dancing, you bloody wanker. Now if you're quite done pestering us, feel free to bugger off and pull the stick out of your arse."

Normally, Velvet's dirty mouth would have had me rock hard. The insults were practically foreplay for her, but sex was the farthest thing from my mind with Raven standing in front of me. As gorgeous as she looked tonight in a tight tank top and jeans, her hair a wild mass of soft waves, I wouldn't allow myself to see her like that anymore. And considering she was rolling with Velvet, I could only imagine what she now thought about me and my perversions.

I took a step back and collected myself. I was going about this all wrong. Making the girl that was already very clearly afraid of me even more petrified would only make things worse.

"Shit, I'm sorry," I said, just loud enough that she could hear me over the music without having to invade her personal space. She gave me a stiff nod and a tight flinch of a smile, and returned to the drink between her fingertips.

I could see the way Velvet was regarding us, her eyes darting from the wariness in Raven's gaze to the regret dimming mine. I didn't want this turning anymore awkward than it already was, so I tried to mask it all with a grin. I was good at hiding behind a manufactured smile. *Shit,* honestly, I was a walking, breathing mirage.

"Hey, let me get you two ladies a drink." I was already signaling Blaine, who had been watching the entire exchange between mixing drinks. Minutes later, he returned with three shots and a few beers. He knew I needed a chaser with tequila. Like I said, damn good bartender. Even better friend.

Velvet leaned in to grab her shotglass, moving in close to my ear. "So what brings Dirty Dom out tonight?"

I nodded towards Blaine and my other friends that were sitting across the bar, watching us like hawks. "My friend owns the place. Kinda like a home away from home."

"That fuck-tastic piece of man is your mate? Bloody hell!" Then pressed in closer, her warm breath on my neck and her straining nipples against my chest. I could feel them pebble against the fabric, as if they were reaching out for me, begging me to taste them, suck them, bite them. I had done all of those things and more, but that was the past. I didn't want to continue on that like that. Not if I could help it.

"You know . . ." she whispered, her voice husky with desire. "If your friend isn't *too* attached to his girlfriend, I wouldn't mind a little naughty fun tonight." I knew when she spoke in that tone, she was horny. Honestly, I'd never spent any length of time with her that didn't involve her naked and me inside her. But there was no way I'd go there with her, especially with another guy, let alone Blaine.

I gently pushed her back so she could see the disapproval on my brow. "No thanks."

"Why not?"

I shook my head. Shit, I didn't want to do this around Raven, but I assumed she already knew about Velvet and me. And it wasn't like the purple-haired vixen was making her intentions discreet. I wasn't ashamed of her. I was ashamed of *me*. And I didn't like her insinuating that Blaine would ever be unfaithful to Kami.

"Why not? Because he *is* very attached to his girlfriend. And if he wasn't, I'd rearrange that pretty little face of his."

She laughed heartily at that, tipping her head back with an air of drama. I looked to Raven to see that she, too, was trying to stifle a snicker. What the fuck was so funny? I snatched up my shot and pounded it, slamming down the glass, and grabbed my beer.

"I fail to see the humor in what I just said," I remarked putting the rim of the bottle to my lips.

"You? Rearrange someone's face?" Velvet scoffed. "You're a handsome bloke, but you're hardly frightening."

I peered over at Raven who was regarding the exchange with a raised brow. "Is that what you think too? That I'm . . . soft?"

She blinked at the question, then went for her own gulp of tequila. "No. Not soft. But not . . . hard either."

"But I was hard enough for you the other night." I took a

swig, my eyes trained on her bemused expression from over the bottle. I knew the wording was crass, but fuck it. I was already three beers in, and that tequila had felt like golden fire in my veins. I signaled Blaine for another round.

"Yeah. You were," Raven agreed. "But it's so hard to tell, seeing as you've dismissed me. For *Cherri,* of all people."

"Cherri!" Velvet trilled. "Oh, for fuck's sake. Please tell me . . ."

I gave her a look that screamed *"don't say another word,"* but I was sure I had been made. Raven wasn't buying it. She knew I had been sleeping with Cherri. Shit. Let's just add her to the list too. I looked around. Was Alyssa the kindergarten teacher going to pop up suddenly? Lauren from the gym? The shopgirl from Neimans? The head cheerleader from 11th grade?

Blaine dropped off the round of tequila sans beer, and I grabbed mine immediately, not even waiting for the girls to touch theirs. Shit. I would need a lot more of these if we were going to play Dom's Dirty Laundry.

"I heard a rumor," Raven said before sipping her beer. "That you were one of Pink Kitty's most valuable customers."

"And who did you hear that from?" I chased the tequila with a slug of beer, even though I didn't even need it at this point.

"Skylar."

My hand was over my mouth just a millisecond before beer went spewing in Raven's face. "Oh shit," I coughed into my hand. "Fuck."

"So it's true?"

"Huh?"

"That you're a whore. That you sleep with any and everyone that'll have you."

Her expression was amused, but I could hear the sharp edge in her tone. And the way those blue eyes bore into mine— unblinking, unrelenting—I knew that she was daring me to spout of some bullshit denial. She wanted to believe I wasn't shit. And who was I to deny her the satisfaction?

"Maybe I am," I shrugged. "Maybe I will."

She grimaced with disgust. "Why do you do it?"

"Why do you care?"

As she glared back at me, her mouth still agape, I knew I had her. Why *did* she care? What was it to her who I slept with? It wasn't like we had ever or would ever have sex.

She grabbed her shot, downed it, and slammed the glass, swaying a little. "I don't."

"Obviously, you do." I looked down at the bar top where Velvet's drink had gone untouched. We hadn't even noticed that she'd drifted over to the dance floor and was grinding all over some dude in a flannel shirt and cowboy boots. Fuck it. I grabbed her shot and drank it. I was feeling some type of way right now, and if Raven wanted to go toe to toe, I was ready.

"About you? Please. You wish I did. I don't need to touch the stove to know it'll burn me. And looking at the company you keep, I'd say you burn pretty good. Am I right?"

I barked out a laugh at her analogy. "Not everything that's hot burns, Raven. But I understand your fear. You talk a good game about taking chances and living outside the box, but ad- mit it—you're a scared little girl." I swayed forward, closing the gap between us until the heat of her body engulfed mine. "And you're fucking terrified of *me.*"

"And why's that?" Her voice was just a whisper a she

195

shifted closer, leaning against me.

"Because of what I want from you. And what you want to give me." It was all just words. All lies. I knew I needed to leave this girl alone, but old habits die hard.

She looked up at me, those bold blue eyes hazed with oblivion. They didn't say, *"Dom, you're full of shit, and I hate you."*

Hate, I could deal with. There was finality in it. Its acceptance would have been easy—cut-and-dried. But nothing was easy with this girl. So she gave me the one thing I didn't need. The one thing that would prove to be the first fracture in my fortress of lies.

She gave me surrender.

Chapter 23

Raven

THERE WERE HANGOVERS.

And there were *hangovers*.

I was *hungover.*

Fuck. Me.

Cracking open an eye had to have taken an hour. Focusing my vision had to have taken a good 45 minutes. And I swear the inside of my mouth was filled with vomit-flavored flour.

How the hell did I get home? And what the hell happened?

I lay there for several minutes, trying to retrace my mental steps. Ok, we were at Dive. We ate, we danced, we drank, we laughed, we saw Dom . . .

We saw Dom!

Shit. Shit on a cracker. Smeared shit on toast. Shit-kabobs on the grill.

That was when everything got hazy. *We were talking.*

There were shots. We lost Velvet somewhere. I needed to sit down. Dom introduced me to his friends. I was laughing my ass off about nothing and everything. Blaine tried to get me to drink water and brought me cheese fries. I hugged the pregnant one. I kissed Angel on the cheek. Angel's a rock star! I leaned against Dom. He placed his arm around my waist. I nuzzled under his chin, relishing the scrape of stubble against my face . . .

Fuck.

And this was why I didn't drink tequila anymore.

With great effort, I looked to the other side of my small, full-size bed, and there he was. Sleeping on his stomach, limbs outstretched and, thankfully, fully dressed in jeans and a rumpled, collared shirt. I felt around, my eyes still closed. Yup. I was dressed too, although I was no longer in my tank and jeans. I had on my ratty lounge sweats, an old tee, and my feet were bare. I was sure my hair would be a rat's nest on top of my head, but it was secured by a hair tie in a messy bun.

What the hell happened after we left Dive? There was no way I could've driven my car from Victoria's. And judging by the fumes coming out of Dom's pores, he wasn't in any shape to drive either. So while my getting home was a mystery, a sleeping Dom was an even greater anomaly. If I was uninhibited enough to invite him to share my bed, what else had I done? What else had I *said?*

Shit . . . if I let something slip in my intoxicated stupor, there'd be no telling what Dom would do. But then again, he was here. And if he knew about my past—*our* past—he'd want to put as much distance between us as possible, the very thing I should have done from the start.

How the hell did I get here, so far off course? Getting to know him wasn't part of the plan. Connecting with him had been a big no-no. And caring for him . . . it would prove tragic for not only me and him, but Toby too.

I forced myself into a sitting position, trying to keep my pained groans to a minimum as to not wake him. The trek to our single bathroom was treacherous, but somehow I managed to make it, only stopping to lean against the wall for support three times. After I had emptied my screaming bladder, brushed the foulness from my teeth and removed the nine pounds of war paint smudged around my eyes, I felt a tad better. Still like shit. But more like a shit salad rather than a shit smorgasbord. I checked Toby's room to find his tiny, twin-size bed empty. I exhaled with relief when I realized that he had stayed the night over at Mrs. Ralston's. The thought of him seeing me drunk and belligerent with his mentor in my bed would probably tip the poor kid over the edge.

I shuffled down the short hall to the kitchen, heading straight for the fridge. After three glasses of water and three Advil to kill the tiny jackhammer on my skull, I started to feel human again, if not a little queasy. There was no way I was sober yet, and I had to be at work this afternoon. The bed was calling my name, whether it was occupied or not, so as quietly as I could, I crawled in beside Dominic, careful not to brush his skin with mine. It was intimate enough that we had slept side by side. I wasn't about to cuddle with him while he was knocked out, like some weird stalker freak.

His face was turned toward me, giving me the opportunity to just take him in, something I hadn't allowed myself to do. He had the longest, fullest lashes I had ever seen on a man, almost feminine, and his lips were naturally pouty. Even his hair looked feather soft and delicate. However, everything about him was undeniably male. Dominic's good looks were almost jarring at first glance. He had the type of beauty that intimidated you because next to him, even Miss America looked like Shrek. But what made him even more attractive was the fact that he made you feel cherished in his presence. He gave you his undivided attention. He listened intently, and he looked at you like you were the most stunning thing to ever grace his sight.

That was why I had fallen for him hard, without him even knowing it. What had meant everything to me had meant absolutely nothing to him. And just like he had that penetrating way of making you feel adored, he also could make you feel two inches tall in the same breath.

I watched him sleep, wondering where to go from here, until I could no longer keep my eyes open. It was early, and I could squeeze in another couple hours before Toby would be up and at 'em. I was just really dozing, taking the detour into dreamland, when I heard what sounded like a garbled cry.

Shit. I must've still been drunk.

I rolled over and squeezed my eyelids together, hoping that the pounding would subside and take the weird sounds with it. But then I heard it again—louder this time—and I knew it wasn't the effects of last night's residual tequila talking. That sound—that strangled desperation—was coming from right next to me.

I turned back over to face him, unsure of what I would find. And what I found was heartbreaking. His eyes still shut tight in slumber, Dominic was . . . crying. Tears streamed from his closed eyes, saturating the pillow underneath his head. He grimaced as if he were in debilitating pain, lips tight over his bared teeth. Had he been hurt last night? Was he sick?

The nurse in me kicked into gear. I did a quick visual scan to see if there were any noticeable abrasions. Gently, I pressed a hand against his sweat-slickened forehead. He didn't seem to have a fever, but his skin was clammy, and his breathing was erratic. As I was debating on whether or not to wake him, his cries became more intense, yet there was meaning to them. He was talking—begging. He was pleading for help, crying for mercy. His whole body was coiled tight, yet every few seconds, jerky convulsions would wrack his frame, and he'd cry out in agony. The horror etched in his tear-stained face was terrifying, and I knew I couldn't wait any longer. I had to help him.

"Dominic," I called out to him, keeping a bit of distance between us. If he was having night terrors, he could seriously hurt me if I tried to wake him too aggressively. "Dominic, wake up."

It was like he wasn't even here. The pain was too real to him. He wasn't dreaming it. He was living it.

As carefully as I could, I gave him a shake, shielding my face in case he lashed out. Still nothing. I shook him again, putting more force into it. He still continued to cry, wincing through it as if he were being hit. Each jerk was an assault inside of his subconscious.

"No! No more! Please!" he sobbed, the desperation in his words causing me to gasp. "It hurts . . . it hurts so bad. Please *tio. No más, por favor.*"

No more, please.

I didn't understand what was going on behind those eye-lids, but I knew I had to stop it. I had to help him. I had to save him.

"Dom!" I yelled, shaking him with all my might with no regard for my own safety. "Wake up! Wake up, please!"

He shuddered under my touch before thrashing from the horror of his dream, gasping for air. "What . . . What hap-pened?" he rasped, out of breath. He scrubbed a hand over his face, then looked at his wet hand with a frown, turning his hard gaze at me. "What did I say?"

It was a simple question, but the way he looked at me—as if I had violated him in some way—was almost frightening. Like I was to blame for the dread that had manifested into a nightmare.

"Nothing," I lied. But the coldness in his eyes challenged me to speak the truth. "Just that . . . You were begging. Beg-ging for someone to stop hurting you. It was just a dream, right? Like, you're okay . . . right?"

He turned his gaze away then and looked down at his trembling hands before folding them into tight fists. "Yeah. I'm okay."

I couldn't describe where the impulse to touch him came from, but I reached out, the tips of my fingers just barely raz-ing his shoulder. He flinched, bounding off the bed in a swift movement. I tucked my hand to my side and looked down. "Sorry."

"Don't worry about it. I better get going."

My head snapped up to his wary expression, and before I could stop myself, I asked, "Why?"

"Because I should. I didn't mean to fall asleep in your

bed. Shit . . . sorry about that."

"Then why did you?"

He ran a hand through his messy, sleep-ruffled hair and shrugged. "You were drunk. And sick. After I managed to clean you up, I was afraid you'd choke or something if you threw up in your sleep. I honestly only meant to stay until I knew you were okay, but . . . I must've dozed off."

"You changed me?" Oh shit. He saw me naked. My muddled mind couldn't remember if the underwear I had on now was the same I had on last night. And I couldn't even think about my bra.

"I had to," he said. "You threw up outside, and some of it splashed onto your clothes. Don't worry; I didn't look."

"Oh." I was relieved. Maybe even a little disappointed that he hadn't wanted to see me naked. I knew thinking like that was dangerous and stupid, but I couldn't deny what I was feeling. "What about Victoria?" Memories of last night were fuzzy, but I remember her coming over to our spot at the bar after she had danced through Angel's set.

He frowned. "Who?"

"Velvet."

"Oh. She's good. Told me to tell you to call her today."

"She got home safely?"

At that, he almost smiled. "Well . . . not exactly."

"Huh?"

"She didn't go home. She was with CJ."

The shock on my face actually made him break into a chuckle, although I did not find this revelation a laughing matter. CJ? Blaine's asswipe cousin? I mean, he was cute and all, in a rugged Taylor Kitsch kinda way, with the longish brown hair and the permanent mischief in his eyes. He and his cousin favored each other with their tall, lean builds and tan skin. But Blaine's body art amped up the hot factor by a good 10 points. Which was why I was surprised Velvet—Victoria—even gave CJ the time of day. He was an idiot, and a guy like him would probably drive her batshit crazy. There was no way she was sober when she made that desperate, last-call-for-alcohol decision.

"So . . . yeah," Dom mumbled, again raking a hand through his hair. It looked like a nervous habit, like he just needed to keep his hands busy. "I better go before Toby comes over. I don't want to complicate things."

Good point. I was just upset that it hadn't been my first thought. "Yeah. You're right."

He looked at the wall, toward the direction of the door. I could tell he wanted to leave, and it had nothing to do with Toby. "So, I guess I'll pick you guys up tomorrow?"

"Tomorrow? Huh?"

"Yeah. Kami invited you two over for dinner. You don't remember? You two talked all night. Even told her how you thought *I* was the father of her baby."

I slapped both hands over my face and fell back into the pillows, surrendering to death by mortification. "Oh my God. Please tell me that's all I said."

He shrugged, a smirk on his lips. "You told Angel she was hot. And I think you made out with her."

"What?"

Another shrug, but he couldn't hide his smile. "I'm sure she'll be ecstatic to discuss the details with you tomorrow. I'll pick you up around 3pm. Tell Toby I said hi."

Wait . . . what? I couldn't go over for dinner. I had already crossed the line with him by having him in my bed, but going to some family gathering would be hurtling over it. This was not keeping my distance. This was not avoiding him. And yeah . . . so he hadn't impregnated Kami and wasn't attached to Victoria/Velvet. That didn't mean that he wasn't a manwhore. And there was such a thing as girlcode, even though Victoria *was* trying to hook me up with him. Still . . . it just wouldn't be right.

"I can't," I blurted out as he turned to walk out through my bedroom door. He paused mid-step.

"Why not?"

"I have to work."

He shook his head. "Not according to Velvet." I could tell he was studying the skepticism on my face, watching me conjure and analyze every excuse I could find. "Look, Kami really wants you there. It would mean a lot to her, and I'm not in the business of disappointing her."

Then, it struck me. Hard. Like a battering ram to the gut. "You love her."

His eyes were clearer than I had ever seen them. "Yes." As soon as the word left his lips, he looked away, once again dreaming of his escape from my quickly shrinking room. "Plus, it'd be good for Toby to be around other people. People that won't judge him or make him feel different. I'll even send you home with a plate for Mrs. Ralston."

He didn't stay to listen to another excuse, and I didn't offer one. I was still too stunned stupid to do much more than sit there on my disheveled sheets that were still damp with his tears.

Chapter 24

Dom

IWASN'T TIRED, AND I couldn't bear to close my eyes even if I was, but I climbed into my bed anyway. Raven had been there during one of my nightmares, and judging by the tears on my cheeks, it had been bad. I'd wanted to run the moment I'd opened my eyes. I'd wanted to escape the concern—the pity—that was so evident in her alarmed gaze. She wasn't supposed to see that. I wasn't supposed to be there, but I couldn't just leave her. Not when she could barely stand on her own.

Undressing her had been problematic, and I was grateful that she had been too far gone to notice my dick straining against my pants, even pressing against her belly as I cleaned her up. She giggled flirtatiously the entire time, touching my face, my hair. Telling me I was so hot . . . I had always been so beautiful to her. She even tried to kiss me when I forced her into bed. Thank fuck I wasn't into macking on inebriated chicks with vomit breath, or this morning would have been awkward for many other reasons. Nope. There was no way I would go there with her like that. Even if she was stone-cold sober, I couldn't do it.

"Hey, I thought I heard you come in," Angel said, stopping at my open door. We rarely closed them here. A habit of living with Kami who was dreadfully claustrophobic.

"Yeah," I remarked, staring up at the ceiling.

"So . . . you gonna tell me what happened last night?" I felt the bed dip beside me as she sat at my side. She was freshly showered, smelling of her expensive perfume and coconut milk shampoo.

"Nothing to tell. She was drunk and sick. I put her to bed and ended up falling asleep myself. You know I wouldn't . . ."

"Yeah, I know. So, are you two cool? I mean, you seemed cool at the bar. Very much so. I can tell she's into you."

I shook my head. "That was the alcohol talking. Raven doesn't give a damn about me." I thought about telling her about what happened this morning, but I didn't feel like rehashing whatever it was that had me shaking and crying in my sleep like a bitch. I was angry at myself for allowing her to see me like that. For allowing those memories to *make* me like that. I hated the hold the past still had on me, and admitting it would only make the ghosts more real.

"Whatever. She does. And it's not only that . . ."

I turned to narrow my eyes at her in suspicion. "What?"

Angel shook her head. "I don't know . . . I can't put my finger on it, but . . . I swear, I know her from somewhere."

"Huh?" I hadn't told Angel about me and Raven's first

meeting, and how I had thought the same, judging by her hostile behavior. But now that I knew she had heard stories about me from the other girls at The Pink Kitty, it had all made sense.

"I don't know; it's weird. Probably nothing," she shrugged. "Well, I'm going to Neimans. You want anything?"

One of the perks of living with Angel was that she loved to shop, and insisted on dressing me, letting her parents pick up the bill. Just another *Fuck You* to them. I never turned down the luxury threads, but now I really had to think about Angel's offer. Raven had mentioned my clothing before, assuming I had money and didn't know the true meaning of struggle. She couldn't be further from the truth, but it wasn't right of me to keep accepting things that I didn't deserve. Angel let me live with her in a grandiose apartment for nearly nothing as it was, knowing I was making a meager salary. Basically, my entire check covered my car note, plus afforded me money to blow on dates and other meaningless stuff. Most nights, I ate at Dive for free, and my scholarship had scrapped the need for student loans. I just had myself to take care of, and here she was— young, in school, and trying to raise a child on a waitress's pay. I felt like a total ass and a phony for flaunting a lifestyle that I hadn't earned.

"No. I'm good."

"You sure? I saw you eyeing those new Gucci loafers."

I shook my head, my mind made up. "No, I don't need them. I don't need anything. You go have fun."

She left, frowning in confusion, wondering what the hell had crawled up my ass and triggered my emo switch.

Raven. And my past. The two things that could never collide.

At 3pm on the dot, I was knocking on the door of her apartment, feeling like a jackass for basically guilting her into coming. Pleasing and protecting Kami had been a tough habit to break, plus it meant I could spend the day with Raven. And that desire was becoming just as difficult to deny.

I half expected her to be lounging in her sweats when she answered, refusing to come. But when she swung open the door, I was momentarily stunned speechless at the beguiling sight before me.

I'd only really seen Raven in her work clothes, whether it was scrubs or booty shorts. And only recently had I seen her in street clothes. But seeing her in a floral print sundress the color of a coral sunset and jeweled sandals, I could only stare, and mentally thank God I hadn't let yesterday's occurrence keep me from being here on her doorstep.

"Too much?" she grimaced, wrinkling her cute, slender nose. Her makeup was light, nothing like the heavy, dark liner she wore around her eyes for work. She had even traded those signature red lips for a shimmery pink gloss. Her hair was tied into a messy braid that fell over her shoulder, while several rogue ringlets dangled around the nape of her neck.

"No," I croaked, my mouth like sandpaper. I cleared my throat and tried again. "No, not at all. Just right."

She was more than just right. She was gorgeous. And I meant that with every cell in my body. The woman in front of me had stolen my breath with her beauty.

"I don't know . . ." She was so uncertain. So insecure. It was like she didn't know of the power she possessed over me.

I took a step forward, until the front of my polo shirt gazed the bodice of her dress, and grasped her bare shoulders as lightly as I could without scaring her. Touching her skin was like holding live wire in my palms, and every second of being shocked just made me hold on tighter. "Well, *I* know, Raven," I told her, looking down into the ocean of her eyes. I held my breath, telling myself to keep swimming. But all I really wanted was to drown in her. "What is it about you? Why can't I leave you alone? Why do I torture myself with wanting you?"

She gasped in my arms, but she didn't move away. Instead, she met my gaze and breathed her own proclamation. "Desire is just concentrated madness of the body and soul," she whispered. "Do you want my crazy?"

"Yes," I replied too quickly to stop myself. Too fast. This was happening too fast, and I couldn't stop. I couldn't keep doing this shit if I was to respect her wishes.

I took a deep breath and closed my eyes, channeling my resolve. Then I let my hands slide from her shoulders, down her arms, and past her fingertips, until I was no longer touching her. No longer entranced by the feel of her skin next to mine.

"But I won't take it. I won't even ask for it." I shook my head, even though I knew I was doing the right thing. "You said so yourself, Raven—I'm a whore. I'm no good. And I have no right to touch you. I'm sorry. It won't happen again."

A door opened from inside the apartment, prompting me to step back to put some distance between us. I could only ponder Raven's disenchanted expression for just a second before Toby walked out wearing a wide grin, and that instantly made me smile.

"Toby, my man!" We bumped fists in greeting before he flashed me a note, thanking me for inviting them. "Not a problem, man. Glad you could make it. Figured it was the least I could do for not being around last week to annihilate you in Battleship."

He made a dramatic gesture, rolling his eyes and waving me off. Both Raven and I laughed, the tension between us gone, but not forgotten. She grabbed a denim jacket, slipping it over the shoulders that had been under my grip just seconds before. I could still feel her on my palms.

The ride to Blaine and Kami's place was uneventful, even a little quiet. Toby seemed to enjoy being in a newer model car, but all I could focus on was the woman beside me, and the words she'd uttered in the doorway of her apartment.

Do you want my crazy?

I did. But I knew she wouldn't want mine. She wouldn't be able to handle it. No one could.

And there lay the conflict. I wanted her. Sometimes I thought she wanted me. However, it wasn't her unattainability that kept us apart. It was me. What I was . . . what had been done to me. It ruled my entire being. It consumed me in a way that made it impossible to be with anyone, let alone Raven. One night stands and back room hook ups were one thing. But a real, substantial relationship? One built on trust and honesty? There was no way. She'd see the ugly in me and go running the other way, wracked with fear and disgust.

When I pulled into the driveway of Blaine's 2-story home, Raven grew increasingly agitated.

"What's wrong?" I ask, cutting the engine. She shook her head and looked down at her hands, which were a nervous knot in her lap.

"I made a fool of myself the other night," she whispered, aware of Toby in the backseat. "I don't want them to think I'm

". . ." I stopped her with my palm over her tangle of twisted fingers. She flinched at our sudden connection, but didn't pull away.

"There is nothing and no one in that house that will hurt or judge you. And certainly not Toby. You're safe here. Both of you are safe here . . . with me."

Every word was true. I meant them with every bone in my body and breath in my lungs. They were safe with me. I just wasn't certain that I was safe with her.

We walked in together to wild hoots and hollers at the television screen. March Madness was still in full swing, and down to the Elite Eight. And just as I had predicted, Michigan was still going strong.

"Who's up?" I called out over CJ and Blaine's trash-talking at the TV.

"Michigan," CJ grumbled. He and Blaine were big Duke fans, and if Michigan took the W today, there was a big chance they'd go head to head in the Final Four.

"Aw, don't be salty, CJ. We won't whoop you too hard next week."

"Fu—" Before he could get out the entire word, Blaine kicked his cousin from where he sat on loveseat, prompting CJ to turn around. "Oh, yeah. Hey, Raven. What's up, little dude?"

"Hey, Raven," Blaine said, standing to shake her hand like the good southern gentleman that he was. "Good to see you again, Toby. You guys have a seat."

"Uh-uh. Raven is coming with us," Kami said, carrying a tray of fresh vegetable with some type of dip from the kitchen. She set it on the coffee table next to the spread of chips and what looked to be a layered bean dip. CJ turned up his nose at the veggies but went for a scoop of refried beans, cheese and guac.

"Where?" I asked, when I felt her stiffen beside me. I understood her apprehension, but I didn't expect her to be this fearful. Raven had been nothing short of bold since the day I met her. Seeing her less than confident made me wonder if it had something to do with Toby.

"In the kitchen," Kami answered before dropping a kiss on Blaine's eager lips. "She can help me and the girls."

"Girls?" Angel was a given—she had left before I headed to Raven's apartment. But who else could be . . .

"Yes. Me, Angel and Victoria. I've got them wrapping lumpia."

Victoria? Holy shit, did she mean *Velvet?*

"You mean to tell me—"

"Yup, that's right. I brought a date, a-holes," CJ explained, with a failed attempt at censorship.

I looked over at Raven, who looked slightly less uncomfortable. Maybe Victoria was a good call after all.

She glanced over at Toby and asked, "Will you be ok?" He nodded eagerly and looked to me, his face breaking into a small smile.

"Of course, he will be," I reassured her, waving him to the couch. Blaine leaned over to smack his cousin on the knee, telling him to scoot over.

Kami came around to where Toby sat, her face beaming with warmth and sincerity. She didn't extend her hand, aware that he may have an aversion to touch. "Hi Toby. I'm Kami. You're welcome to anything here. Would you like a soda?"

Toby looked to his sister before nodding.

"Great! I'll have your sister pick out your favorite. Sound good?"

Another nod, this one accompanied by a blush. I totally understood. Pregnant or not, Kami was absolutely beautiful. Especially when she smiled at you and made you feel like the tallest man in the world. I had to give it to Blaine—he had made her happier than she had ever been. She was glowing from the inside out.

I gave Raven a nod and a reassuring grin as Kami led her to the kitchen, where the mouthwatering aromas of fried vegetables, stewed meat and noodles filled the air, along with feminine laughter. Minutes later, Angel emerged with a Sprite for Toby and a beer for me. I kissed her on the cheek as she left to rejoin the ladies, causing Toby's face to catch fire one more time. To most people, it just seemed like a normal, pubescent boy response. To me, it gave me the confirmation I had hoped for. Toby's reactions to the opposite sex were deemed healthy. He didn't seem overtly interested nor repulsed, both signs that could have meant sexual abuse. And he seemed comfortable with sitting with the guys too and not insistent on clinging to his sister. I inwardly rejoiced. If I was wrong about him—and I sincerely hoped I was—then I could not find a better reason to be.

Once we were left to our manly devices, I tried to focus on the game, but my mind kept wandering to the kitchen where I knew Raven was being scrutinized. Not in an awkwardly in-tense way, but I was certain that both Angel and Kami had questions for her. They were just as protective of me as I was with them. I was just thankful that CJ had brought Velvet—er,

Victoria. Still hard to believe she had hooked up with *him*. Even harder to believe that she had stuck around now that the beer goggles were off.

Surprisingly enough, CJ was able to keep the trash talk to PG-13 with Toby there, with only a few slaps and kicks from Blaine. Michigan had just scored the winning shot, much to their chagrin, when the girls filed out of the kitchen, and lined the dining table with several covered dishes.

"Ok, you Neanderthals. Time to eat!" Angel announced.

"About time," CJ grumbled, jumping to his feet. "I'm starved."

He made a beeline straight to Victoria—dressed modestly in skinny jeans and a flouncy blouse—and kissed her passionately, eliciting a squeal. Even her purple hair seemed less shocking with its soft waves slicked back into a ponytail. She looked . . . pretty. Soft and delicate. And I momentarily felt guilty for never choosing to see her like this. For never choosing to see *anyone* for more than a waste receptacle for my doubt and pain. Except for Raven. And that was only because I knew we would never go there. I couldn't use what was not at my disposal. And shit . . . I didn't want to.

We settled around the dining room table, a new addition since Kam had moved in nearly 6 months ago. She had always wanted a place for all of us to be together, especially with the baby coming. She was worried about failing at something she was already a natural at. And between me, Angel—hell, even CJ—that little one would be the most spoiled baby in the world.

"So, Raven, how long have you lived in Charlotte?" Blaine asked before filling his mouth with a forkful of rice and marinated pork.

She reached for her glass of wine and took a sip before answering. "About a year. I moved back to take care of Toby." Her eyes nervously darted to where he sat beside her as she answered. As if she wasn't used to talking about him.

"So you lived here before?" I knew Blaine was just making small talk and trying to be polite, and honestly, I was thankful for it. These were things I had wanted to hear from her lips, and not from a file. I knew she had lived in Virginia previously, and had transferred from her nursing program at Virginia Commonwealth in Richmond. But I hadn't known about her living here in Charlotte in the past. Interesting.

"Yeah," she answered without meeting his friendly gaze. "When I was younger."

"Oh, cool. So how do you like it so far?"

Raven shrugged, pushing food around her plate. "It's all right. Not much has changed, honestly. The economy still sucks anywhere you go, so work has been less than great."

"Raven is one of the waitresses at the club I work at," Victoria chimed in from beside CJ. "Haven't you seen her?"

Blaine's eyes flared as wide as his plate before he choked out a cough. "No," he croaked, reaching for his beer. "Can't say I have." Kami was tight-lipped beside him, and CJ was cackling like a hyena at his cousin's dismay.

"Oh, I'm sure you have," he jibed. "Remember that one night?"

"*Oh wow,* the fried rice is amazing. Kami did you do something different?" I piped up, hoping to save both Raven and Blaine any further embarrassment. But Victoria hadn't taken the hint, no matter how burning Raven's stare was.

"Actually, she's one of our best waitresses. Much too good to be working at a dump like that. Especially with Sal cutting hours."

"You got your hours cut?" I asked, my voice soft beside her. I didn't want to draw more undue attention to her, but I knew how badly she needed the money. If she couldn't pay her bills and fell behind on rent, the state could take Toby out of her care. And DCFS probably wasn't too thrilled about her working in a strip club as it was.

"Yeah," she shrugged. "No biggie. It'll pick up again, or I'll be able to find something else."

"I don't mean to be presumptuous," Blaine interjected, after recovering his voice. "But if you're looking for something else to supplement your hours . . ." At that, Raven lifted her gaze, genuinely interested. "With me and Kam preparing for the baby's arrival, I don't see myself wanting to be behind the bar as much. And we already lost her on the floor. So I was thinking about promoting one of our waitresses to bartender, leaving a spot open. I can't guarantee how many hours, and it may be pretty busy on weekends—"

"Yes!" Raven blurted out before he could even finish.

"Yes? Honestly, you'd be saving me the headache of trying to find someone."

"Yes," she repeated, looking over at Toby, her eyes filled with some unnamed emotion. "We'd love to."

"Great! Come by tomorrow, and we'll take care of everything."

Just before we all turned back to our plates with gusto, I saw Kami look up and Blaine and smile, which he happily returned. She leaned into his shoulder, positioning her forehead

217

right at his lips. And with eyes closed, his heart open for all to see, he kissed her.

I envied that small display of honest affection. I wanted to touch someone so unguardedly . . . love someone so un-selfishly. They had what I had always wanted—unconditional, uninhibited love. And that yearning was only made greater by wanting that with someone who didn't want it with me.

"I'm just happy to finally have a few more ladies around this place," Angel said, as she reached over to snag another lumpia. They had wrapped and cooked a good three dozen and we were already down to the final few.

"I'm sure you are," CJ muttered with a snicker.

"Don't make me bring up some of the trolls I've seen you with, *Craig,*" Angel threatened, pointing her deep-fried roll at him. "Vic here is a definite upgrade from the butterfaces we've had to endure. You better not screw it up. Because I can't tol-erate another scarecrow."

"Scarecrow?"

Angel tapped her temple. "All the necessary parts yet no brain."

"Well, you don't have to worry about me, love," Victoria winked. "I've handled blokes much cheekier than him." She reached over and pinched CJ's cheek, causing him to blush scarlet from neck to brow as he damn near purred into her palm. The simultaneous clank of silverware falling onto plates around the table was deafening. CJ? Blush? Surely we had to be witnessing an act of divine intervention.

After dinner, we cleared the table and covered it with a Monopoly board, and the room crackled with childish glee. I had already filled in the gang on Toby's affinity for board games, and Kami thought it'd be a great way to make him feel welcomed. Since he was mute, Raven read his cards aloud for the group at first. But after a few turns, Toby pulled out his notepad and shorthanded the instructions. It took longer and probably made his hand cramp trying to scribble things down as fast as he could, but he wanted that piece of independence. And, thankfully, no one denied him that.

We were a good hour into the game when both Raven and I had gone bankrupt, along with CJ and Angel. That left Blaine, Kami, Victoria and Toby to battle it out for victory.

"He's really good," I said to Raven as we watched from a few feet away.

"Yeah," she smiled thoughtfully. "I remember playing games with him when we were younger. Candy Land. Trouble. Sorry. He was always quick, even then."

"How old was he when you left?"

I watch the way her throat moved as she swallowed the bitter taste of remembering. "Too young."

I wanted to press for more, but not here. And I seriously doubted she wanted me rummaging through her past with everyone present, having a good time. But I wanted to talk to her. I wanted to be near her. I just didn't know if she'd let me.

"Hey, you wanna go for a drive?"

"Now?"

I shrugged. "Why not?"

She nodded towards Toby, who was snickering as he took Blaine's money. "I can't leave him alone."

"He's not alone. I'd trust Kami and Angel with my life. Blaine too. And oddly enough, as crazy as CJ is, he's a good guy." Just as I said it, he leaned over and whispered something

219

in Victoria's ear, causing her to squeal and smack him on the shoulder. If someone could learn to feel something for him within the span of just a few days, surely he couldn't be all bad.

"I don't know . . ."

"We could take him with us."

She grimaced with uncertainty. "I don't know if he'll want to leave."

I should have let it go but I wanted time with her more than I wanted my pride. "Well, we could . . ."

"Oh, just go, you two lovebirds," Victoria called out from the table, surprising us both.

Raven's face blushed deep rose, her blue eyes wide with embarrassment. "Huh?"

"He's fine here with us, Raven," Kami chimed in, a sheep-ish smile on her face. "We'll take good care of him. Plus, I'm sure Toby doesn't want to miss dessert."

"Oh, yeah, buddy. Kami's brownie sundaes are the shiii—uh, the best," CJ added.

Raven looked at the eager faces around the table, each one sharing looks of reassurance. "Are you sure?" she asked her brother, leaning down to meet his eyes. He gazed back with complete certainty and nodded. Then he did something that caused tears to shine in her bright blue eyes, as well as every eye in the house. He placed his palm against her cheek.

I knew what that simple gesture meant to her—to them. Toby had been so closed off since she had come back into his life. And here he was, trusting again. Telling her that she could do the same.

"Ok." She stood upright and turned to me, her gaze full

of apprehension, but something else too. Maybe fear. Maybe hope. Maybe a mixture of both.

We were mere steps from my car when she said, "Wait. I'm not going." I stopped in my tracks, my heart sinking into my gut.

"What's wrong?"

A sly smile stretched itself across her face. "I'm not going anywhere with you. Unless I drive."

Shaking my head, I fished my keys out of my pocket and tossed them at her. She liked to be in control, and I liked letting her take control. It was a win-win for us both.

"So where are we going?" I asked as we pulled out of Blaine's quiet, suburban neighborhood.

"You'll see."

I reached over to fiddle with the radio, eliciting a slap on my fingers. "Driver picks the music, Trevino."

I put up my palms in surrender, letting her have her way with the music dial. I was more than surprised when she stopped it on an oldies station.

"Were you even born when this song came out?" I asked as The Bangles' "Eternal Flame" played through the Bose speakers.

"Were you?"

"Good point."

Silence hung between us for a long moment before she murmured, "My mom liked this song."

"Before she . . ."

"I didn't know her before she died. Not anymore."

I didn't know what that meant, or what to say. So I went with the one thing that felt appropriate. "I'm sorry."

She shook her head. "It's not me you should be feeling sorry for."

I turned to study her profile in the setting sun. She didn't look at me, her focus trained on the road, but I could see the regret in her haunted eyes. She didn't want my pity, and I had none to give her. "I don't feel sorry for you."

I thought she might be offended by my words, but instead she nodded, understanding what I had meant. "Thank you."

Minutes passed as she drove, the sounds of Michael Jackson, the Eagles, Cheap Trick and the Bee Gees filling the silence. She sang along quietly to some, loudly with others. I watched her with rapt attention, amazed by this woman who commanded all of my senses. She was gorgeous without trying, unintentionally funny, and her energy was infectious. I couldn't look at her without smiling. I couldn't be near her without wanting to be closer still.

When we pulled onto a dirt road and began to follow a steep path uphill, I knew exactly where we were going. Back in the day, we called it Lookout Point. It was the place us high school kids would go to drink cheap-ass Boone's Farm and hook up under the stars. I had taken my fair share of impressionable young girls there, but I hadn't been in years. Especially with someone I actually gave a damn about.

"Here we are," she announced, putting the car in park. Then she reached behind the seat and grabbed her purse. "I'm glad you suggested a drive, Dom. It'll make this a whole lot easier."

Confusion settled on my brow. "Make what a lot easier?"

When Raven's gaze collided with mine, I knew that bringing me to a dark, secluded area wasn't by chance. She had a purpose—a mission. And that mission was me.

"Get out. I'm going to shoot you."

Chapter 25

Raven

THE LOOK OF SHEER horror on Dom's face when I opened my purse and pulled out my weapon of choice?

Fucking hilarious.

Of course, we were both in stitches when he realized that it was a camera in my hand, not a gun. But after our last time together on the roof of my building when he joked about me pushing him off, I just couldn't resist.

"Ha Ha, very funny," he grumbled. "I knew you weren't going to *shoot me*-shoot me."

I was still in hysterics. "Oh really, Trevino? So you just walk around sporting a what-the-fuck face? Come on. I want to get this shot."

I positioned him just a few feet from the cliff drop, causing him to groan with nerves.

"Do I have to be so close to the edge?"

"Yes," I insisted. He didn't really, but I liked to mess with him. Dom was just too easy to screw with. "Ok, now act natural."

He frowned, and I couldn't deny myself the chance to capture it on film. "Natural? I thought that's what I was doing?"

I shook my head, grinning. He was just too damn adorable. "Just be loose. Stop thinking about the fact that you're in front of a camera. Haven't you ever modeled before?"

"Uh, no," he said running a hand through his hair. Click click click. Another one for my collection. "Why do you ask?"

"Just seems like you'd be the type," I shrugged. The type being insanely hot.

"Nope. Sorry to disappoint you."

"Who said anything about being disappointed?" I asked, zooming in on the way his lips sat in a natural, naughty smirk. Nope. Not disappointed at all.

When Dom grew tired of being my muse, he insisted he have a turn with the camera, making me his reluctant subject. I was used to being behind the camera, not in front of it. Seeing yourself through someone else's lens seemed so personal, so intimate. I was afraid of how Dom saw me. Maybe even a little afraid of how I saw myself.

After he was done torturing me, we leaned against the hood of the car, watching the city lights spread out below us. I don't know why I had brought him here. Maybe I had secretly hoped it would trigger a memory . . . something he had buried deep inside a long time ago. Maybe something he wanted to make right after all these years.

But . . . nothing. And I couldn't say I was upset about it. I hated to admit it, but I was actually starting to like the guy, especially after seeing him so dejected yesterday morning. It made him seem more human to me. More *real.* Not the cold-hearted bastard I had told myself he was, when I stayed up late plotting my revenge. Planning all the ways I could hurt him just as he had hurt me.

"Thanks for getting me home safely," I blurted out, not really knowing where it came from. I couldn't remember if I'd thanked him, but I knew I was eternally grateful. He could have left me at the bar, piss drunk and sick. But instead, he showed me compassion. Something I hadn't shown to him despite all his attempts to be kind and generous.

"Don't worry about it," he remarked, with a shrug. "We've all been there. Some of us more than others."

I nodded, and fell back into listening to Foreigner sing about a love that felt like the first time. I closed my eyes and tried to block it out . . . the hurt, the humiliation. I was torturing myself. It was like I wanted to suffer more than I already had. More than *we* already had.

When Dom spoke next, his voice was pensive, almost regretful, as if he didn't want to go down this line of questioning, but it was inevitable.

"What happened to Toby . . . before he found your mom? Was something done to him?"

I shook my head, because, honestly, I couldn't answer that question. Nothing and everything had been done to my little brother. After I left, and Adel had fallen apart completely, he was neglected. She stopped caring for him, stopped feeding him, stopped cleaning him. So eventually, he had to learn to do it himself. He was nine then, so he was old enough to figure things out. But that was before the alcohol started. Then the drugs. Then the men. And by the time I came back for him, after learning about my mother's death, it was already too late. He had lost his voice, along with what little hope he had left. Just as she had lost her will to live.

"He's never told me himself," I said to the moon. "But the doctors believed he had endured so much mental anguish through her years of drug use, that her death had tipped him over the edge. She was a shitty mom, but after I had left, she was all he had. And finding her . . . dead . . . face down in her own bile, it broke him. That little boy crumbled right there on the ground beside her dead, rotting body. By the time anyone found them, it had been three days. He stayed next to her corpse for three days and didn't say a word. Or maybe he said his last words to her."

My chest squeezed so hard, that I didn't think I'd be able to choke it all out. I had never told anyone that story. No one. I was disgusted with myself for not being there. I was angry at her for allowing herself to die. And I was heartbroken for Toby. He was the real victim in all this. He was the one who had hurt the most.

I didn't tell Dom about Toby's stint in a mental hospital after he had gone mute, considering that he probably already knew. At first they believed he was in shock, and maybe he was. But it never got better. He would just sit and stare out the window for hours, never saying a word, barely moving. Sometimes I'd fear that his hope was to stop breathing. That way, he and Adel could be together.

Once they had decided he wasn't insane or suicidal, they granted me full custody. I never told him that his own father, Gene Christian, had refused to take him. He had a new family, one that didn't bring him shame and tarnish his good name. And taking in the poor mute kid that he abandoned, just didn't fit into his life.

"I failed that little boy," I found myself whispering. "I failed him. I failed myself."

I felt his hand grasp mine, the warmth of his skin radiating up my arm and touching the cold place inside me. The place I had kept hidden from the world, locked up tight. The place he created, yet didn't even know it. Yet, here he was, thawing it with his touch. Reclaiming the space he deserted so long ago.

His voice was full of secrets and thick with emotion. "You didn't fail, Raven. You saved him. You saved . . ."

I looked at him then, needing to see his eyes. So much conviction there, yet he gave nothing away. I wanted him. Godammit, I wanted to give him my crazy. I wanted him to remember what it felt like to want me too. I just didn't want him to remember *me*. Not like that.

"Be still." Only our heated breath lay between us.

"Ok," he murmured, leaving his lips parted. When he ran his tongue over the top of his teeth, the wind left my body. He had stolen it with that one, insignificant move that would serve as the straw that broke the camel's back. The straw that broke me.

"You won't touch me." It wasn't a question.

"If you knew about me. If you only knew the . . ." It wasn't an answer.

We sat there for much too long, our lips much too far apart, breathing each other in as if that were some type of re-placement for the one thing that we both wanted, yet refused to have. It was like being on a diet. You see the cupcake—you

AFRAID to FLY

want it—you know it'll be good . . . but you know it'll be bad for you. And while it may be the best thing you ever put in your mouth, you know the guilt and shame will be twice as intense. And you'll hate yourself for being too weak to deny that fucking cupcake.

He was the first to pull away. He was always the first one. And when he did, I still felt the guilt and shame. And I didn't even get the satisfaction of eating the cupcake.

"I'll drive," he said, moving to the driver's side. I fished the keys out of my jacket pocket and handed them to him. I didn't have it in me to argue or demand he let me take the wheel. I wasn't angry at him. Just the opposite, really. I respected his restraint. I only wished I had had an ounce of the same.

I'm lying, I thought to myself as we made our way down the hill and onto the priority road. I'd been lying to myself this entire time.

I was angry. I wanted him to want me. I wanted him to want me so bad that it kept him up at night. I wanted him to need me to the point that I would invade his every waking moment. I wanted the madness of yearning. I wanted full blown, out-of-control, uncontained desire. I wanted his crazy, his ugly, his agony. And I wanted to give him mine in return.

It was a special thing to give yourself over to the one person who had destroyed you. Maybe I was sick in the head. Maybe this was a case of Stockholm syndrome, and I had merely fallen in love with my captor. The only difference was, he didn't want to keep me.

We pulled into the driveway of Blaine's house, and I was out the car before it even came to a full stop.

"Wait," Dom called out, just as I took the first step leading to the porch. I had no plan once I got inside the house. He was our ride home, and I wouldn't make a spectacle of myself just because my stupid, girl feelings were hurt. So I turned around, careful to school my features in its usual passive guise. He wouldn't see me care. I wouldn't let him.

He took his time reaching me, and for a second, I thought he was toying with me. But he was stalling. Whatever he needed to say, he didn't want to, but he needed to. The same way I had felt before when talking about my mother.

"The other morning . . ." he began, catching my undivided attention. I had worried myself sick about what I'd seen. I didn't want to bring it up; I didn't think it was my place. I figured if he wanted me to know, I would know.

And now . . . he wanted me to know.

"My life wasn't—isn't—what it seems. And when I was younger, there were things done to me . . . things I can never talk about. Things that would terrify you, Raven. And I don't want you to be scared of me. I don't ever want you to feel like you have to guard yourself from me. So I'm not touching you because I don't want to. I'm not touching you because once I do . . . I can't stop myself. I can't be with you, and be *me* at the same time. And I won't do that to you."

His face looked so pained, so defeated, that I couldn't stop myself from touching him even if I tried. It was just the brush of my hand against his cheek, but when my skin met his, he groaned. As if the contact physically hurt him. I was hurting him. I had dreamt of doing that very thing, yet there was no satisfaction in it. There was no feeling of victory. Only this overwhelming need to take every ounce of his pain away.

I cupped his cheek with my other hand, feeling the soft scratch of stubble against my palm. He closed his eyes and groaned again, his jaw clenched tight. I moved my fingers to trace the angle of his chin all the way up to the shell of each ear. He shuddered under my touch, but it wasn't enough to make me stop.

To make me stop hurting him. To make me stop healing him.

I was still standing on the step, putting us at eye level, and giving me full view of every single wince and tremor. It empowered me to know I could affect him, yet it was he who controlled me. This unattainable man that made me absolutely crazy with wanting what I shouldn't have.

"What are you doing?" he gasped when I slipped my hands into his hair.

"Touching you." I didn't even recognize my own voice. It was too heavy with passion. Too desperate, too raw.

"But I told you—"

"You told me you wouldn't touch me. You never said anything about me touching you."

I'd like to think it was me who made the first move and closed the distance between our panting lips. But in reality, we met somewhere in the middle of resolve and resignation. And in that space, where two breaths became one, and all that existed was his taste on my tongue, I surrendered myself completely to the very man that I had vowed to hate. I let his hands run the course of my body, sliding up the backs of my bare legs, and wished he'd part them and wrap them around his waist. I let him lick and suck my tongue into his mouth, and I imagined they were my pebbled nipples, bruised pink with his hungry kisses. I let him pull me closer into his body, close enough for me to feel the growing hardness against my belly, and I longed to have it deep inside me, filling me with pleasure . . . filling me with pain.

If our past had hurt me, maybe our present could heal me. Maybe Dom could cancel out the ugliness of those memories by fucking me so beautifully that there would be no room to harbor my resentment. I would be too full . . . too full to feel anything but him.

When we pulled away, breathless, I was only partially aware of my dress fisted in his palms around my waist. He was blocking my front, but if anyone came outside or looked out the window of Blaine's house, they'd get a full view of my white, frilly thong.

Dom gingerly smoothed the dress down over my hips, touching me so gently, it was as if he was afraid to make a mess. I could see it in his eyes—the panic. His regret was closing in, but I couldn't let it take him. Not now. Not when I just got him back.

"Hey," I smiled, causing him to look at me and abandon the task of fixing my clothes. "I'm all right. *We're* all right. See?" I smiled so he could see just how happy he had made me. Because I was. I was fucking happy. And I didn't want to apologize for that. I didn't want to feel bad for having one goddamn thing for *me*.

"Are you sure?" he asked warily.

"Positive," I replied, before kissing his lips one last time. He tasted just like I remembered, maybe even better. Age and experience had done him well, even if it had cost him his dignity.

"God, Raven," he gasped, when I pulled away. "I want you so badly. But it's hard for me . . . it's hard for me to be with someone and . . ."

"Yes?" What was he saying? That he was incapable of having sex? I knew that was bullshit. So why was he making excuses? When we both knew he had already screwed half of Charlotte.

"It's hard for me to be with someone and . . . *care.*"

"Care?"

"Yeah. I don't . . . feel . . . what most people do when they have sex."

"Then what do you feel?"

"Nothing. Numbness. Well, my body feels it . . . obviously." He sheepishly looked down between us at the erection that was still straining against his jeans. My mouth watered involuntarily. *Shit.* "But inside, I can't. I'm not there."

"Then where are you?" I was trying to understand, but damn if I wasn't frustrated. I didn't get it—was he trying to scare me away? Giving me reasons not to sleep with him?

"Anywhere else." His voice was so small, I didn't think I heard him at first. But then he lifted his face to mine, and looked at me with those hazel-green eyes shrouded in secrets and lies. And I saw something I recognized. I saw hurt and shame and hatred. I saw myself.

I took his hands in mine, and did something I told myself I would never do. I broke my last cardinal rule. And I chose to trust him.

"I want to be anywhere else too . . . with you."

Chapter 26

Dom

THERE WAS A REASON why people hated Mondays.

It was the reset button.

The proverbial flush of weekend bliss in order to make room for the following week's fresh pile of bullshit.

I had gone into my Monday with an open mind and an open heart, two things I never imagined could coexist within me. But Raven . . . Raven was my monkey wrench. My plot twist. She flipped the switch on my pessimism and gave me a renewed sense of hope. So, I looked toward the future. I was excited to go into work Monday morning. I was thrilled with the prospect of seeing both her and Toby again. I was optimistic. That is, until I arrived and remembered . . .

It was fucking Monday.

Helping Hands had been broken into over the weekend. The entire place was trashed. Papers littered every inch of the floor, computers were smashed, and food was smeared all over the snack bar, the stench giving us a warm welcome when we came in this morning. The place was destroyed, and thousands of dollars—and even more hours of work—had been lost.

Insurance would help us recoup some of our losses, but it wouldn't replace the children's art projects and science experiments. We prided ourselves on providing them a safe environment, and now, it seemed none of us were safe. How could they thrive in chaos?

The whole team worked tirelessly to clean up as much as we could while Amber worked with the police. We didn't have the funds to hire a cleaning crew, especially now, and with cops everywhere, it'd be wasted anyway. As second in command, I made the call to prepare the gymnasium for after school activities, since it seemed the least destroyed. We cleaned up the floor and walls, removed all the trash, then set up groupings of table and chairs for tutoring sessions. The bleachers could be used for private mentoring and individual activities. I even planned to order pizza for their after school snack out of my own pocket. I didn't want the kids to see this as a tragedy. A stumbling block, yes. But we would make the most out of it.

"What happened?" I heard a familiar voice gasp from behind me. I turned around to find Kami taking in the scene, her eyes wide with shock. Shit. I had forgotten about our lunch date, and with all the commotion, hadn't thought to call her.

"Break in," I answered before leaning forward to greet her with a peck on the cheek. "Damn, my bad. I should have called before you came all the way down here. We're swamped here."

Her gaze grew wide with panic. "A break in? Are you ok?"

"I'm fine. No one was here. Just a mess is all. Probably

some neighborhood punks. Wouldn't be the first time."

"Oh God. Anything I can do?"

"Nah. Just let Angel know that I might be home late tonight."

After I walked her back to her car and kissed her goodbye, I thought about texting Raven to let her know what was going on. I didn't know where the impulse came from; I didn't check in with anyone outside of Kami and Angel. But, I thought . . . maybe she'd care. Maybe she'd want to know I was safe. Maybe she wanted to hear the sound of my voice through those typed letters, just as I craved to hear hers.

I grabbed a broom and continued to sweep instead. Because . . . maybe she didn't.

As we anticipated, the afternoon was complete pandemonium. The kids were worried, many of them shaken by the shift in routine. The pizza helped, along with a promised game of basketball after the allotted hour of study time, but I could still feel their anxiety. Especially Toby's. Uncomfortable with such a large crowd convening in one enclosed space, when he arrived, he made a beeline for the highest level of the furthest bleacher. I made it a point to save him some pizza, and once everyone was settled in their designated groups, I took it over to him.

"My man," I said placing the flimsy paper plate beside him. "Sorry about the craziness. Trust me, it sucks."

He shrugged a shoulder and looked down at the textbook he was holding. Math. He had math tutoring today, but he was too upset to go to his tutor. It meant exposure in front of everyone.

I gestured towards the book. "Hey, I can help you with

that if you want me to. I mean, I don't know how good I'll be, but maybe we can figure it out together."

He looked at me, and just a little of the carefree boy I saw last night playing Monopoly peeked out. The corner of his mouth turned up, and he nodded.

"Ok, cool. Why don't you eat this slice before it gets even colder, and I'll try to explain what we're doing without totally confusing you."

He chuckled and nodded again, handing me the book and picking up the plate. I turned to the page that was bookmarked by the homework worksheet.

"Ok, dividing decimals by whole numbers . . ."

Somehow, some way, we survived 6th grade math. At least one day of it. Well, one hour.

As promised, the kids got to play ball until it was time to go home. And while Toby didn't want anything to do with it, I did manage to get him to come down to the bottom of the bleachers to watch and listen to me play coach. I was almost sad when parents started arriving to pick up their kids. In the past, I had given serious thought to coaching little league sports, but I didn't have children of my own, and I didn't want to risk someone thinking I was a predator. So it was nice to be able to do something I was passionate about without dealing with certain assumptions.

"Hey, Coach Trevino." Even though the sound of her voice had been echoing in my head all day, it was still no replacement for the real thing. Not even close.

I made myself not turn around too quickly, and forced myself not to smile too widely. But the moment I took her in—wearing blue and yellow duck scrubs—all my restraint went out the window.

"Hey," I grinned. Oddly enough, she was beaming too.

"Hey."

"Good to see you." It was the appropriate thing to say in front of a gym full of kids, teachers and even a few parents. But what I really wanted to do was scoop her up in my arms until her blue, Croc-covered feet no longer touched the ground, and kiss every bit of that perfect mouth.

"Love what you've done with the place," she remarked, taking in the makeshift classroom/basketball court.

"Yeah. Looks like some kids got in over the weekend."

She frowned and shook her head. "Anything get stolen?"

"Not that we can tell. Lots of damage though."

"Then I doubt it was just kids."

Damn. She was right. All the iPads, computers, hell, even game consoles . . . something should have been stolen.

I needed to talk to Amber, find out if there were any particular political or social groups that would have something against inner-city youth getting ahead. But I wasn't quite ready to leave Raven. Not yet.

"Um, uh . . . do you think I can see you? Tomorrow?"

She looked back at Toby who seemed overly interested in a thread on his sleeve, and rolled her eyes. He was listening. He was always listening.

"I'm training at Dive tomorrow. But only for a few hours. Maybe . . . after? We can pick up dinner, since I won't have time for Hashtag Spaghetti Tuesday."

"Or . . . how would you feel if I cooked for Hashtag Spaghetti Tuesday?"

She raised a cynical brow and put a hand on the curve of

her hip. "You want to cook spaghetti?"

"Come on, how hard could it be? Between me and Toby, we got this." The kid lifted his head at the mention of his name and smiled.

"Ok. If you think you two can handle it . . ."

"Piece of cake. Sauce, meat, noodles," I said with a wave. "And if you're cool with it, I was thinking I could save you a trip by just letting Toby hang out with me until I get off. Then maybe you could meet us at my place?" Her body went visibly rigid at that thought, so I hurriedly tacked on, "Only if you're comfortable with it. If not, no biggie."

"Um . . . ok. Yeah. I guess that'd be ok," she nodded. "Yeah, that's fine."

"Great. So . . . see you tomorrow?"

"Yeah. Tomorrow."

Tomorrow couldn't come soon enough.

Ok, so I lied. I could not cook spaghetti.

I couldn't even boil noodles without them clumping together. And you're supposed to brown the meat *before* adding the sauce?

Toby was no help. He was more excited to get to ride in my Charger again. Then when he saw Angel's pimped-out pad, I pretty much lost him to the 85-inch flat screen with every channel known to man, plus our PS4, Xbox One and Wii U.

"A little help here?" I called out, trying to figure out why the sauce kept splattering everywhere.

Toby walked right in the kitchen, turned the range's dial and walked right back out without so much as a look in my direction. I looked at the mess around me, myself included. It was a good idea and a valiant effort, but I didn't want to serve Raven this crap. Hell, I wouldn't serve a dog this crap. So I called in the big guns.

"Kam, how fast do you think Mr. Bradley can whip up a few orders of his Cajun shrimp and chicken pasta?"

"I don't know. Want me to ask?" she answered over the Dive Happy Hour background chatter.

"Please. And tell him I need it as quick as he can. It's an emergency."

"Does that emergency start with an R?" she teased, excitement in her voice.

"Yes. And a failed attempt at spaghetti with meat sauce."

She made a tsking sound and laughed at my pathetic culinary experience. "Should have called me."

"I know. So can you make sure it gets done? And if one of the bus boys can drive it over by . . ." I looked at the clock. Shit, less than an hour. " . . . seven o'clock, tell him there's twenty bucks in it for him."

"You got it Wolfgang Puck."

"Haha. Love you. And don't tell anyone it's for me!"

At 6:57pm, I was tipping Dive's bus boy, Gary, his twenty and thanking him for the food, while Toby watched the entire exchange over the Xbox controller in his hands. I was still trying to hide the Styrofoam evidence when the buzzer sang for the second time in five minutes.

"It's . . . me? Raven?" she stammered, when I answered through the intercom. I could see her through the security monitor, fussing with her hair and applying another coat of lipgloss. I was tempted to just stand there and watch her for a few more moments.

"Come on up," I said, smiling to myself.

I had to play it off like I wasn't waiting impatiently by the door for her, but when I looked over at Toby and caught his smirk, I knew I'd been made.

"Oh, hush. Give it a few years, and you'll be doing the same."

He shook his head, trying not to laugh, as if to say, *"Yeah, right, dude. Not me. I'd never be that whipped."* To which I shot him a look that said, *"Oh, you just wait. Some girl will come along and put you flat on your ass, struck stupid but happy as hell."*

When Raven knocked on the door, breaking us from our unspoken conversation, I braced myself for the worst. One: I had never brought a woman here for any reason other than sex. Two: I had never taken a woman anywhere without it either leading or following sex. And Three: I had never given a damn whether they had children, siblings, pets, whatever. That wasn't my concern.

But here I was, Dirty Dom, serving pasta to a woman I'd only had the pleasure of kissing, and said woman's kid brother. And I had never been so excited to be so square and *normal* in my life.

"Smells great in here," Raven remarked as I took her light jacket and purse, and hanged them up. Her wide eyes roamed the palatial, ivory-hued space with the same awe and amazement that most people did when they visited for the first time. I inwardly cringed. God, I hoped she didn't think I was a pompous douche.

I felt like I should apologize, or some shit, for an apartment that wasn't even mine. But before I could, Raven spun around and said, "Nice digs, Trevino. Compensating for something?"

I exhaled a nervous chuckle and shook my head. "No. Not at all. But you should probably ask Angel. According to her, she's got the biggest . . . *ego* . . . ever. And will threaten bodily harm if you try to test it."

"Oh, God, do I even want to know?" she laughed.

"Probably not. Unless you know Tyrone."

"Can't say that I do, Trevino."

"Good," I jibed, wiping faux sweat from my brow.

We took our playful banter to into the living room, where Toby was still parked in front of the TV, game controller in hand.

"Hey kid," she greeted him, ruffling his hair. He flicked his gaze up at her and gave her a nod.

"Sorry. Seems I've created a zombie."

"S'okay. I'm sure it's a nice change from the board games. How about the grand tour while he finishes up?"

I extended the crook of my arm and bowed. "Certainly, m'lady."

I showed her the necessary rooms—the bathrooms, the dining room, Angel's studio (she got a kick outta that). Of course, I saved my bedroom for last. It was the last room down the hall, but I also had my own reasons.

"Nice," she mused, checking out some of my old sports trophies from high school. "You still play?"

"Not unless I want to embarrass myself," I replied, shaking my head. I was good in my day, but not pro good. And honestly, I only took up sports because I thought that was what

242

I was supposed to do as a *real* man. As a *straight* man. I never bet on actually liking them or even being good.

"And let me guess," she gestured toward my king-sized bed, decked out in a royal blue duvet and half a dozen pillows. "The throne in your den of iniquity."

"More or less," I shrugged. She knew my reputation, yet she was here anyway. No use in playing coy now.

Raven ran her fingers over the slick satin of the bedspread before turning to face me, the backs of her thighs touching the foot of the bed. "Nice."

"It's all right, I guess."

"Have you changed your sheets lately?"

"I don't know, is there a need to?" I didn't bother to mask the suggestive edge in my voice as I moved in closer.

"I'd say. You never know what may come up." The edge of her lips lifted into a naughty smile.

Another step forward. "Ms. West, are you flirting with me?"

"That depends, is it working?"

I chuckled, shaking my head, but I was still closing the distance between us. "I think someone has been recording those cheesy pick-up lines from the club."

"Well, those cheesy pick-up lines got me alone with you in your bedroom, now didn't they?"

We were toe-to-toe now, so close that I could inhale every one of her breaths and covet them as my own. I don't know what I was waiting for—a sign, permission—but I let the moment linger, allowing it to build and evolve into something greater than desire. More tangible than lust.

She licked her glossy bottom lip, and the sight of her pink

tongue was the only signal my body needed. Fingers tangled in her dark tresses, I cradled her head in my hands as I crushed my lips to hers. She opened for me willingly, sliding her tongue against mine with the same hunger that raged deep in my gut. The very same hunger that had me lifting her by her waist to sit her on the bed. Her legs found my hips, fitting themselves around my body, pulling me closer into the warmth radiating between her thighs.

This was easy. Physical intimacy was damn near instinctual to me. But as I settled on top of her body, her heat melding with mine, I forced myself to remember that it was Raven I was touching. Raven I was kissing. Raven I wanted to be so deep inside of that she would become molded to me.

I could do this. I could be present for her. If I closed my eyes, I wouldn't lose her like I had lost everyone before. My heart and mind wouldn't be ruled by the sensations of my body. I could do this for her. I could be normal for her . . .

"Wait, Dom. Stop."

I froze and opened my eyes, only to find that I was no longer settled on top of her body, eagerly kissing her lips. I was hovered over her with my hands up her shirt, teasing her breasts as my tongue licked a path from one hipbone to the other, stopping to dip inside her jewel-studded navel.

I had done it again. I had gone too far. And this time, I hadn't even noticed. This time, I hadn't even been there.

Chapter 27

Raven

"OH GOD." DOM RECOILED and jumped to his feet like my skin was on fire. He looked down at his hands and frowned before stuffing them behind his back, as if he were admonishing them for touching me. "Raven, I'm so sorry. Oh God, I'm so sorry."

"You're sorry?" I questioned, sitting up and adjusting my shirt. I was ready to go the fuck off. He was rejecting me— again. But then, I saw the dejection on his face. The look of pure defeat. "Why? Because I'm not."

He opened and closed his mouth half a dozen times before responding with narrowed eyes. "Wait . . . you're not?"

"Hell no." I stood up and placed my arms around his neck, keeping him from backing away any further. "Why would I be sorry, Dom? I wanted that. I wanted *you.* It's just . . . Toby is in the other room, and I'm really not trying to have the awkward talk with him."

I could see he wanted to run; I could feel the rock-hard tension bounding the muscles in his back. He was shaken, and it wasn't just about him getting caught with his hands up my shirt. There was something deeper in his forlorn gaze. Something darker.

"I'm sorry, Raven," he whispered. "I lost myself. I thought I could be stronger than . . . I'm sorry." I felt the burden of guilt lift from his shoulders marginally, but not completely. He closed his eyes an exhaled before leaning his head forward to touch it with mine.

The defeat in his voice was so heartbreaking, that I couldn't do much more than pull him into my arms. I started out on this journey, believing that Dominic Trevino was the aggressor—a predator—when in reality, he was anything but. There was something fragile inside him, something that could be easily broken. And I knew right then, with his eyes shut tight and his forehead pressed to mine, that I had the power to shatter it completely. To destroy him, just like he had destroyed me.

I didn't want to think like that, but that had been all I had ever wanted for years. All I had ever dreamed about. To make him feel all the pain that he had given me. And here it was— the opportunity to make him pay. To restore the dignity I had lost that night so long ago. I didn't know what to do. I cared for him, and I wanted to believe he had changed. But would that make up for the person he was? Could that overshadow what he'd done?

"Can we try again?" he whispered, our lips just centimeters apart. It was like he had heard my internal battle and was providing me with a truce. *Let's try again.* Oh, how I wished it were that simple.

"Try what again?"

"Tonight." He lifted his face and pinned me with his molten gaze. "Dinner. Us."

"Sure." I could rewind tonight, if only for tonight. But the same couldn't be said for our past.

"Come on. We're missing Hashtag Spaghetti Tuesday."

He led me back to the living room, where he left me to go finish up dinner. Toby was flipping through channels like a kid on Christmas, hopefully oblivious to what had been going down just down the hall and to the left. I didn't know how to do this. Was there some special protocol to follow when dating a new guy? Should I have asked for his permission? I knew he liked Dominic, but that didn't mean he would be cool with *me* liking Dominic.

"Hey, kid," I said, grabbing his attention from some TV show featuring dumb stunts posted on the internet. He looked over at me and raised his brows. "So you know . . . Dom . . . and me. You're good with that, right?"

Toby shot me a look that I could only describe as one part mocking, one part amused, as if to tell me, *"I already know what's going down, and it's cool. Please just spare me the details."*

"Ok," I said in response. "Just wanted to be sure."

Seconds later, Dom announced that dinner was served and led us to a dining room table that was much too grandiose for the three of us. Sparkling crystal and china covered a linen tablecloth that boasted some type of intricate lace detailing on the sides. Everything was so white and clean and intimidating.

I couldn't eat here. I'd be too afraid of splattering spaghetti sauce on one of the linen napkins that probably cost more than an entire day's pay.

"This is stupid, isn't it?"

I looked up at Dom, wondering if I had heard him correctly. "Huh?"

"This room. It's stupid. No one ever eats here. And when we do, it takes like half an hour to move all this crap." He stood up and grabbed the covered dish that sat in the middle of the table. "Come on."

After putting the food back in the kitchen, we piled our plates high with pasta, bread and salad and moved to the living room floor. While it was still nicer than any floor I'd ever sat on, it was much less daunting than the formal dining room.

"So what do you think?" Dom asked before slurping up a noodle. "Did I just slay Hashtag Spaghetti Tuesday or what? And don't feel bad. Not everyone can be great at everything. Unless you're me."

I twirled a bite around my fork and inspected it before bringing it to my lips. "I have to admit, it is delicious. My compliments to the chef. I'll be sure to thank him Thursday during my shift at Dive."

I tried to keep a straight face, but his expression of shock and embarrassment was just too rich. We both nearly fell over into our plates with laughter. Even Toby was chuckling with a hand over his mouth.

"Dude! Did you think I wouldn't notice? I was in the kitchen when your order came in!"

Dom could barely keep it together. I was almost afraid he'd choke on one of his noodles. "I'm gonna kill Kami! I told her to keep it a secret!"

"Well, it didn't help that I passed the busboy in the hallway."

He shook his head, trying to regain his wits. "I'm getting my $20 back. See. This would have never happened if you liked tacos like the rest of the world. The only people who hate tacos are terrorists and people who take awkward cat portraits."

I gasped, clutching my imaginary pearls for dramatic affect. "You hate cats?"

"You *like* cats?"

"That's it. This relationship is over."

We shared another laugh, enjoying the ease and comfort of just *being*. Dom was easily the sweetest, funniest guy I had ever known, and I enjoyed being around him. It was like being outside on a warm day, and the sun shining just for you. I tried to keep reminding myself that it could be a ruse; he'd had so much experience with gaming girls that he had become a pro at it. But I wanted to believe in something more than his shadowed reputation. I wanted to believe in *him*.

"So how did those pictures you took turn out?" he asked before popping a shrimp into his mouth.

"Good, from what I can tell. I haven't had the chance to edit or anything."

"Well, I'd love to see them. You have a good eye. I can tell."

I shrugged it off and focused on my plate. Talking about myself and my love for photography—the one thing my mother and I had in common—always made me feel self-conscious. It was that piece of me that I had never shared, yet for some reason, I had shared it with him. So in essence, I was showing him the tiny fragment of Adeline West that I carried with me. It was like exposing my darkness and trying to pass it off as beauty.

After dinner, I offered to help him clean up the crime scene in his kitchen, while Toby enjoyed his last taste of cable TV. I picked up a congealed clump of what used to be pasta, with a set of tongs.

"Um, we need to talk about this before we move further."

I looked up from the burnt meat and sauce he was trying to scrape into the trash and grimaced. "Yeah, uh, about that. Home Ec was not my strong suit."

I let a glob fall back into the pot with an unceremonious *plop!* and cringed. "What? No secret family recipes?"

I watched as the light dimmed inside his eyes. He shook his head, his focus turning back on his task. "No. I don't. Secrets, yeah. But no recipes. And no family."

I stayed quiet as I watched him scrub the pan furiously, the muscles in his forearms flexing with every violent scrape against stainless steel. There was something there . . . something lurking in that admission. We all had secrets—hell, I should know. But no family? Dom was an orphan?

My voice was small when I spoke next. "What happened to them?"

He took his time walking the pan over to the sink and dumping into a sudsy pool of hot water. "Died when I was little. Car crash."

"Both of them?"

"Yeah." His voice was flat, devoid of emotion, as if the subject had turned him cold.

"What happened to you?"

His shoulders hunched forward, like he was shielding himself. I knew that move. I'd seen Toby do the same when I first came back into his life. The doctors told me it was an act of defense, common in children who had experienced trauma.

"I became numb."

I stepped forward. "What do you mean?"

"I mean, I learned to deal." He turned to me, grinning as if we weren't just talking about his parents' heart-wrenching death, and shrugged. "I'm fine, Raven. Really. People die. You and I both know that."

"Yeah, I know . . ." Shit, did I ever. Physically, my mom had only been gone a year, but she killed herself off a long time ago in my heart. When I moved away, she somehow thought that meant I was no longer her daughter. She was happy to leave my elderly grandparents with the task of dealing with her little slut of a daughter. And honestly, leaving her home was the best thing that had ever happened to me. But it was the worst thing that ever happened to Toby.

I went back to gathering the rest of the pots, pans and utensils and dumped them in the sink. Shoulder to shoulder, he washed and I rinsed, our movements synchronized, as if we had known each other in another life. And in that life, we hadn't been orphaned, and we didn't have secrets that threatened to tear us apart. And the man I was starting to fall in love with wasn't the monster that had triggered every terrible thing that had ever happened to my little brother and me.

Chapter 28

Dom

WEDNESDAY WAS RAVEN.

Calling her after she got off work, and talking on the phone until 3 in the morning. Telling her about my pipe dreams to change the world. Listening to her bucket list of places she wanted to visit.

Thursday was Raven.

Watching her waitress at Dive as I sipped beer at the bar with CJ. Pulling her into my arms as she walked by. Stealing kisses whenever she had a free moment.

Friday was Raven.

Meeting her for lunch near her school. Daring her to take a bite of my taco until she relented. Tasting her lips as I pressed my body into hers at her car, nowhere near ready to say goodbye.

Every day was filled with her, yet it wasn't nearly enough.

The yearning for contact had been steadily growing stronger, and while I didn't want to rush her, I knew myself. I knew what my body needed. And it was becoming harder and harder to stifle its urges.

This whole thing was new to me. And considering we hadn't even put a label on our . . . *situation* . . . I honestly didn't know what was appropriate. I knew I didn't want to fuck it up, that was for sure. But I also knew that I couldn't keep denying the side of me that craved contact. And the fact she hadn't made it known that she needed it—needed me—made me start to doubt what was between us. Maybe I was delusional, playing myself into thinking that we were actually together. Shit, it wasn't like we'd made things official.

But still.

I cared about her. I couldn't lie to myself. And for that reason, I was reluctant to take this to a physical level, no matter how badly I wanted her. In my fucked up, convoluted head, sex wasn't a show of intimacy that was attached to emotion. It wasn't an act of love and affection. It was confirmation—a necessity to feel solidified in my manhood. It was the only way I could go to bed at night and feel somewhat okay in my own skin.

I didn't want to use Raven for my own selfish needs, but . . . fuck . . . I needed her. I needed her bad.

In my bones, I knew that being with her would break my resolve in two. I knew my fortress of fantasy would come crumbling down the very moment I fit myself between her thighs and pushed inside her. Not falling for her wasn't an option, because I had already fallen. Fallen deep and hard and fast. Too fast. And nothing that happened that forcefully could be good for me. But, being the indulgent motherfucker I was, it just made me want her more.

I was in my room getting ready for the evening ahead, when Angel stopped inside my doorway, her guitar case in tow. "You coming tonight?"

I shook my head. "Raven worked the lunch shift today, so we've got plans."

"Oh?" She watched me button up a crisp, linen shirt before making a suggestive sound in her throat. *"Ohhhh.* I know what tonight is."

"I don't know what you're talking about, Ang."

"Bullshit, you don't. The clothes, the sexy cologne, fresh haircut. You're about to give her the Dirty Dom Special with extra sauce."

"You're ridiculous," I muttered, shaking my head.

"Dude, you act like I don't know all your tricks. Hell, I *taught* you all your tricks."

"Um, I remember that happening much differently," I scoffed.

"Whatever. You were okay before me. I made you great. *Leg-end-ar-y.* You'll go down in history books as the guy that took Angel Cassidy's V-Card and the only peen this puss has ever seen. Be proud, young grasshopper."

"You're talking about yourself in third person now? What's next? Rushing random stages and giving fake honors to Beyonce?"

She rolled her eyes and waved a hand dramatically. "Puh-lease. Beyonce thinks they should give all awards to me."

We shared a laugh and a kiss on the cheek before she went to rock the masses, leaving me to contemplate my next move.

Raven and I had plans tonight, but she didn't know it yet. And if I was going to do this . . . if I was going to take this step, I had to do it the right way. No matter how much it terrified the fuck outta me.

An hour later, I stood in the middle of her tiny apartment, nervous as hell and rethinking everything I had done to get to this point. Shit, what if this was a mistake? What if she saw this as yet another violation? What if I was being presumptuous and all this would prove comical to her? I wanted to call Kami and unload on her, but that wouldn't be fair. She was happy, she was in love, and if she could go through hell and back for the person she adored, I could too.

Toby was only too eager to help me out with my odd requests, without truly knowing the nature of them. Of course, that was after I lent him my PS4 for the weekend. Since he usually stayed over at Mrs. Ralston's when Raven worked late, after hooking up the game system and providing them with takeout, I was left to prepare.

Angel was partially correct—this was *the night.* But there would be no Dirty Dom. I wouldn't try to fuck her brains out, only to get up, dress and leave right after. Not if I could help it.

Two dozen candles flickered around the room, the wine was chilled, and soft music played. In my mind, this was the corniest thing I had ever done. But in my heart, I hoped that the sentiment would not be lost on her. I wanted her to know that I had not only listened to her dreams, I cared about them. I cared about her. And sometimes you had to do corny shit to prove that you gave a damn about someone.

I held my breath when I heard the key slip into the lock of her front door. It felt like hours instead of mere seconds before the handle twisted and she stepped inside. But when she lifted her gaze and took in the scene in front of her, I thought . . .

This.

This was what I had been waiting for.

The wonder in her eyes. The look of complete and utter amazement. This was what I wanted more than anything. Maybe even more than sex.

"Oh my God," she gasped as she realized what I had done. "How did you . . . ? How did you do this?"

"I've got friends in high places," I smiled. "I hope you don't mind."

"Mind? Holy crap, Dom. I never thought . . . I never even imagined . . ."

She stood speechless with a hand over her mouth as she gazed at all the beauty that was seen through her lens. All the beauty she had captured and reflected.

Although it had taken some time and a couple bribes, I was able to get ahold of all of Raven's undeveloped photos. Luckily, most of them were in a shoebox full of USBs in her closet, but some were still on old-school rolls, before the days of digital. I was amazed by how deep her passion ran, and how truly talented of an artist she was. And I wanted her to see just how amazing I thought she was. Toby had let me know that the printing could be expensive, and Raven could rarely afford it now that she was a full-time working parent and student. So, I took it upon myself to take care of it, and display her works on every wall, surface and space in the living area of her apartment.

There were black and white photos of random people in their rawest, realest forms, all traveling on different paths.

Some were homeless people around in the heart of the city. There were photos of stoic business people in power suits, barking into cell phones. Pictures of women cradling babies, lips pressed to chubby cheeks. Portraits of children playing, laughing freely without a single care in their world. Shades of happiness, anger, sadness, desperation and love were all displayed on her walls. It was honest. It was life.

"There were a lot. More than I had space to cover. So I placed them in a folder for you." I stepped beside her and handed her a glass of wine.

"Thank you," she said before taking a sip. "This is incredible, Dom. I just . . ." She paused to collect herself, taking a breath. "I kept telling myself that one day . . . one day I'd do it, and I'd get to relive all those special moments frozen in time. And then maybe their beauty would erase all the ugliness in my past. They would rewrite my history."

I slipped the glass from her hand, placing it on an end table nearby. Then I pulled her into my arms. "If I could replace every hurt you've ever felt, I would. I would take it all and bottle them up forever so you would never suffer again. But then we wouldn't be standing here. I wouldn't feel for you the way that I do. And you wouldn't be looking up at me with the most gorgeous blue eyes I've ever seen. So while I would erase your past if I could, I want to keep it too. Because without it, we would never have this present. And we'd have nothing to hope for in the future."

She smiled at me, and I felt my insides heat. "When did you get so poetic?"

"I don't know. I think a girl had something to do with it. She's the artsy fartsy type."

When she laughed, eyes closed and head dipped back, I felt like the luckiest man in the world. Because I had made her happy, if only for a little while.

"Sometimes I think I know you, Dominic Trevino," she whispered. "And then I realize that I was wrong."

"Not as bad as you thought, huh?"

A Cheshire grin crept onto her lips. "No. You're much worse."

Her mouth was soft and warm against mine, her hands delicately firm as they slid up my neck and into my hair. I could taste the longing on her tongue, sweet yet tart from the wine, and I drank it in like an elixir. She intoxicated me. Beguiled by the beauty of her soul. I felt like I had just woken up from a lifetime of detachment, and now I lived to feel *everything*.

I could have kissed her forever—and I wanted to—but I forced myself to pull away in an act of selflessness. There was something she needed to see. Something she needed to know about me.

"Come with me," I said, my voice husky.

I took her hand and led her over to where that framed photo of her and Toby sat. I had paid special attention to this section, decorating it with some of the oldest photos I'd had developed. The pictures that her mother had taken. I didn't want to upset her, so I put most of them in a folder for her to look at later. I only showcased a few shots of her and her brother, ones that would only evoke happiness in her when they called on a lost memory. She gasped aloud as she touched each one, remembering birthday parties, bike rides and forts made of blankets in the family room. I wanted her to see that not all past was pain.

When she came to a more recent photo, I awaited her re-action without breathing.

"How did you get this?"

"Last weekend after dinner . . . you let me take a few photos."

"You said you didn't know what you were doing."

"I didn't. You did it all for me."

Her back was to me in the photo, her arms outstretched and head to the sky as she stood at the cliff's edge. She was unguarded and completely uninhibited. In that moment, she was as free as a bird.

"Turn it over," I told her.

When she read the inscription, the words I had fashioned just for her in my scrawl, an undefined feeling filled my chest. Maybe it was pride. Maybe it was lust. Maybe it was fear.

All the beauty in the world has been captured in your eyes.

Raven, you reflect life.

Then she looked at me, and I realized, it was none of those things at all. Not even close.

Chapter 29

Raven

I DIDN'T HAVE THE words to say thank you. There was nothing in the English language that could verbally define what I was feeling at that exact moment. So I didn't say a word. Instead, I showed him. With every single part of me, I surrendered myself to what I felt for Dominic Trevino and kissed him like my dying breath lay on his lips. And everything I had felt before—before pain and abandonment and humiliation ever played a part in our story—was resurrected. All those emotions rose up within me and took flight. And in his arms, I was soaring.

As if it were choreographed, we began to shuffle towards the hall, towards the bedroom. I wasn't even sure who initiated the move, but I knew I wanted to. I knew I wanted him. And judging by the feel of his body against mine, hard and hot in every place my fingers touched, he wanted me too.

He wanted me.

After everything that had happened . . . all the rejection, the disgust . . . *now* he wanted me.

I don't know how I was supposed to feel about that. I had changed so much since then, and so did he. We were different people now. And *this* Raven had never known what it felt like to have *this* Dom kiss her with so much passion that her knees nearly collapsed under her. She had never had every stitch of clothing peeled off her body so agonizingly slow by him. And *this* Dom had never let his hands worship every single solitary inch of her frame with the barest of caresses.

For *this* Dom and *this* Raven, it would be the first time. There would be no memories to overshadow it.

His hands touched me everywhere, his lips and tongue following their path. He was a blind man that could only see me through physical contact, and he needed to learn every freckle, curve and dimple. I shuddered when he dipped his head and wrapped his mouth around my nipple. I arched my back into the sensation of his gentle sucking, needing each wet, greedy draw. He gripped me around the waist, pulling me closer into the reverence of his tongue and teeth, moaning with gratitude. When I felt the sheets hit my back, he moved down further, reacquainting himself with the jeweled barbell in my navel. His short fingernails gently scraped up and down my rib cage as he kissed every bit of my torso, sending tingling warmth to my core.

The sounds I was making were indecent, raw and unbelievably erotic, but they didn't compare to the gruff moans and growls that rumbled in his throat as he savored my body. He seemed to take pleasure in making me squirm under his touch, as if it were enough for him. As if all he wanted was to make me pant his name as he spread my thighs, my flesh, and tasted me.

I held onto his hair, because not holding onto something wasn't an option. I knew he had experience—much more than me—but I never imagined he would be this *good*. Then I began to wonder if he made every woman feel this way . . . this alive. I wondered if he made their knees quiver like this while propped up on his shoulders. But as the roughness of his tongue stroked the softness in me, I couldn't find the strength to care.

I was so ready for him, and when he moved onto his knees, I could clearly see that he was just as ready for me. He was still fully dressed, and I felt a pang of guilt for not giving his body the attention it deserved. Against the tremble in my joints, I sat up and kneeled in front of him on the bed.

"What are you doing?" he asked as I began to unbutton his shirt.

"What does it look like?"

I frowned a bit, but it didn't deter me. "I wanted this to be about you tonight. I want to take care of you."

I fumbled with the last button then slipped the garment over his shoulders. "You do. You have. But now it's my turn. I've waited too long for this chance, and I'm not going to waste it."

His chest and abs were spectacular, as I knew they would be. Deep cuts of muscle under smooth, bronze skin were like marble underneath my fingertips. A short dusting of black hair ran from his belly button and disappeared into the waistband of his slacks. I leaned forward and kissed his chest, the skin like heated silk under my lips, and went for the clasp of his pants. I kissed him again, this time wetting a small, brown nipple with the flick of my tongue. He groaned and gripped the back of my head, spurring me on. I licked the other one, then raked my teeth down to his abs. I wanted more of him. I needed every glorious inch of the man I'd longed for since I was just a girl.

"Lie down," I demanded, guiding him onto the bed.

Once he was flat on his back, I crawled up his body, resuming my tour of his torso. I laved each nipple thoroughly. I kissed every mound of muscle on his abs. Then I followed the little trail of dark hair with my tongue.

I worked on the buttons of his pants and moved them down his legs. His boxers were next to go, and he was only too eager to ease the strain that jumped and pulsed in my palm when I took hold. I put him to my lips, tasted the slickened skin from root to tip. His whole body trembled, and his breaths were reduced to short, jerky pants.

I had power over him. I was controlling his pleasure. And that revelation within itself was nearly enough to send me over the edge.

I worked him with my mouth and hands until he begged me to stop. And even then I tortured him a bit more. We laughed when he pulled me up from between his legs and flipped me over.

"You're asking for trouble, aren't you?" he grinned lazily, tousled hair falling into his eyes.

"If your name is Trouble, then yes. Yes, I am."

He kissed me deep and long and so thoroughly that it was like being fucked. I couldn't breathe, and I didn't want to. I had surrendered to his sensual asphyxiation, had offered my life in exchange for his passion. It scared me how badly I wanted this—how desperately I needed him. He was my greatest fear and my most erotic fantasy, stripped raw and melded into one.

He was Trouble. And I wasn't asking for him. I was begging.

Chapter 30

Dom aka ~~Dirty~~ Trouble

I'D LOST MY VIRGINITY before I could read.

By the time I finished high school, I'd slept with more than half of the entire female student body, earning the moniker Dirty Dom.

In college, I had lived up to it, and then some.

But in this moment, with Raven's body under me, all over me, I felt like I had been born again. I was renewed by a feeling so foreign and overwhelming, that I knew I would never be the same. Not after tonight.

I died inside her. I died and came back to life, only so I could live for her.

Every stroke was a gasp of air. Every kiss was a heartbeat. And every touch was seeing for the very first time.

I'd had wet. I'd had warm. But I'd never had this. Not with anyone. There was something undoubtedly innocent about her, although she obviously knew what she was doing. She touched me like she wanted every caress to count. Like she wanted her body—her soul—imprinted to mine. No one had ever wanted me like that. There were women that wanted to covet my body, my attention, my cock, but no one had ever made me feel like they wanted *me*.

She touched my face and looked at me as I surged inside her. My first instinct was to close my eyes or look away, but I couldn't. She wouldn't let me. There was a peace in her glassy eyed-gaze, as if she could see the ugly inside me . . . could see the shame and regret and pain . . . and find beauty in it. Find life worth saving in all the rot and decay. She saw me in that ruin. And with her hands grasping my shoulders, her back arching to its peak, she saved me.

And I was *there*.

Every second, every minute. Every sigh and gasp and groan, I was there with Raven. I felt her touch and kiss. I felt her softness surrounding me, sucking me deeper into bliss. I didn't have to block it out—I didn't want to. I was there because I wanted to be. I was there because I loved her.

We lay tangled in sheets damp with sweat, our bodies still glistening in afterglow. Everything felt different now, maybe because *I* felt different now. This would have been the part when I'd grab my pants, kiss the chick on the forehead and get the hell outta there. If I was feeling romantic, I'd bring her a washcloth. If I was hungry, I'd offer her a meal. It was always on my terms, always about what I wanted. And now, my needs were the furthest thing from my mind. No, that wasn't true. My needs were wrapped up in pleasing Raven.

"What are you thinking?" she whispered, her voice raspy

with exhaustion and strain. I liked that she wasn't afraid to be vocal, yet she didn't feel the need to be dramatic about it, in an attempt to stroke my ego. Most women I'd been with were like that. They thought that if they screamed the loudest or came the hardest, I'd somehow be encouraged to stay.

I rolled onto my side, propping myself up on an elbow so I could look at her. "Nothing. Everything."

"That's awfully vague."

"Well, would you believe me if I said I was thinking about you?"

"And that's awfully corny."

She laughed, and I realized what a great laugh it was. It was the throaty kind that made her voice sound super sexy. And now that it was tinged with a touch of hoarseness, it was even more erotic. Damn, I could feel myself getting hard again.

"Seriously. I am. I'm thinking about you, and how that was beyond anything my imagination could have come up with."

"Well, what did you think? That I had a third boob like that alien broad in *Total Recall?*"

I gave a one-shouldered shrug. "No, but if you did . . ."

"Don't even say it," she shook her head. "Because if you say tri-boobs gets your rocks off, I'm gonna have to ask you to leave."

I let my fingers trail up her belly to caress the underside of her breast before pinching the nipple. "No, you wouldn't."

"Oh yeah? What makes you think I won't?"

I guided a pebbled bud into my mouth while simultaneously moving between her legs. "Because I've got a few good reasons why you'd want me to stay."

Saturday was Raven, and so was Sunday.

In truth, I wanted her to be everyday ending with Y.

But Monday . . .

Monday would not be claimed. She was a bitch that relented for no one. And even though I was still high off Saturday night, plus three times on Sunday, that internal solitude would not last. It wasn't mine to keep. I should have known better.

Raven had picked up an evening shift at Dive, so I offered to drive Toby over after work. I could see he had something on his mind. The kid wasn't stupid; he knew what his sister and I had been up to. And while he seemed okay with it, I needed him to know that my intentions were pure.

"So, you know I really care about your sister," I said to him on the drive over to Dive. He cut his eyes at me and shrugged. "And you know that I would never do anything to hurt her or you." A single nod. "I guess I just want you to know that I'm serious about her, and I want to be in both your lives. But if you're not cool with it, just let me know. Okay?"

He nodded again, and then went for his pen and pad a minute later. When I was stopped at a red light, he passed me the note.

She said we would try to do #TacoTuesday tomorrow. I like tacos. So thanks.

I smiled and nodded my head. It wasn't the most traditional blessing, but it told me everything I needed to know. Toby approved. And that was all that mattered.

The usual Dive Happy Hour crowd was in full swing, and it felt good walking in that evening. It felt like I was coming home, as corny as it sounded. It wasn't the place; it was the fact that everyone that I loved was under one roof. Raven, Toby, Angel, Kami and yeah, Blaine. Hell, even CJ was part of this dysfunctional group that had become my family. And considering he was still seeing Victoria—a record for him— maybe she would be too.

I swear it was like we were a support group for the hopeless and dejected. Orphaned? Abused? Abandoned? Rejected? Molested? Misunderstood? We'll take you in!

That was how it was, and how it should be. Even the broken needed a place to belong.

"'Sup, Dirty . . . little dude," CJ said to us in greeting. "Catch the game last night?"

"Please, stop with the Dirty crap," I muttered, bypassing him to give both Kami and Angel a peck on the cheek. "And no. I was busy."

"Busy, eh?" His brows danced suggestively, to which I pretended to ignore. "Oh, come on! Don't leave me hanging!"

"Will you shut up?" Blaine chimed in after filling a drink order. I gave him a head nod in thanks. "Hey, Toby. Mr. Bradley, our cook, has got steak nachos on special tonight. I'm sure I could snag an order if you're interested. Sound good?"

Toby nodded eagerly before scribbling down, **Yes, please.**

"Cool. I'll have your sister bring 'em over when she gets a sec. Sprite, too?"

Toby nodded again, even allowing a small smile to break through. Blaine grabbed a glass for his soda then looked over to me. "Beer?"

"Definitely. Thanks, man."

"What kinda guy brings a kid to a bar?" a familiar voice

said from behind me.

When I turned around, I didn't bother hiding my smile. There was no way I could. Hearing her voice, seeing her face . . . it was if someone had hooked me up to a defibrillator and brought me back to life. I didn't care who saw, I had to feel her body against mine. I hopped down from the stool and scooped Raven into my arms, spinning her around. She squealed out a laugh, which I hungrily swallowed with a kiss.

"Missed you," I said against her lips.

"You just saw me. Less than 24 hours ago."

"I know, but still . . ." I released her for only a split second to lean over and grab a bag I had brought in from the car. "I have something for you."

"A paper bag. You shouldn't have."

"Just open it."

As she pulled the item from the bag, a dimple set between her brows. "A coffee cup?"

"Read it. Kitschy mugs are kinda my thing."

When her eyes caught the sketch of the little camera with the words **I Shoot People** over it, she burst into a fit of laughter. "Sounds about right. I did shoot you, after all. And you liked it."

"I did. Shoot me anytime." Then I kissed her so deeply and held her so close to me that her feet were three inches clear off the ground.

I was so wrapped up in the feel of her . . . the taste of her . . . that I didn't even realize the entire room had gone silent. Slowly, I set her down and turned to face my friends who all wore varied shades of shock and amusement. They'd seen me with women—lots of them—but never like this. And I was never with anyone. We were either fucking or we weren't. But Raven . . . even with her clothes on, I wanted to be around her. Her and Toby. I wanted them both in my life. And not just for a day or a week. I wanted them because they were like me—they had been forgotten. And only someone who was equally as lost knew what it meant to be found.

"Wow," Kami gasped.

"I know, right?" Angel whispered back.

"Dude, you are so whipped!" CJ chortled, slapping his hand on the bar. "I'm not saying that's a bad thing. I know how it is!"

I shook my head and laughed right along with him, because, hell, he was right. The beautiful woman in my arms had me so whipped, you could put me on a sundae.

"So sorry to break up the pow-wow, gang, but I thought we should catch up."

I swear it was like a record scratched and flew right off the turntable. We dropped the happy smiles and laughs and turned toward the sound of the saccharine-laced southern drawl. Amanda stood before us, hand on her boney-ass hip and her boobs mashed together like two rotten grapefruits. None of us had seen her since Angel dropped the proposal bomb two weeks ago, so we assumed she had crawled back under whatever rock she had been hiding under. Yet, here she was, dressed to the nines in Trailer Skank Couture, smiling like she just hit the lotto.

"What are you doing here?" Blaine asked, his voice devoid of its usual friendly tone.

"Oh, just was in the neighborhood. Don't worry; I won't keep you long. But I came across some interesting news, and

I thought, what kinda friend would I be if I didn't share it?"

"You're not a friend, bitch," Angel muttered.

"Well, after you hear this, you might think differently. Such a shame . . . you think you know somebody, only to find out that they're harboring an ugly secret. Apparently, one of *you* isn't a friend either."

"Oh, for fuck's sake, get to the point!" CJ huffed out. None of us even admonished him for the F-bomb slip. We were all sick of this episode of Lifestyles of the Poor and Desperate.

"Gladly." She reached into her purse and pulled out a beige file folder, making a show out of flipping it open. "Since someone had such an interest in people's personal info, I thought I'd do a little fact checking. And, boy, did I hit the jackpot! One of you has some explaining to do."

I felt Raven tense in my arms, her whole body growing hot. She looked pale, her eyes wide with horror. What was going on? What could she possibly fear from Amanda? And what the hell could Amanda have on any of . . .

"Dominic Luis Trevino, born May 26, 1990, orphaned when he was barely four years old. He was taken in by his uncle, Hector Trevino, who was convicted of sexually assaulting Dominic until he was the age of twelve. Hector, who is up for parole later this year, argued the defense that Dominic *wanted* it. That he *loved* it. That he even *ejaculated* when they had sex. After Dominic was taken from his uncle, he was placed in a group home, where he began a sexual relationship with another *male* resident there, which lasted until he moved here from Florida. After that, Dominic posed as a straight male, sleeping with close to a thousand women, when he's really nothing but a *fake* and a *fag.*"

No one spoke, no one moved, no one even breathed. The least of all me. How . . . How had she found out? Those records were sealed! Where did she get—

"Funny what you can find out when you fuck a lawyer or two. And just in case you all don't believe me, read it for yourselves." She pulled several photocopied sheets from the folder and tossed them at our stock-still bodies, causing paper tears to rain down on us.

When her gaze went to Toby, I knew where this was going. I knew what she would say, yet I was too stunned to stop her. "Kinda scary that a liar and a fraud like him is working around children, especially young boys. Wonder if your employer knows it. Oops! I bet they will now."

Then she stepped in close, pinning her vicious gaze on Raven. This was the kill shot. This would be the one to end us . . . to end me. "Statistically, most pedophiles were molested as children. Be a shame if that happened in this case. Careful."

I couldn't breathe. I couldn't speak. But I knew I had to go. I had to get far, far away from this. I was covered in the bloody filth of my past, and now they all saw it. They all knew what had happened to me. They knew what I was. I could feel their eyes on me, could hear the whispers around the room. I knew what they were saying.

Faggot. Queer. Freak. Sissy. Pedophile. Rapist.

They were talking about *me*. They could see *me*.

Through the numbing cold in my veins, my legs carried me toward the door. I was running. I was bursting through the exit. I was speeding away, and never coming back.

The ugly had found me. My eyes had found beauty, but it wasn't enough. I wasn't strong enough to hold on to it. I wasn't worthy enough to keep it.

What was wrong cannot be made right.

What was broken cannot be fixed.

What was dirty cannot be erased.

Chapter 31

Raven

KNEW I SHOULD have said something—done something.
But I couldn't. Or I just . . . didn't. My first thought was
that it couldn't be true. But then he ran. He left us and he
ran. And that was all the confirmation I needed. Dom was molested. And Dom . . . No. I couldn't believe he was gay. Could
I? Could the women be a front for a secret life?

There was a shrill scream and a scuffle, breaking me from
my reverie. Angel was trying to lunge for Amanda, but CJ had
her by the waist. So no one thought a thing when Kami slowly
rose from her seat and walked towards her, her round belly
leading the way. That's why it came as a shock to us all when
Kami reeled back with all the power in her little body and
punched that sadistic bitch in the face, sending her sprawling
backwards onto the floor, her nose gushing blood.

"If I ever see you around my family again," Kami gritted

out, leaning over so Amanda could hear her loud and clear. Blaine flashed to her side and gently tried to pull her away, but the tiny warrior wasn't having it. "I will kill you. Do you hear me? I will fucking kill you."

Amanda scrambled back, holding her face, until she was out of reach. Then she jumped to her feet and ran for her life. Kami was serious. And she knew it.

"She's getting away!" Angel cried. "How dare she! I will end her!"

The entire bar had witnessed the whole thing, and now everyone was whispering. Some had even pulled out their smartphones and were recording it.

While CJ was trying to calm Angel down, Blaine was comforting Kami, who was still fuming as well. I started to go to Toby, fearful of what I would find. He was just a kid and all this was much too heavy for all of us. This would shatter his world. And it was still on the mend from the last time it had been broken.

"Raven?" I turned to see a still-shaken Kami and an equally worried Blaine. He had his arm around her waist, but it seemed like he was holding her up on shaky legs. She looked to him then looked back to me, wearing a pained grimace. "I think my water broke."

Those five words zapped me back into reality, and I sprang into action, letting my instinct and training guide me. I looked down and sure enough, there was fluid running down her leg, along with a good amount of blood. Shit.

"Let's get her down. Blaine, call her obstetrician. Kami, are you having any pain?"

Cringing, she nodded, as CJ slid a chair under her. "Yeah.

Cramping. I thought it was gas all day, so I didn't say anything."

I gently pressed against her belly to check the baby's position. "What about now? Any pressure?"

"Yeah, um." She leaned in as close as she could. "In my butt. It feels like I have to poop."

I looked up at Blaine's wide, worried gaze. "We have to get her to the hospital right now."

"What do you need me to do?"

"Carry her to the car. I'll stay in the back with her to make sure she's okay. Angel, if you can, grab me some clean towels and some gloves from the kitchen."

He reiterated everything I said to the doctor on the phone, telling her we'd be there in ten minutes. I was just praying that this baby would hold on until then. I had studied this stuff, and observed, but I had never actually delivered a baby.

"Here, take my car. It's faster," CJ insisted, who oddly enough seemed just as somber. "I'll ride over with Angel and the little guy."

Shit. Toby.

I only had a second to turn to him to ask him if he was okay. He shook his head furiously, gesturing me to go.

"Okay, Blaine. Can you get her to the car?"

Before I even got the question out, he gingerly lifted Kami into his arms like she weighed next to nothing. CJ jogged to the door and held it open for us. Then he did the same with the backseat of his car.

"Here are the towels and gloves!" Angel exclaimed, running to catch us. She kissed Kami on the face and promised to be right behind us.

I thanked her and climbed into the back with Kami. "Ok, Blaine, keep the doctor on the line and put her on speaker-phone."

He did as I ordered, and within seconds, we were peeling out of the parking lot.

"Doctor, I'm Raven West, and I'm a CNA. I have your patient here who has been having mild contractions throughout the day, and has experienced PPROM at 34 weeks gestation less than five minutes ago. No meconium present that I could see, however there is some blood."

The doctor asked us both questions. How far apart are the contractions? About five minutes apart. On a scale from 1–10, how bad do they hurt? A 7. Maybe an 8. Any loss of mucous? Not that we could see.

"Ok, Raven, I'm going to need you to check her. Can you do that?"

I was already spreading out the towels and pulling the latex gloves on my hands. "I can."

I took a deep breath and closed my eyes for a beat. I could do this. I had to. When I reopened them, Kami was smiling at me, her lips tight as she tensed with the next contraction. "I trust you, Raven. You've got this. Don't be afraid."

I nodded, accepting her words of encouragement. She was right; I had this. Kami and Blaine had been good to me . . . had been good to Toby. I wouldn't let them down.

"Just breathe, Kami," I said softly as I measured her cervix. "Take deep breaths."

"You're doing great, baby," Blaine said from the driver's seat. "Almost there."

"Doctor, we're looking at five centimeters dilated," I

called out. "And about 20% effaced."

"Ok, I've got my team waiting at the emergency entrance, prepped and ready to go. What's your ETA?"

"Less than two minutes," Blaine answered.

"Ok, good. We'll be waiting."

The second we pulled up to the hospital, we were cast into a whirlwind of commotion. Kami was wheeled to L & D, with Blaine right beside her. I offered to park the car and meet him in there, giving me a chance to reevaluate the last twenty minutes. Everything happened so fast. If Kami hadn't gone into labor, I could've gone after Dom. But would I? None of what happened to him was his fault, but I couldn't deny that it left me with a lot of uncomfortable questions.

Who was Dominic Trevino?

Many years ago, I thought I knew, only to find out that I was wrong. And now, it was happening again. Having a tainted past wasn't a deal breaker, but being gay and not telling me? Yeah. It was. And was he, in fact, at risk of becoming like his uncle? Was he already having urges?

God, what had I gotten us into?

"Oh, thank God!" Angel exclaimed when she saw me walking from the parking lot. Toby and CJ stood beside her, just as anxious. "How is she?"

"She's good. In good spirits. Shouldn't be long now." I turned to Angel, hoping she would detect the message in my words without alerting Toby. "Have you spoken to him?"

She shook her head. "He's not answering. I don't know what to do. He's hurting right now, but asking him for answers may not be wise right now."

"So . . . you knew? About him?"

"Yes," she nodded. "At least about the parts that were actually true. Just wait until you speak with him before you judge him, okay?"

She was right. I couldn't make any snap judgments. Not until I spoke with him. What had happened to him was not his fault. He needed compassion and understanding right now. Not accusations.

I pulled out my phone and sent him a text, telling him where we were and what had happened. I hoped he knew how much he was wanted—needed—by the people who loved him, myself included. He would hate himself if he missed this, probably more than he already was right now.

Being a CNA had its perks, so I was able to get us back into the delivery ward. CJ stayed in the waiting room with Toby, while Angel and I quietly crept inside Kami's room. After I identified myself, the doctor nodded in my direction and thanked me for my help.

"You're doing great, Kami," she said while examining her. The nurses around her were hurriedly getting her hooked up to monitors and an IV. "Deep breaths."

After her exam, and some observation of the baby's vitals, the doctor turned to her team and instructed them to prep. I knew what was coming and quickly told Angel to step aside.

"Kami, we're going to have to prep you for an emergency C-section. The baby is in distress, but don't worry. Everything will be fine."

"What? What's wrong?" Kami grasped Blaine's hand even tighter, frantically looking between him and the doctor.

"Nothing for right now, but we have to move quickly."

A nurse ushered Blaine away to change while the rest of

the team moved into action. Angel and I could only step aside and let them do their jobs.

"Is she going to be okay?" she whispered after Kami was wheeled down towards the OR. I felt her hand search for mine between us. She was scared and needed physical comfort, and while that really wasn't my thing, I laced my fingers with hers.

"Of course, she will. She'll be fine."

"Because . . . I can't lose her. Dom is . . . and now her . . . I can't lose them both."

I wanted to ask her what she meant about Dom. What was he? He wouldn't actually *leave* would he? Not without saying goodbye, right?

Panic rose inside of me, and the need to see him grew more urgent. He couldn't disappear. He had to get through this, if not for me, then for Kami and Angel. They needed him. They loved him. And he needed to stick around for Toby. That kid admired the hell out of him, and Dom had been the only one to break through to him.

"Come on. Let's go wait out here," I said to Angel, leading her towards the waiting room.

I needed to try one more time. I needed to believe that all hope was not lost. Not when I had just finally found it.

Chapter 32

Dom

I HAD ALREADY BOOKED a one-way ticket to Nowhere when I got the text from Angel.

Kami's in labor. Emergency C-Section. You need to be here.

That was just one of many, but it was the only one that made me pause. Kam was in surgery? What had happened? She wasn't due for weeks. Was the baby all right?

No. I couldn't let myself care. Not anymore. Caring had only brought me pain and humiliation. Loving had only labeled me a monster.

What if Amanda was right? It was true—most pedophiles were victims of sexual abuse. And what happened between Matthew and me when I was a kid . . . it only further proved that I was a sexual deviant. I knew what I was doing then, and I knew that I didn't like it, but the need to be loved had been so overwhelming that it eclipsed my judgment. Maybe I was a fake and a fraud. Maybe I was doing Raven a disservice by being with her. I didn't want to embarrass her more than I already had.

I called the airline and had them hold my ticket. I had to say goodbye to Kami and Angel. They deserved that much. Then I would say goodbye to Toby and Raven, and exit their lives for good.

Another text came in, and while I had been able to thwart the others, this one caught my eye.

Please talk to me. I'm here for you. Don't shut us out.

Us? Us?

Didn't she see I was doing this for them? To save her and Toby from having to endure more pain?

I couldn't take it anymore. I couldn't allow myself to give a damn about how they felt. I powered down my phone and locked the door to my room. I'd stay long enough to see that Kami had made it through surgery all right, but then I was gone. For good.

It had to have been close to midnight when the pounding started. I heard voices, both male and female, telling me to unlock the door. I wished they'd stop worrying about me. I wished they'd go away altogether. Just give up on me already.

I grabbed my remote and clicked on the TV, turning up the volume as high as it would go.

There. I didn't off myself.

That seemed to appease them.

The next round of knocks came early in the morning, but it was only Angel this time.

"Please Dom . . ." the small, muffled voice said from the

other side of the door. "Please don't do this."

I could hear her sink down to the hardwood, could see her shadow underneath the door. She sat there for a long time, waiting, sometimes crying. Thankfully she gave up around noon and left. Good. She was one step closer to letting go.

I slept so I wouldn't think. And when I couldn't stand to close my eyes, I drank, courtesy of the stash I kept in my closet for whenever I had company (Angel got sick of me walking to the kitchen ass naked for booze). And when that wasn't even enough, I dipped into my stash of antidepressants that were probably long expired but still did the trick. I didn't want to feel anymore, and the one thing that got me out of my head was a no-go. I couldn't fathom going through the motions for some random, faceless chick. I didn't want to see anyone. I couldn't even look at my own damn reflection.

I flipped on the news after my haze of dejection had lifted. It was Wednesday morning. I had buried my head in the sand for two days. I needed news about Kami—that was the only reason I had stuck around. Then I needed to make a move to get the fuck outta here.

"Dom? You awake?" It was Angel again. She must've been listening at my door. "Come on, open up."

I didn't say a word. I just went over and unlocked the door. She stepped inside and quickly covered her nose, trying to stifle the offending odor of booze, sweat and tears.

"Dude, what the fuck? We've been worried sick about you." She spied the empty bottle of liquor and pills. "Are you okay?"

I flopped onto the bed, my entire body still sore with fatigue. "Peachy-fucking-keen. What do you want?"

"Kam had the baby."

"Are they okay?"

"They're fine. Healthy. She wants to see you. She's worried about you—we all are."

"Don't."

"Seriously, you need to see her. It's not healthy for her to be this upset about you, and you know it. She just went through a traumatic experience. Don't put her through anymore strain."

I ran a hand through my greasy hair and heaved out a sigh. "Fine. I'll see her." I'll see her, then I'll go. That's all the closure I could give them.

"And your job . . . they've been calling. I told them what had happened with Kami and how you were refusing to leave her side. Amber needs to speak with you a.s.a.p."

"Fine." Little did she know that my conversation with my supervisor would be no more than an apology and a resignation. Word traveled fast. Amber knew that I had had a rough upbringing and had been adopted. But she didn't know the details. Since I was a minor when it all went down, those records had been sealed. Or so I thought. Now I knew exactly why Helping Hands had been ransacked. Amanda must've gotten some of her dumpster juice friends to help her get some dirt on me after my little DCFS threat. Well, they found it.

She left me to shower and dress, and when I emerged, she handed me a sandwich. I was starving, but I wasn't sure my body could keep down anything. It was too full of grief.

The ride to the hospital was silent for the most part, except when Angel brought up the one topic that I had been desperately trying to avoid.

"Raven has been calling you. She came by a few times. She's worried about you."

"So?"

"So?"

"She should worry about her own problems and leave me alone with mine."

"That's not fair, Dom. She cares about you. So does Toby. Why would you think otherwise?"

Because I'm not worth it. They were better off without me.

"Look, let's just get this over with."

Once at the hospital, she led me to the NICU where Kami would be. It was an entire process to get in there. You would swear we were going to visit an inmate in prison or something. Sure enough, we found Kami rocking in a chair, singing softly to the tiniest bundle I had ever seen. Blaine stood beside her, completely enamored by the mother of his child and his brand new daughter.

The moment she saw me, her face broke into a smile so wide that she nearly broke me right then and there. Tears welled up in her eyes automatically as she signaled for Blaine to take the baby, while Angel gingerly helped her to her feet.

"Thank you. Thank you for coming," she cried, wrapping her arms around me and squeezing as tight as she could without hurting herself.

I choked down the knot in my throat and forced myself to hug her back. It wasn't that I didn't want to. It was because I did. I wanted to hold her. I needed to. And I was bad for her. I was bad for everyone.

She pretended not to feel the stiffness in my body when she pulled away, her soft smile still in place. "Come on. I have someone I want you to meet."

She took my hand and led me to where Blaine was cooing over the tiny, pink bundle in his arms. He was in love, insanely so. Which made me want to back away and run even more.

"Dom, this is Amelia, named after Blaine's mother," Kami beamed proudly. "Amelia Dominique Jacobs. This is your goddaughter."

Goddaughter? Amelia *Dominique?*

I took a step back, shaking my head. No. Why were they doing this? They knew how much I loved them . . . how much I would love her. They knew that little girl would become my entire world.

"It's okay," Kami whispered, refusing to let me go. "It's okay, Dom. I know . . ."

She did. If anyone knew my headspace, it was her. She knew what it was like to feel unworthy . . . unlovable. She understood what it was like to be terrified to feel for people because people hurt you. They left you. They ripped you apart.

I let Kami pull me back to her and her family. Our family. They had made me a part of it whether I liked it or not.

"Here, man. You should hold her."

I could see that Blaine hated to give her up. I would be too. Amelia was absolutely the most beautiful, most precious little thing I had ever seen, even with the plastic tubes in her tiny little nose. Kami had me take her seat on the rocking chair, where they set her in my arms. She was warm and so tiny. She had a head full of dark brown hair, and her soft skin was the color of cream. I loved her already. How could I not? And ev-

287

ery day of her life, that little girl would know that she was the most cherished child in the world.

I hated them for doing this—for forcing me to stay—but I loved them for believing in me enough to allow me this gift. They knew what I was . . . what I could turn out to be. Yet, they were trusting that I wouldn't grow up to be the same kind of monster that turned me into a victim. Maybe they were stupid. Or maybe they were exactly what a real family was supposed to be.

"Hi, beautiful," I whispered down at her as she slept. "I'm your *tío* Dominic. And I'm going to be your guardian angel. All beautiful girls get a guardian angel."

Out of the corner of my eye, I saw Blaine pull Kami closer and kiss the top of her head. Angel came over to kneel beside me, equally as enamored by Amelia.

"Isn't she adorable?" she squeaked. "I want one."

"She's not a doll, Ang. You can't just pick one up from the store and dress her up."

"I know that. But still . . ." She leaned in close and stroked one of Amelia's tiny fingers. "You know, you have Raven to thank for this. They only allow immediate family in here, but since she sometimes works this department and knows the nurses . . ."

"You can thank her."

"Dom," she sighed. "You have to talk to her some time. She cares about you too."

"She'll get over it."

"But what about Toby? Will he get over you too?"

She had a point, but thankfully I wouldn't have to tell her so. A nurse entered to inform us that little baby Amelia would need to rest now. Kami was welcome to stay, but she said she was feeling weak and wanted to lie down a while. When we got back to her room, Blaine decided to grab a coffee, and Angel joined him. I knew what this was. They thought they were slick by leaving us alone. They thought leaving me with Kami would help me get my head together. Sneaky bastards.

I helped her back into bed, then dimmed the lights. She looked amazing to have just had a baby, but I could tell she was tired. The fact that she was up moving around after all that trauma was incredible.

"Come," she ordered gently, grimacing as she tried to scoot over in her hospital bed.

"Kam, you need to rest."

"I know. Come rest with me for a little while."

I heaved out a breath and did as she requested. Denying her was still difficult for me. She was tiny, even though her belly was still pretty swollen, so we both fit just fine in the bed.

"I want you to know . . . you are beautiful to me, Dominic Trevino. And before your head gets any bigger, I'm not talking about the exterior. You know why we chose you as Amelia's godfather?"

"No." I didn't. I was the last person I expected, especially now. I didn't even have the balls to show up to the birth.

"Because no one knows pain like you. And no one will ever fight as hard as you to keep her from it." She leaned her head on my shoulder and grasped my hands with hers. "I don't care about the sins of your body. I only see the light of your soul and the fullness of your heart. That's all I've ever seen. Even that day you saw me—shaking like a leaf in front of that crisis center—I knew that I would grow to love you. Because there is just something inside you that makes it impossible not to. That's why I let you take my hand—a stranger that I didn't even know from Adam. And that's why I vowed to keep holding your hand until the day I died. I needed you then, and I need you now. And I'm not the only one, sweetheart. You are so needed. You are so loved."

I didn't even realize I was crying until I tried to speak, the words catching on a sob. "I don't want to be like him. I don't ever want to hurt anyone. You know me. I would never . . . I would never . . ."

She turned my head to face her and touched her forehead to mine. "I know that, baby. And you won't. You are good, Dominic. You hear me? You are the best person I know. And you deserve so much love that it smothers you . . . that you can't breathe from all of it. So don't push it away. Don't run, please. I need you, Amelia needs you, Angel needs, and Raven and Toby . . . they need you too."

"No." I tried to shake my head, but she was still cradling my cheek. "No one needs me, Kam. I don't want anyone to ever have to wonder if I'm . . ." I couldn't even say it through the tears—hers and mine.

"We don't wonder. And neither should you. You listen to me, dammit. You are not your past. You are not your pain. You are kindness and strength and beauty. You *are* love."

We cried together in that hospital bed until exhaustion lulled us to sleep. And I realized that the love I felt for Kamilla Duvall was completely different from the emotional connection I felt for Raven. Kami was a mother—she always had been. And I had clung to that quality inside her all these years, because I'd never had that. I had never felt that type of love.

And now, I would happily surrender it to the person who need-ed it more than me. The person who had changed my entire world the moment I felt her tiny frame in my arms and forced me stay. My goddaughter.

Chapter 33

Raven

I HAD BEEN WORKING the trauma unit for the last two days, but made it a point to check in with Kami and the new baby. Blaine hadn't left her side, so CJ and his dad, Mick, were running the show. I also gave up my day off to help out at Dive in his absence. Toby didn't mind. CJ had hooked up an Xbox in the back room, so he was pretty occupied the entire evening anyway. There was also a couch back there that he dozed on when it got late. Everyone was ridiculously nice to him and made sure he stayed stocked on food and drinks while I tended to the tables. It was weird. No one had ever been that kind to us. But then again, I hadn't really given anyone a chance to.

I had a 15 minute break, so I jogged up to see how Kami was doing, hoping that she had heard from Dom. But what I found was even better. Sorta. Actually, I didn't know what to think about it.

I found Blaine standing outside Kami's recovery room, looking through the window. His expression was pensive, and after a couple days without shaving, he looked even more dangerous. But I knew better.

I followed his eyes and saw the source of his concern. I gasped aloud, disturbing him from his thoughts, and he turned to me with a tight smile.

"How long have they been like that?" I whispered.

"A while." He looked down at his cold coffee, then back at his girlfriend holding Dom as they slept. I didn't understand why he wasn't upset, but he wasn't. He looked more relieved than anything.

"It doesn't bother you?"

He shook his head, the long, chocolate brown layers of his hair falling into his eyes. "No. I've seen worse. It's how they are."

How they are? What kind of relationship did they have?

I watched with him for a while, trying to wrap my head around it. I didn't believe Kami was interested in Dom like that, but I couldn't help the pang of jealousy that shot through me. Still, she somehow got him to come out of hiding, and for that, I was grateful.

"How do you do it?" I whispered to Blaine, our eyes still glued on the scene before us.

"Do what?"

A gestured a hand toward the scene inside the room. "Handle . . . that. Handle them?"

He chuckled quietly to himself and shook his head. "I don't. It's not my place to. People like them feel more than everyone else. They may not show it, but they do. And some-times, it's all too much to trust one person to handle. But they—Kami, Dom, and Angel—are each other's safe houses. They trust one another because they know that whatever ugly they've faced, they have each other to show them the beauty. People like you and I have been fortunate enough to never have to face the horrors that still haunt them. So we wait, and we hope, and we love them enough to try to make them see that they're safe with us too. And we thank God when they finally do."

I could only turn to look at him, wondering where the hell that had come from. Blaine was so much more than a hand-some face. He was a good guy, and Kami was damn lucky to have him.

"I meant to tell you . . ." he began after a few moments of my awkward staring. "I received everything from your back-ground check. Your name . . ."

"I use my middle."

"I saw that." He was silent for an uncomfortable beat, be-fore taking a deep breath and speaking again, his voice hollow. "When I was in high school, I heard of a girl at a rival school. Her first name was Melanie too."

My face grew hot, and I could feel sweat bead all over my body. No. No, it couldn't be. I wanted to beg him not to say another word. I wanted to tell him to shut the fuck up and mind his own business. He couldn't know this. He just couldn't.

"I grew up with CJ after my mom died. And he was a jackass even then. One night he showed me these pictures . . . told me about this girl . . ."

"Please don't." My voice was so weak that I barely heard

it over the blood whooshing in my ears.

"It's not my place. But if you think it's something he should know, you should tell him. Tell him before he's exposed even more. You know all his secrets, and if you want him to trust you like he trusts her," he said, nodding towards Kami, "you have to be honest."

He was right, and I had half a mind to break down in tears and tell him so. If Blaine knew about me, who else did? Kami? CJ? How long would it be before my past caught up to me and destroyed the life that I had built for my brother and me? And what would *he* think of me then?

"Don't worry. No one else knows," Blaine said.

"Thank you."

I looked down at my watch to find that I had to get back to work, shaken or not. I was just about to bid him goodbye when Dom began to stir in the bed next to Kami.

"Talk to him. If he finds out from someone else and is humiliated again, we'll lose him for good." Then Blaine stepped around me and went into the room. I watched him wait patiently as Dom gently untangled himself from Kami's hold. He stood up and the two men exchanged a few hushed words before bro-hugging.

I had wanted to see him for days. I needed him to know how I felt about him—how I didn't believe what Amanda had said. But now that *my* secret was out, I wasn't so sure.

When he stepped into the hall, momentary surprise touched his sleepy eyes. But just as fast as I saw it, it was gone. He was cold . . . detached. It was like he was looking right through me, not seeing me at all.

"I called you." My voice was barely a whisper.

"I know."

"I need to talk to you."

"Now's not a good time, Raven . . ."

"Please." I took a step forward, aching to touch him, but I refrained. I was afraid of him. Not because I thought he would hurt me, but because I knew I had given him the power to.

"Look, you don't want to talk to me. You've already heard everything. What more needs to be said?"

"The truth." I took another step, close enough to breathe him in. "My truth."

He looked away and scrubbed a hand over his face before taking a deep breath. "Fine. Just come over after work."

"I work at the club tonight."

He shrugged. "I'll be up."

The rest of the day crawled along, as anxiety built. I was going to tell Dom the truth about me—about us. I was going to reveal how I had hated him for years, and how I blamed him for all the bad shit in Toby's life and mine. I was going to reveal how I had once dreamed of hurting him, yet had fallen in love with him instead. He had to know that he wasn't alone in his pain. I shared it with him.

I got to his apartment around 2 am, nervous that I'd wake him and Angel. But when I buzzed their place, he let me through immediately without saying a word. That was okay. I just needed him to listen. Listen and understand.

The apartment was dark when he opened the door, but I was glad for it. My neck felt flushed, and my palms were sweaty. As calm and cool as I tried to act, I couldn't shake the nervousness, but it was too late to turn back now. He expected an explanation, and I would give him one.

Dom led me back to his room and shut the door. I heard music coming from Angel's room, which didn't surprise me. She was probably just getting in too. Wednesdays were Open Mic Nights at Dive and AngelDust played for the contestants. The thing that did surprise me, was that she wasn't alone in the room. There was another female voice, and it didn't sound like they were playing Yahtzee.

"So . . . talk," he said, flopping down on his bed. He seemed so angry . . . so hateful. I didn't understand what I had done to him. Hell, maybe he already knew.

"Are you upset with me?"

"No. I'm not." He ran a hand through his tousled locks. He wasn't as groomed as he usually was, and a good amount of stubble was on his jaw. Still, he was gorgeous. He'd always be gorgeous to me.

I took a deep breath, and closed my eyes for a beat. Here it was . . . this was the pivotal moment I'd waited for. The moment I'd expose him for what he was. I just never expected to be dreading it. Honestly, I would have taken this secret to my grave if Blaine hadn't called me out.

"Dom . . . I went to Pine High."

He frowned. "Okay. When were you going to tell me we went to the same school? Are you trying to say we may have known each other?"

I shook my head. "We did know each other. At least I thought we did."

He huffed out an irritated breath. "I never knew anyone named Raven at Pine. What are you talking about?"

I had to push myself to keep going. I had to do it now or I'd lose my nerve. "That's because my first name is Melanie.

And up until a few weeks ago, I was convinced that you ruined my life."

"What? Wait . . . what are you saying?"

I wrapped my arms around myself defensively, preparing for the assault. Once he knew about me . . . once he knew the truth, he'd hate me. He'd hate me like I had hated him. He'd be repulsed by me, just like my mother had been. Just like everyone had been.

"I saw you every day. You were a junior at the time. You had U.S. History down the 9th grade hallway, right next to my locker. One day you said hi to me and smiled. I thought it was love at first sight." I chuckled nervously at my pathetic, childish notion. "I was a mess. Jacked up haircut. Braces. No one smiled at me. But you did."

Disbelief was etched on his face. "Raven—Melanie . . . I don't get it. Why didn't you tell me this before?"

I held up a hand. "Because that's not all of it. Soon the smiles turned into winks. Then you introduced yourself. I already knew your name though—everyone did. I heard what the girls said about you. Some were heartbroken. Some were in love. Some said you were the best sex they'd ever had. I didn't care. I just knew that I couldn't stop thinking about you. I lived every day to see you in the hallway. It was all I looked forward to."

Dom scrubbed a hand over his face and shook his head. "Look, I was seriously fucked up then, okay? You can't believe I knew that I was leading you on by being nice. I was nice to everyone."

"No. You did lead me on. You led me on, and I let you." I looked down at the knot of my fingers in front of my lap and tried to steel my resolve. I had to tell him. I had to tell him what he'd done so we could fix this. "You invited me to a party at Lookout Point. It was the end of the school year, and everyone would be there. You said I had pretty eyes, and that I better save you a dance. It was the best day of my life. I thought you liked me. At least that's how you made me feel.

"I showed up wearing my favorite skirt. When I spotted you in the crowd, you were surrounded by people. They clung to your every word. The girls all looked at you like you were a god. You had been drinking—everyone had—but that only made you more charismatic. It was like you were the sun, and we were all planets, rotating around your every move. Desperately hoping to be in your light.

"You saw me and came right over. You hugged me tight to your body, told me I looked beautiful. And I believed you."

Dom squirmed uncomfortably like he knew what came next. He had no idea. No clue of the damage his actions had caused. "Raven, I'm sorry. I was an asshole then. You have to forgive me."

I nodded. "Oh, I do. For that, and for what happened after. You took me to a vacant car. I think it was Angel's, because I remember the smell of new leather. Even if it was a beat up Pinto, I was glad to follow you anywhere. I knew what you were about. You weren't taking advantage of me, Dom. I wanted you. I knew what I was doing."

His shoulders seemed to sag with relief, but I knew it was premature. In a few minutes, he'd be repulsed, and I'd lose him.

"You were my first kiss, but I wanted you to be more than that. I wanted you to be my first everything. You laid me down in the back seat and kissed me so gently . . . touched me like I was made of glass. I felt so lucky to be there with you. You made me feel so . . . loved.

"When you put it in, it was like you didn't know. You didn't understand why I had screamed. And I didn't expect it to hurt so bad. You looked down where we were connected and . . . you covered your mouth and jumped out of me like I was on fire. You barely made it outside the door to puke, grabbed your shit and ran. You just left me and didn't come back."

He climbed to his feet, fresh tears shining in horrified eyes. "Oh my God, Raven. Oh my God . . . I'm so sorry. Please believe me, it wasn't you. I swear, it wasn't you."

I held up a hand, prompting him not to say any more. "That wasn't the best part. You left the car door open, and these guys . . . they saw me. They came in and whipped out their phones and . . . and . . ." The knot inside my throat cracked in half and fat, salty tears rained onto my cheeks. "I was the talk of the town. Don't you remember? *Nasty chick fucks on her period. Bloody Bitch. Slut forgets her tampon. Backseat Blood Bath. Threesome with Aunt Flo. Code Red. Bloody Melanie.* They said that I was so disgusting, some poor guy had puked right on me. My mom and stepdad saw them. Gene lost his job, because his boss felt it could be harmful for the company's image. They fought all the time about money, until Gene ended up leaving us. My mother hated me after that. She said if I weren't such a nasty slut, Gene would have stayed. And Toby would have his father.

"After that, I went to live with my grandparents in Virginia. I had to. I couldn't show my face in public again. I started using my middle name . . . tried to change my appearance. I thought I had left it all behind, but what I really left behind was Toby. If it weren't for those pictures . . . if you hadn't left me there, none of that would have ever happened. Was I so disgusting then? Were you that repulsed by my body?"

"No!" he shouted, grasping my shoulders. "No, never! I swear, Raven . . . I didn't know. I didn't know it was you."

"Then what was it? Why did you leave me?" I was shouting too. Screaming and crying and blubbering like a fool. "What did I do to make you physically sick? What happened? Tell me! Help me understand!"

He let go of my shoulders and dropped onto the bed, his hands covering his face. He was shaking, but so was I. I fell to my knees in front of him and grasped his wrists. I needed answers. I would never find peace if I didn't know why.

"Please, Dom," I whispered. "What did I do?"

"Nothing," he croaked. "I . . . I see blood . . . there. I can't . . . hurt someone . . . there. It takes me back. Takes me back to when I was bleeding and crying and hurting like that. It makes me feel like a monster. Like him. I get sick. I always got sick when he did it. I would vomit and be left to lay in my own blood and bile. I'm so sorry. I'm so, so sorry."

Oh my God.

Oh my God.

I was wrong. All these years, I hated him for intentionally hurting me, and he hadn't. He was still hurting himself.

I couldn't help myself. I wrapped my arms around his trembling frame and held on tight. I couldn't lose him now. He had seen my crazy, and I had seen his. There was no reason to pretend anymore.

"I love you, Dom. I love you and I'm sorry."

"No," he whispered.

I lifted my head from his knee. "Huh?"

"No," he repeated, louder this time. He moved out of my grasp and scrambled to his feet. "No, Raven. You can't love me. Look at the pain I've caused. Look what my . . . *affliction* . . . has done to you. To Toby. You don't need me in your lives. You need someone safe and honorable. Someone normal."

I was on my feet too, angrily dashing away tears. "What are you doing? I told you I love you, and you tell me *I can't?* Screw you! I don't care about your past, Dom. We all have skeletons. And here I am, saying that I'm cool with yours. Shit, I'll bring mine—they'll hang out. I don't want someone normal. I want *you.*"

He shook his head and looked away. "I'm sorry."

"You're sorry? For what?"

"I'm sorry . . . but I don't want you. Not anymore. I regret hurting you, and it pains me to have to do this, but I have to end this now." When he turned to look at me, his bloodshot eyes were empty and cold, exactly how I felt at that moment. "I don't do relationships, Raven. I thought you understood that. They call me Dirty for a reason. Just ask your friends at the club."

I sucked my teeth, my nostrils flaring with anger. "I know what you're doing, Dom. I won't let you do this. You're not going to push me away with that Dirty Dom bullshit. So fuck your reasons. I won't let you do this."

"Do what? I fuck whoever I want, whenever I want, Raven. That's who I am. What . . . did you think you were special? You were a challenge, I'll give you that, but now that I've had it, I have no purpose for you anymore."

"Shut up! I won't let you say these things . . . these lies! You're not like that, Dom! Stop pretending!"

"Pretending? Sweetheart, I've been pretending my whole life. Haven't you heard? Didn't Amanda make that abundantly clear? But I'm not pretending about this. Raven, you're cute. But cute isn't enough. We had fun, I'll admit, but I've moved on. So should you."

"Moved on?" Here came the fucking tears again.

"What? You thought I was alone those two days when I wasn't answering your calls. I was busy, Raven. Busy with someone else. Sorry."

I covered my mouth with trembling fingers, feeling like I would hurl at any moment. This wasn't supposed to happen. How could I be so stupid? How could I think for one minute that he could love me back? When he was incapable of even loving himself?

He wasn't like he was in high school. He was worse. He *knew* what he was doing now, and he didn't give a fuck.

"Now, if you'll excuse me, Angel and her friend are expecting me. You should go. Unless you want to join, of course."

I forced myself not to break apart in front of him. I wouldn't let him see that he'd hurt me again. Not anymore. It would probably get him off. That was what sick son of a bitches like him reveled in—destroying others.

I went over to where I had dropped my purse and picked it up off the ground. Then without a word, I reached inside and pulled out the peace offering I had brought for him, setting it on his dresser. I should have thrown it at him or shattered it in a million pieces, but I wouldn't give him the satisfaction. And I didn't want to keep it. I didn't want any trace of him in my life.

Dominic Trevino had done it again. He had ripped me apart without an ounce of remorse. And this time I had let him.

Chapter 34

Dom

I WAS A LIAR. No. I was worse than that. I was a murderer. I had killed the only thing that mattered to me outside of my family. I had killed my only shot at happiness.

Years and years of lying had made me good at it. Raven believed I could actually move on so quickly. That I could even *see* any girl but her. I had to tell her that. I had to make her see that I was defective. That I would always be flawed. And she didn't need that in her life. Not after what I had already done to her.

I vaguely remembered that girl in high school. After the incident, I had fallen into a dark place, completely humiliated and disgusted with myself. I never fucked virgins. It was a policy of mine. I had only made an exception with Angel, but that was a different circumstance. We were both fucked up, and just needed . . . someone. Something to ease the pain. And after, we both cried together. She knew she was a lesbian, no matter how badly she tried not to be. And I knew that I'd never have a normal relationship without that monster looming over me, watching, waiting for me to show weakness.

I knew I was drunk that night at the party. Drunk and horny and desperate. Honestly, I didn't even remember Raven's face. She could have been anyone. That was how fucked up in the head I was. I just needed a warm, wet hole. I had absolutely no self-respect.

My legs were like jelly, but they somehow carried me over to my dresser where a coffee cup sat. I thought she had returned the one I gave her, opening a fresh wound from the countless scars of rejection, but then I turned it around. And the sentiment . . . the idea that she had thought about me . . . it was enough to make me stumble backwards until I had collapsed onto the floor in a heap of misery.

It was a colored drawing of a smiling taco, and with it were the words **Let's Taco 'Bout It.** Through tears, I laughed out loud. Even when she hated me, she made me happy. I didn't deserve her; I never had. Maybe I was playing myself into thinking I could somehow change for her. That I could be someone I wasn't. How foolish of me to tell myself those lies.

It was late, but I didn't want to sleep, so I fashioned my resignation letter to Helping Hands and emailed it Amber. Even if I was staying, I couldn't work there. I was no good to those kids. They needed a role model, not a liability.

I could hear Angel and her date across the hall. I had no idea who it could be; probably some chick she picked up at Dive during last call. She was hurting, and like me, mindless sex was the anecdote. It didn't cure us. It just numbed the pain.

I thought about doing the same . . . finding some hole to purge my sins and bury them deep until they could no longer be seen, if only for a little while. But the thought of touching another person—kissing another person that wasn't Raven—disgusted me. But the fact that I couldn't imagine being intimate with a woman—couldn't do the one thing that made me a man—terrified me even more.

I grabbed my keys and coat, and all but running out of the apartment. I didn't know where I was going, let alone know what I would do once I was there. I drove around, searching for something I would never find. I drove until the city lights began fade into the greys and blues of dawn. Until I found myself on that cliff that overlooked the city. The cliff where I took Raven's virginity so many years ago . . . ruined her in the backseat of some stranger's car. But it was also the place where she had driven us to use me as her muse. She joked and giggled as she snapped photos of every one of my awkward poses. Then she looked to the sky, arms spread wide, and basked in the moonlight as I captured every smile, every laugh, every flutter of those dark lashes.

Why had she taken me here, when it held such a negative connotation for us both? It was as if she wanted me to remember. And then what? Forgive and forget? Or maybe her plight was to push me away all along. Like she had tried in the beginning.

This was what she wanted; she just didn't realize it yet. But soon she would see that it was for the best. She would see that she couldn't allow herself to be caged by my failure. I loved her too much for that. I had to set her free.

So I bit back my fears and approached the cliff's edge.

With arms stretched wide, I lifted my tear-streaked face to the heavens, and I said goodbye.

Thursday was a faceless girl from the bar on the corner.

I didn't have the guts to go back to Dive yet. I wasn't ready for the stares and whispers. Everyone knew what I was now, and they would never look at me the same.

The girl was cute enough, a barista at a local coffee shop. She was out with her friends, drinking cheap margaritas, looking for someone to warm her bed, and eventually her heart.

I couldn't do it. I tried, but I couldn't. She ended up sucking me off until her lips were sore before giving up. I blamed it on the alcohol, but I wasn't drunk. She told me to call her. I smiled and kissed her on the forehead.

Friday was Lauren from the gym.

I chalked up my failure to launch on the fact that I was in a strange place with a strange woman. So running into Lauren on her way to the sauna was a happy coincidence. At least that was what I told myself.

It started out fine at first. She took me to a storage closet, whipped off her itty-bitty sports bra and pushed her tits together. I licked and sucked them like a starving man, willing myself to focus on the sensations coursing through my body. But I couldn't help thinking that Raven's breasts were so much nicer—soft and natural and the perfect size to fit in my palms. And I couldn't help but notice that her lips were not as full and plush as Raven's. And her body—while fit and toned—lacked the curves that I had worshipped the night when I made love to Raven.

I couldn't stop seeing her . . . feeling her. I couldn't make myself stop wanting her. And I knew what I had to do. I had to make her hate me. Hate me more than I already hated myself.

Saturday was Cherri. Even if it killed me.

I showed up at The Pink Kitty well after midnight, after all the dumbass frat boys and bachelor party douchewads were already drunk and broke. I knew she would be here—Cherri always worked Saturdays. She was a headliner and Sal's pretty little cash cow.

I expected her to be pissed at me for blowing her off, but Cherri was more than happy to see me. She bounded over to me and placed her thong-clad ass on my lap before kissing my lips.

"Oh my God, baby, where have you been?" she squealed.

"Busy."

"Yeah? Too busy for me?" Her hands were in my hair, and it felt like spiders crawling all over me. I grabbed her wrists and held them to her lap.

"That was then. I'm here now. Let's go somewhere more private and talk."

The smile on her face could've split her face in two. She hopped onto her platform heeled feet and tugged on my hands. "Come with me."

And I did. I would.

Chapter 35

Raven

I WAS EXHAUSTED—BOTH MENTALLY and physically drained. I hadn't slept a wink since I left Dom's apartment three nights ago, and keeping food down was a bust as well. I was only surviving on pure will at this point, and the sheer need to pay our bills. My hours working as a CNA paid the rent, but my tips paid for everything else. Raising a kid wasn't easy, but it was a job I was proud to do. Toby was the only family I had left, and I had to do right by him, no matter how wholly I suffered.

"Get some rest, love. You look positively knackered."

Victoria wrapped her arm around my shoulders and kissed my cheek. She and CJ were planning a trip to Myrtle Beach next week, and she wanted to make up the days she'd lose. Quite frankly, I was astonished they had lasted this long. It was obvious that CJ was crazy about her, and while he was good-looking, he was pretty dim-witted. However, he had surprised the hell out of me when Kami went into labor. To offer his car without second thought, and sit with Toby without a single gripe . . . maybe I was wrong about him. It wouldn't be the first time I misjudged a guy.

We had enough girls on shift for me to cut out early. Even with my foul attitude, I had made enough in tips tonight to cover the rest of the light bill. I just wanted to crawl into bed and shut my eyes. Just shut out the world for the rest of the night and pretend the last 72 hours never happened. Maybe even the last week.

I was almost at the hallway headed for the exit, when I heard the most annoying laugh known to man. I'd gone nearly the entire night without running into Cherri—a rare gift when I needed it the most—but I guess my misery was inevitable.

If I were ever to haul off and backhand her, sending her flying right off her clear plastic hooker heels, this would be the day. I just didn't have an ounce of patience left in me to deal with her smug attitude. So I took a deep breath, counted to five and stepped into the hall.

And froze.

He had her pushed against the wall, clawing her fishnet-covered thighs while he laved her neck with his tongue. He seemed so hungry for her, so desperate to get inside the skimpy lace boyshorts that did nothing to cover her ass cheeks. She pulled his hair, bringing his mouth to hers. When they kissed, I felt my whole world shatter into a million broken pieces. But that wasn't the worst part. Far from it. Because while she stroked her tongue with Dom's, she opened her eyes and looked at me, her gaze so icy, that I felt my blood run cold.

When Dom finally pulled away and wiped the red lipstick from his mouth, Cherri decided to twist the knife in my heart turning to me with a mocking grin. "Grab us a bottle of champagne, will ya? But knock before you come in."

I visibly saw Dom's back stiffen before he slowly turned his head to face me. His brow was furrowed at first, but then it smoothed into that impassive stare he had pinned on me the last time I saw him. The same look he wore when he told me he didn't want me anymore.

"Hey Raven," he said, his words empty as if he were talking to Joe Shmoe on the street. I couldn't even answer. If I did, I would cry, and I'd be damned if I let them see me so broken.

When I turned around to walk the other way, I heard Cherri mutter, "How pathetic," under her breath before laughing. Then there was the sound of a door closing.

I had hoped that being honest with him would draw us closer. I thought maybe—just maybe—he would understand what it was like to be beat down and humiliated. But I was wrong. About him, about us, about everything. I was wrong.

I had no more fight left in me. No more left to give. This was it. It was over.

Fuck that.

No, the hell it wasn't.

I spun on my heel and marched to the backroom with a fire lit under my ass so hot that the rubber of my soles could have melted. Fuck knocking on the door. I would kick this bitch down if I had to. Luckily, they were both too stupid to lock it, so I swung it open and walked my happy ass inside, hitting the lights on the way in.

"What the hell?" Cherri screeched, scrambling up off her knees and covering those water balloons she called tits. "Get the fuck out!"

"No, bitch. You get out. I need to have a word with my boyfriend."

"Boyfriend?" She laughed like she was an evil villain in a cartoon. "Dom isn't anyone's boyfriend, especially not to some gutter rat. Now get out. We're busy."

I stepped in so close to her that I could feel those disgusting ass salt-filled sacks against my chest. "I may be a gutter rat, but at least I wouldn't open my mouth and my legs for any guy with a few singles. Is that all it takes, Cherri? Does George Washington get you hot?" I fished out a couple of ones from the tips I had stuffed in my back pocket and threw them at her. Dammit, I needed that cash, but I wasn't about to back down now. "Here you go, sweetie. Now drop to your knees like a good pussycat and pick them up with your teeth. I know the floor's dirty but you're used to putting filthy things in your mouth."

"You jealous little cunt," she retorted. "You wish you could be me. Now go get me a drink. My throat is parched, and I need to get back to blowing your *boyfriend.*"

I don't even know what set me off—her calling me a cunt or her talking about blowing Dom. But the minute I felt my palm connect with her jaw, it felt like my arm had been yanked from my body and was being wielded by someone else. And dammit, it felt *good.*

"You stupid bitch! How dare you!" Cherri screamed, holding her cheek. There was a tiny droplet of blood in the corner of her mouth but other than that, nothing but her pride was hurt.

"I told you to get out once," I said, my voice dead calm and my glare just as eerie. "Don't make me say it again."

Cherri scrambled to collect the rest of her clothes, taking what was left of her dignity, and damn near ran to the door. "You are so fired! Hope you like Ramen noodles, slut!"

"I happen to love Ramen noodles. Probably as much as you like baby gravy with every meal."

Flustered and bleeding, she slammed the door so hard that the entire room vibrated. I didn't feel it though. My whole body was already trembling with rage and adrenaline. My jaw clenched, and my hands balled into fists, I turned to the real cause of my fury.

"Boyfriend?" he grinned smugly as if his life weren't in danger. "Since when did I become your boyfriend?"

"Since when did you become a dick?" I shot right back at him.

He finished zipping himself up before running a hand through his mussed hair. "Raven . . . you knew what I was about. You knew how I was before we hooked up."

"I knew you were a manwhore, yeah, but you were never an asshole. Must be a newly acquired trait."

He shrugged. "Things change. People change."

"Bullshit. You're good—I'll give you that. You almost had me fooled for a minute."

He huffed out an annoyed breath. "Fooled about what?"

"About you not caring. About you just slipping into your old ways. Dom, we're both flawed, okay? We've both been hurt and abused. But you don't see me trying to bury my pain in some cheap skank, now do you? Get over yourself. You've had it rough—I get that. And I am truly sorry for everything you have been through. But that doesn't give you the right to mistreat the people that care for you—that love you. You're so afraid of becoming a monster . . . so scared of hurting people. Well, what the fuck do you think you're doing to me—to Toby—right now?"

He made a frustrated noise in the back of his throat and began to pace the floor, his hand tangled in his hair as he tugged violently.

"You don't get it."

"Get what?"

He didn't answer. He just kept stalking in a circle, his jaw so tight, I thought his teeth would break.

"Answer me, Dom! What is it that I don't get? That you're a liar? A cheater? A user? Please enlighten me. Tell me all about your deep, complex feelings that require you to fuck strippers. Come on. You were so bold back in that hallway. Tell me what I—"

"You don't get that I fucking love you!" he shouted angrily, fists clenched at his sides. Then he was moving toward me so quickly, I only had time to move back into the crushed velvet padded wall. He pinned me between his arms and pressed his body into mine. The weight of him was so scary yet exhilarating, I couldn't bear to breathe. I was too possessed by the intensity that swirled inside those hazel-green eyes.

"I'm in love with you," he whispered. Dom was panting . . . shivering. I wasn't sure if it was from restraint or rage. "And that's why I can't do this. I'm weak, Raven. I'm tired, and I'm scared, and I'm weak. You deserve better. I'm not a good influence for Toby, and I could never be a good man for

315

you."

"Why not?" The words broke on my tongue.

"Because I'm not a good man. Sometimes, I'm afraid that I'm not even a man at all."

The despair in his voice was so real that it brought tears to my eyes. "Don't say that . . ."

"It's true!" he shouted, barely two inches from my face.

I gasped in fear. He was losing it, and I didn't know what he would do. I never thought he would physically hurt me before, but now, with him so desperate to be heard, I didn't know what to expect.

"Don't you see what I am? Can't you see what I'll become? I'm already half-way there." He laughed sardonically, tipping his head back. "You are so blind. I can't tell which one of us is more pathetic. I've ruined your life once. Why the hell would you let me do it again?"

I hated to admit it, but he was absolutely right. Why was I holding out hope for someone that deemed himself hopeless? He had told me time and time again that this wasn't what he wanted. That *I* wasn't what he wanted. And even if he did love me like he said he did, how was he proving that by hooking up with Cherri, and God only knew who else?

I met his eyes, mustering all the courage I had left in me. I was exhausted, and while the feel of him against me set my soul on fire, his actions had turned me cold.

"I don't know. I must be crazy." I dipped under his arm, freeing myself from the cocoon of his body. "But not anymore."

Just before I hit the door, I turned back to find him still leaning against the wall, his head down. Now . . . this was it.

Now it was over.

"Was it ever real?"

He was quiet for so long that I wasn't sure that he had heard me until he answered, the sound of his voice provoking the first tears to fall from my eyes. "No. Because I'm not."

"Goodbye, Dom."

"Goodbye, Raven."

I had once stood at the very edge, face to the sky, longing to feel the wind in my hair.

I wasn't afraid of flying; I feared the fall. But, pain had made me strong, and life had made me brave, yet love had made me weak.

So I stretched my wings and flew. *I soared.* Only to come tumbling back down to earth. And I vowed that I would never fly again.

Chapter 36

Dom

THE FUNNY THING ABOUT being at rock bottom was that you had nowhere else to go but up. I didn't think I had hit it yet, but I had been pretty damn close. However, there was one girl who had ensured that I didn't completely spiral down into the abyss of regret. And while she was barely six pounds, and her fist was the size of an acorn, she commanded my best. And dammit, that was all I would give her. Even if it hurt.

I spent every day trying to reclaim my life. I smoothed things over with Amber, who refused to let me quit. She told me to take a leave of absence to get my head straight. And when I was ready to come back to Helping Hands, my job would be waiting for me.

I surrounded myself with the people I loved, which meant I spent most of my time at the hospital with Amelia or at home with Angel and Kami, who had been released already. Being separated from her baby was hell, so at least I was distracted by the task of entertaining her.

I still hadn't found the balls to go back to Dive though. The wound was just still too fresh. And Dive meant that I could run into Raven.

"You're sortof a dumbass, you know that?" Angel remarked to me as we sat in the waiting room. Baby Amelia was being released today, and we had showed up for the occasion.

"Why, thank you. I love you too, pumpkin."

"I'm serious. You're a dumbass. You have a shot at something real . . . something whole. Yet, you're letting it slip away. For what? Slumming it with me every night? Trolling for chicks that we'll never see again? Bitch, please."

I took an exasperated breath before diving into all the reasons why I had chosen to walk away from Raven. "Look, you know I can't be with her. You know why I can't allow her to stay with someone like me."

"And why's that?"

"Because. I'm not . . . right. I'm not . . ."

"Oh bullshit. Sounds like a cop out to me. A whiny ass, baby cop out." Then her voice spiked into a shrill, mocking tone, the emphasis on *whiny ass baby.* "Oh boo hoo. I have a beautiful woman who knows all my darkest secrets, but loves me anyway. But I'm too emo and broody to see it through my dark cloud of pity. *Wah wah wah.* Oh God. Cue the Britney look-alike and cry me a fucking river."

I rolled my eyes. "You know it's not that simple."

"Oh, really? Explain the part that's difficult. Explain what's so hard about understanding that we're all flawed, and we all come bearing our own bags of bullshit, yet we deserve a chance at happiness. What's so hard about letting someone love you instead of punishing them—punishing yourself—just because they can see the beauty in all the wreckage? The exact same thing you've been trying to project your entire life?"

Oh shit.

She was right.

Ever since I was a child, I'd always strived to please people, hoping to gain their love and affection. And I had done that, minus the façade and fauxness. I had made Raven love me just by being me. Granted, I was my best self when I was with her, but not because I felt I needed to be to gain her heart. I wanted to be. She demanded it with her no-nonsense attitude and aversion to my bullshit. She made me laugh over the silliest things. She made me dig deeper and really think about what I was putting out in the world. She was artistic, soulful, sarcastic and free-spirited, and I loved everything about her. Yet, I had let her go. No. I pushed her away, ensuring that she would abandon my realm of regret for good. My misery didn't love company. It required my full, undivided devotion, guaranteeing that I would never desert it for anyone and anything else. It had been all I'd known, and that was the way I liked it.

But now there was Raven. And Toby. And I had seen that there was so much more to the endless emptiness. I could *feel* again.

I turned to peer at Angel, whose mouth was turned up into a knowing smile, her eyes fixed on the hospital linoleum. "Make your move, loverboy," she said, as if reading my mind.

I leaned over and kissed her on the cheek. "Thank you."

"Don't thank me yet. Your little stunt at the club got her

fired. So you've got a lot of ass kissing to do. Pack your Chapstick."

Raven was fired? Shit. I wasn't surprised. Everyone knew Cherri was Sal's pet. Unless Raven was putting out, he'd have no qualms about giving her the boot.

Angel and I waited in amicable silence, until Blaine and Kami finally emerged with baby Amelia in tow. She was a strong little thing, and had hit all her milestones within a few weeks, resulting in her early release from the NICU. Since Kami's baby shower never happened, the girls were planning a baby viewing instead, and only inviting close friends and family. No way were we going to allow complete strangers to breathe on her. Hell no.

"Please tell me you don't have one of those Baby On Board signs," Angel huffed, as Blaine and I fumbled with the car seat cradle. Holy shit. When did babies get so damn complicated?

"What's wrong with those?" Kami asked, frowning. She totally had one. I had seen it poking out from the diaper bag, and she was just itching to slap it on the window.

"What's wrong with it?" Angel derided. "So just because a person has a baby, they're allowed to drive like an effing 90-year-old grandma? *Oh, go ahead and cut me off. You have a baby. Yes, you can go 30 in a 55. I understand. You're a breeder. You pushed a pot roast out of your cooch. I get it.* Eff that."

I couldn't help but laugh. At least someone was making an effort to not curse around the baby, as if she could even understand.

"I'm just saying, Baby On Board signs are just another way of saying *look at me, look at me, I had unprotected sex!*

And frankly they're tacky. Yellow? Ew."

Kami caught my eye the same time mine sought hers. We both smiled. Angel bitching about anything and everything was a good sign. It meant things were getting back to normal. Things would be all right. Our family was not only still intact, it had grown and blossomed into something rare and priceless. And for that, I felt something I'd thought was lost. I felt hope.

Chapter 37

Raven

"TOBY! COME ON. WE don't want to be late!"

I double-checked to make sure I had a new SD card and all my lenses stashed in my camera case. Blaine had asked me to take photos during the Sip and See at Dive in honor of their new daughter. I was more than happy to oblige; I had been dying to get some shots of that precious baby girl, plus it was the least I could do for all of Blaine and Kami's generosity. After Sal fired me for slapping Cherri, it felt like everything I touched turned to dust. My relationship—whatever it was—with Dom was officially over. Toby was heartbroken that he had disappeared from our lives and from the center. And now I had to figure out how to make up for the lost income.

I wanted to curl up in a ball and die, but instead, I made a fool of myself by getting teary eyed during my shift at Dive.

Blaine had stopped in to check on things, but had caught me in the backroom where we kept our purses and coats. He pulled me aside and asked me what was wrong, and I completely fell apart.

I told him about Dom, about Cherri, and about losing my job. I told him that I didn't think I was cut out for this parenthood stuff and had considered sending Toby to our grandparents, who weren't fairing much better than me. I wanted to give up. Being a grownup had just become too overwhelming. I'd had it with *adulting*. That shit sucked.

After patiently listening to me sob like a blubbering idiot, he handed me a box of tissues and told me—not asked—that I would come work at Dive full time. He even said that Toby was welcome to come into work with me anytime, and could even earn a few bucks by helping with minor things, even though it was illegal as hell. I understood what he was doing—he was giving me a home. A place to belong. A family, even if it was just a work family. And that made me sob even harder.

So doing a good job today was important to me. I wanted to capture every precious moment on their special day. And that started with showing up on time.

Toby bounded down the short hallway, his brown hair a wild mess of curls. He needed a haircut, and I made a mental note to ask CJ about a good barber. He had gotten over my kitchen haircuts real quick.

"Hey kid, let me take a look at you." I finger-combed his nearly shoulder-length mane, fixed his collar and straightened the wrinkles from his polo shirt. My little brother was growing into a handsome young man. It wouldn't be long before the girls started noticing him. I just hoped they wouldn't see his verbal aversion as something weird or wrong. I didn't want him to be hurt by anyone, ever. And nothing stung worse than being rejected by someone you cared about.

We arrived at Dive just before the first guests began to file in. Before it got too crowded, I quickly snapped some shots of the party décor—pink and vintage gold with old fashioned signage and paper pinwheels. There was a sipping station set up in the bar area, featuring mimosas with assorted fresh fruit purees and garnishes. Adjacent to that was a buffet table lined with chaffing dishes, including a dessert bar showcasing mini cupcakes, cake pops and chocolate-covered strawberries, all dressed in pink.

"Isn't it lovely?" Victoria gasped, sidling beside me. "Such a beautiful day for a beautiful baby."

She was absolutely right. Kami and Blaine had spared no expense, and I had a feeling Angel had a hand in the planning as well. It was Sunday, so Blaine had decided to close up shop for the private affair. Hard to believe that just last night, this place was packed with wall-to-wall patrons, chugging beer, pounding shots and rocking out to AngelDust.

The place was gorgeous, but something was missing. Although I didn't want to see Dom, I had mentally prepared myself to be in the same room with him again. He hadn't been back to Dive since that incident with Amanda, and I wasn't sure he would be here today. I wanted to ask, but I had my pride. He'd made it abundantly clear that there was nothing left between us. Asking about him would be pouring salt in my own wounds.

Once the party was in full swing, I busied myself by snapping photos of guests meeting baby Amelia for the very first time, along with congratulatory praise for the proud parents. Most of the partygoers consisted of Blaine's relatives and Dive employees, along with the members of AngelDust who would be performing some occasion-appropriate cover songs a little later. Everything was perfect, but still no Dominic. And while it was sad that Amelia's godfather wasn't in attendance, I thought maybe it was for the best. All eyes were on the happy family, as they should be. And factoring in him and all our would-be drama would detract from today's purpose.

The music started, AngelDust taking the stage to play their version of Paramore's "Ain't It Fun." They were amazing—maybe even better than the original—and I happily bopped around, capturing images of the guests dancing and singing along. Surprisingly, I even caught Toby nodding his head, his eyes glued to the stage and Angel Cassidy. She looked down at him and winked, causing his face to flame bright red. Huh. He had a crush on her. I wasn't surprised; straight or gay, Angel Cassidy had always been a stunner. I imagined she had more than her fair share of male attention.

If his adolescent male affections weren't enough of a revelation, I was momentarily astonished by yet another discovery about my baby brother. His mouth . . . was *moving*. He was singing along. And that filled me with a sense of maternal pride and hope that I didn't think existed inside me. There was a chance he would come back to us. It may have not been today, or tomorrow, or even this year, but there was a chance we'd get him back.

The band played a few more songs before Angel requested that Blaine come to the stage. Smiling, he cradled his daughter to his chest and made his way to the front. And as Angel belted out the first few notes of Bruno Mars' "Marry You," her raspy tone giving it a rock edge, I knew exactly why she had called him up. Oh my God, Blaine was proposing. My camera whirred at lightning speed as I captured the bright smile on his face as he held his baby close. I searched through the excited crowd for Kami, hoping to get her reaction as she realized what was happening, but she was nowhere to be found. However, as the band transitioned into the verse, she was definitely heard.

Kami stepped onto the stage, leading the song with a voice that completely left me gobsmacked, as Victoria would say. She was *singing*. And she was *incredible*. And by the perplexed look on Blaine's face as he looked up at her, this was not the plan. For the second time in 60 seconds, I was left with a WTF face. Blaine wasn't proposing, at least he wasn't anymore. *Kami* was.

After the verse, she sang her way down to the dance floor area where Blaine stared at her in awe. Too engrossed in the enormity of the moment that they had chosen to share with us, I had to remind myself to take pictures so they could relive these memories for years to come. Watching Kami sing to him, and to their newborn daughter, had to be the sweetest thing I had ever seen. She had always been somewhat reserved—although friendly—so seeing her so beautifully exposed, pulled at my heartstrings a bit.

I moved around the room to get every angle, careful not to intrude on their intimate moment. But after the song ended, and Kami dropped to her knees. And with my mascara running, I got in as close as possible. The look on her face as she looked up at Blaine, his own eyes watery with overwhelming emotion, was like seeing true love on display in its most raw, vulnerable form.

"Blaine," she said into the mic, her voice quavering. "You've given me safety, security, patience, understanding and unconditional love. And now, you've given me the honor of being a mother. And while these things are absolutely priceless and immeasurable, I must ask you for one more thing. Your last name. So, if you would have me, I would gladly give you the rest of my life in return. Marry me?"

There wasn't a dry eye in the room as Blaine dropped onto his knees right in front of her, holding their baby tight between them. The way he pulled her to him and kissed her . . . it was like their love radiated throughout the room and touched the most hollow of places. You could feel it expand in your chest, making it hard to breathe through the knot of emotion in your throat. It was exhilarating, it was scary, and it was completely real. And I thought, *This is what it must feel like. This is what it's like to fly.*

"I've wanted that since the day you came tearing in here. From the very first look, the very first smile, the very first shot of tequila, I've wanted to make you mine until the rest of our days. You don't have to ask, baby. I'm already yours. And if you'll have me, I promise to make you happy. You and our daughter, and the other eight children I can't wait to make with you," he chuckled, causing a ripple of laughter around the room, even a few hoots and hollers. "I love you, Kami. Yes. A thousand times yes. Let's get married."

The crowd erupted into cheers, and I even found myself shouting with glee between snapping pictures. The happy couple—well, trio—eventually got off the floor and resumed celebrating with family and friends. After Angel gave them each hugs and kisses, she jumped back on the stage to finish AngelDust's set.

"Since this is Make Angel Cry Day, we have one more special request."

She didn't say any more than that. The band just began to play, and I recognized the song instantly. Apparently, it was Make Raven Cry Day as well. A dozen memories ran through my head as Angel sang the first verse of "Eternal Flame." Memories of my mom when she was happy and healthy. Memories of knowing what it felt like to be someone's daughter, to belong to someone who loved you because they created you. Memories of her singing those words to a tiny Toby as he smiled and laughed. Memories of his first words, and the way he used to call me Mawwy in his adorable toddler talk. And most recently, memories of riding down the highway at the wheel of Dom's car, singing at the top of my lungs, feeling wanted by him, and wanting him too—as scary as it was.

I missed being Melanie. I missed having a sense of security. I missed belonging. And I missed him.

Even when I thought he was a piece of shit, he was still a part of my life. I had held onto him all these years, lying in wait, hoping to come face to face with the monster that had destroyed me. Except he wasn't a monster. He was a beautiful, tortured soul whose only crime was feeling too much . . . hurting too much.

I almost didn't see him through the tears in my eyes, when he stepped into view. But when I did, all the fight, all the resistance in me dissipated. My shoulders sagged, and my camera bag slipped past my arms. If it weren't for his quick reflexes, my camera would have been the next to go. I fell into him, surrendering all the pain, all the anger to him. I let him hold me and tell me that he was there to catch me. I let him be what he had been all along—my safety net. Tethering me to this life when I wanted to fly far away.

"Why are you here?" I managed to say.

Dom looked down at me with compassion and caring in his eyes. "For you, Raven. I've always been here for you. You're bigger than my fear, bigger than my pain. You're the most perfect part of me," he whispered, a smile on those perfect lips. "Besides, we have so much to *taco* 'bout."

With eyes shut tight and my head tipped to the sky, I laughed until it hurt. And I laughed because it hurt to keep denying how much I loved him.

"Tuesday night?" I asked, gazing at him through tears and stars in my eyes.

He squeezed me tighter and nodded. "Tuesday it is. And every day until eternity."

"Eternity seems like a mighty long time."

"Only when you're not having fun."

Then, he kissed me for every broken promise, every lonely night, and every anguished cry. He kissed me like I belonged to him . . . like I'd always belonged to him. And truth be told, I always had.

Chapter 38

Dom

I GAZED DOWN AT the woman in my arms and prayed to the gods of heaven and earth that this wasn't a dream.

Last night had been insane. Kami and Blaine got engaged in front of all their friends and family, and I'd made it my mission to win Raven back, even if I made a fool of myself. Even if she rejected me at every turn. Even if she had listened to all my fucked up, convoluted reasons why we shouldn't be together, flicked me the bird and walked out of my life for good.

Why?

This right here.

Having her in my arms, her naked, perfect skin dewed with the remnants of sex and sweat. Getting to kiss her mouth, her neck, and her shoulders as she slept. Watching the glow of sunrise touch her paleness, causing it to warm under my touch.

I did it all for this. For her. Because I loved her more than I hated me. And because I loved her—really, truly loved her—I found that hating me wasn't nearly as easy as it used to be. Because if this beautiful being could love someone like me, despite all the ways I've hurt her—past and present—and despite all the ways *I've* been hurt, then I couldn't be all that bad. She saw something in me. She saw beyond all the exterior bullshit, the slick lines and cheesy anecdotes, and I became transparent in my feelings for her. And like I'd always believed, she captured the beauty . . . the beauty in *me*. The parts of me that had been buried so deep within my pain and loathing that I could no longer find it. I could no longer *feel* it.

Now, here we were, a tangled web of arms and legs and sex-mussed hair. And I'd never felt more alive, more loved, and *free*. Freer than I ever thought possible. Freer than people like me—and her, and even Toby—probably deserved.

Her love for me made me weightless. It made me daring. And every time I looked in her eyes, I felt the wind beneath my arms and the sun at my back. I tipped my head to the sky and tasted the sweetness in the air. And with her and Toby at my side, I *flew*.

The End . . .

Or is it?

"**Y**OU'RE SURE ABOUT THIS?"

Raven looked at me with a smirk on her plump, kiss-ravaged lips. I couldn't keep my hands off her, and my need for physical contact seemed to be amplified whenever she was around.

"I'm sure," she nodded. "I appreciate that you're worried about us, Dom, but I won't let you take care of us. I am not a kept woman."

Despite my better efforts to make her stay, Raven had insisted on going back to her apartment. I had already talked it over with Angel—there was plenty of room here for her and Toby. Ang had even agreed to tone down the wild antics. I guess we'd both been getting burnt out from the steady stream of faceless women that had once graced these hallways. Hell, the hardwood was damn near worn from so many walks-of-shame.

"You know it's not like that," I assured her, trying to pull her back into bed with me. God, I could never get enough of her. I was starting to think I was borderline addicted, itching like a fiend for my next fix of Melanie Raven West. She was my disease, and the cure to my ailing body and soul.

She looked at the watch on her slender wrist and cursed

under her breath. "Shit, I gotta get to my shift. Tonight, ok? The three of us can watch movies. We might even spend the night. Depends on if you're a good boy."

I made a low noise in my throat that ended with a groan. "Good boy? I thought you liked me because I was trouble."

She leaned forward to sweep her tongue across my lips, tasting my desperate need for her. "I like you, because you're trouble. But I love you, because you're you."

That was all the motivation I needed. With one swift movement, I grasped her by the waist, pulled her back into bed, and pinned her body under mine.

Five more minutes. Blaine would understand.

Toby

THEY WERE AT IT again.

Well, I couldn't hear them, or any gross crap like that—ew—but I knew what sex was, and I knew couples liked to do it. Duh. I just didn't get why. Seemed totally sick to me. Yuck.

But Mel was happy, and that made me happy. I knew it was difficult for her having to raise a kid alone, working day and night, plus finishing her nursing degree. She deserved to be with someone that made her smile. And I couldn't think of anyone better than Mr. D. He was the best. And Mel only deserved the best.

Plus all her "visits" with him allowed me to play Xbox and PS4 whenever I wanted. We never had video games growing up—we couldn't afford them after my dad left. So that was awesome. And...it meant I could see Angel.

God, she was gorgeous. Like, if I was ten years older, or she was ten years younger, I would totally want her to be my girlfriend. I'd never imagined I'd ever want that with someone, but I wanted that with her. It was stupid—I know. Even if she was my age, I couldn't even freakin' speak to ask her out. And who would want some head case like me? Not a freakin' rock star.

But, for the sake of dreaming, maybe I would ask her. Maybe I could speak...for her. Or someone like her. Beautiful, and nice, and funny, and totally cool.

Mel had worked through her crazy to be with Dom, and I believed that no one else but him could break through to her.

So maybe there was someone out there for me too? Someone to give me reason to swallow down my fear and sadness, open my mouth, and say...

"Hi. I'm Toby."

Acknowledgments

I've always felt that writing acknowledgments was right up there with writing blurbs—hard as hell. Not because I'm not grateful—Lord knows I am. But because there is absolutely no way to sum up my gratitude into words that could ever express what my supporters mean to me. So yeah…acknowledgments suck. But the people in my life don't, so I'll do the best that I can.

I first want to thank Mia Sheridan, Emmy Montes and Rebecca Shea for making sure my ass was on point with capturing this emotional story. Thank you for being gentle and kind with Dom, and giving him a swift kick in the pants when needed. I love you all!

Thank you to the JFJ Girls for all your loyalty and support from the very beginning! Extra special love & hugs to Shanta, Louisa, Alicia, the Jennifers (Diaz & Noe), Andrea, Sandy, Holly, Martha and Sofia for all the shares and pimping. You girls are amazing!

I also want to thank my PR & Marketing team, Sassy Savvy Fabulous PR for all their hard work and dedication. Sharon and Melissa, you have been incredible, and I respect and appreciate everything you have done for me.

Big hugs to The Rock Stars of Romance for all their help in promoting Afraid to Fly. Lisa, you have been so professional and helpful. Thank you for all your hard work in giving ATF wings! And Milasy…what can I say, babe? I heart you more than salted caramel cookies, and I am so thankful for our friendship.

To my amazing editor, Tracey, who has been with me since FOF… Woman, we've done it again! Thank you so much for being such an important part of this process. I am so happy to have you on my side. And to Kara, my proofreader, I am so glad to have the chance to work with you! You're awesome, woman!

My formatter, Stacey, is incredible at what she does, and I am thankful to work with her once again. So glad to have met you! Hang Le, you are amazing and so crazy brilliant. Thank you! And to Regina, who has kicked ass with yet another unbelievable cover…Girl, your talent never ceases to amaze me! I love you!

I want to give HUGE props to Mo. Honestly, there is no amount of thanks I could give to properly encompass how much you mean to me. I am so grateful for all your dedication and friendship. And your hair. Because, let's face it—hair is important. #priorities

Thank you to all the wonderful readers, bloggers and reviewers who have supported me through this journey by sharing, posting and reading ATF. I could not do this without all of you!

Lastly, I want to thank my family for sticking it out through the craziness. When I set out to write ATF, I honestly didn't know what I was signing up for. And I absolutely love you guys with all my heart for having my back and loving me through all the chaos.

To anyone I may have missed, please chalk it up to my head and not my heart. It's the Friday night before release week and I'm literally running on fumes, coffee and liquor. Please believe that I am truly grateful for you all!

Xoxo,
-S

About the Author

Most known for her starring role in a popular sitcom as a child, S.L. Jennings went on to earn her law degree from Harvard at the young age of 16. While studying for the bar exam and recording her debut hit album, she also won the Nobel Prize for her groundbreaking invention of calorie-free wine. When she isn't conquering the seas in her yacht or flying her Gulfstream, she likes to spin elaborate webs of lies and has even documented a few of these said falsehoods.

Some of S.L.'s devious lies:
FEAR OF FALLING (a Fearless novel)
TAINT (a Sexual Education novel)
TRYST (a Sexual Education novel)- *coming in 2015*

THE DARK LIGHT SERIES
Dark Light
The Dark Prince
Nikolai (a Dark Light novella)
Light Shadows

Meet the Liar:
www.sljennings.com
www.facebook.com/authorsljennings
Twitter: @MrsSLJ
Instagram: instagram.com/s.1.jennings

Made in the USA
San Bernardino, CA
25 June 2015